The Unforgetting

ROSE BLACK

ORION

First published in Great Britain in 2020 by Orion Books,
an imprint of The Orion Publishing Group Ltd
Carmelite House, 50 Victoria Embankment
London EC4Y 0DZ

An Hachette UK Company

1 3 5 7 9 10 8 6 4 2

A CIP catalogue record for this book is
available from the British Library.

ISBN (Hardback) 978 1 4091 9061 5
ISBN (eBook) 978 1 4091 9063 9

Typeset at The Spartan Press Ltd,
Lymington, Hants

Printed and bound in Great Britain by Clays Ltd,
Elcograf S.p.A.

www.orionbooks.co.uk

'It is wonderful that five thousand years have now elapsed since the creation of the world, and still it is undecided whether or not there has ever been an instance of the spirit of any person appearing after death. All argument is against it; but all belief is for it.'

James Boswell, The Life of Samuel Johnson

Author's Note

In the spring of 1851, I returned to live with my older
brother in the house in which I was born. I was almost
thirty years of age and wanted only to forget the past.

Not long afterwards, Lily Bell entered our lives. Her
arrival and soon her untimely 'death' marked the beginning of the events that I relate here, events that rendered
forgetting impossible. Those happenings that I didn't
experience at first hand, I have used my imagination to
describe.

Whether or not I acted correctly, or as a woman
ought, I leave to the reader to decide. I have in mind
one reader in particular. I hope that she may one day
read these words and understand. Perhaps forgive.

This novel is dedicated to her.

FS, Nether Hall, 1854

One

Lily Bell opened her eyes. Her trunk stood on the floor
at the end of the high iron bed. The other bed was empty
– neatly made, as if it hadn't been slept in at all – and
the air tinged with the smell of burned toast. She lay
back on the pillows, considering her new circumstances.
They'd arrived late the previous evening and had walked
to the lodgings in the darkness, going from the harbour
up a steep path, a carter following with the luggage. The
wind had blown her along, turned her skirts into a sail,
and clutching her hat with both hands, breathing in
the clean, salty air, Lily had forgotten the rigours of the
journey and felt only excitement. In the first-floor room
she was to share with Faye Salt, she'd lain awake on the
lumpy mattress imagining herself on stage – Cordelia in
green velvet, Ophelia in dripping purple satin, or Juliet
in any costume at all. The roar of the audience rang in
her ears as if it were real. Later, Lily realised that it was
the sound of the sea. The sea lent itself to tragedy, she'd
thought contentedly, drifting into sleep.

The events of the last few days were still so surprising that Lily couldn't be certain even now that she hadn't dreamed them. On Tuesday, she'd stayed up late, listening to the night-time creaks of the house, staring into the embers, imagining the life that lay ahead of her if only she could find a way into it. Next morning, she'd been on her way down the stairs when she heard raised voices coming from the kitchen.

'Over my dead body,' her mother said.

'I told you, Ruth. It's settled. The thing is done.'

'Then undo it.'

'Can't. I signed a paper. It's out of the ordinary, I don't mind admitting. She's going to— Ah, there you are.'

Alfred Bell was at one end of the table and her mother at the other, her face pallid.

'I'm going to what?' Lily said.

'Tell her, Alf. Tell her how you plan to dispose of her. And don't omit the reason why.'

Lily could make no sense of the speech her step-father gave. 'Erasmus Salt ... burden of debt ... ghost machine ...'

She moved into the scullery to run a glass of water. It was Jennifer's day off; the floor needed a sweep and the stone sink was stacked with pans waiting to be scoured. 'And you, my dear child—'

'I'm not your child,' Lily interrupted, from force of habit.

'Will be the human actress in Professor Salt's—'

'Actress?' The word had seemed to hypnotise her, to

4

cast a spell over her that would pull her out of the life she'd known and into the world where she longed to be. Staring out of the window she didn't see the bud-laden boughs of the apple tree swaying in the March breeze or the makeshift workshop that occupied most of the garden. She saw herself, on stage, in the beam of the limelight.

Her mother began a furious riddling of the coals, clinkers flying down into the pan, the cat leaping from her lap.

'There's a sister, Ruth,' Alfred Bell said. 'Spinster, I suppose. She'll keep watch over her. Salt gave me his word.'

'Tell him, Lily,' her mother said. 'Tell him that you won't so much as consider it.'

'There's money in it,' Bell continued. 'The debt written off and a salary as well.'

Turning back into the kitchen, aware that she played the first major role that life had offered her, Lily pulled her Chinese silk wrapper around her and stood very straight. 'I shall go. My mind's made up. I'll send my wages straight to you, Mother.'

'Yes, Lily, but—'

'I'll be launched on the stage. It's what you wanted for me.'

'Not under the direction of Erasmus Salt.'

'Mother, don't you remember? I met the professor, a few months ago. He was charming. He helped us.'

Her mother seemed to choke on the rising plume

of ash. 'And now we know his price,' she said, flinging down the poker.

Despite the chill in the air, Alfred Bell was sweating, his skin shining. He mopped at his forehead, addressed the foot-hollowed brick floor. 'She leaves tomorrow, early. It's all arranged.'

Mother had slumped back down onto her chair. 'This will be the death of me,' she said. 'You mark my words.'

Lily had imagined that when, the following morning, she and her stepfather arrived at the coaching inn on the south side of the river, the professor would audition her for the role. But Erasmus Salt had barely spoken to her. In the yard of the inn, by a hired coach and four, he'd looked at her with bright eyes and – in a gesture so unexpected, so uncouth, that Lily wondered now if she'd imagined it – reached out and taken a lock of her hair between his fingers. 'She'll do,' he'd said. 'Do even better than I recalled.' He let go of her hair, passed something to Mr Bell and in moments her trunk had been roped onto the roof, her stepfather had handed her up inside the vehicle and they'd set off through the archway and onto the street.

The coachman whipped the horses to a fast trot and outside the window a succession of shops, public houses and small factories rushed by. Sitting opposite Lily, Professor Salt stared at her – as if he could see through her black velvet jacket with the red camellia pinned to the lapel, right to the very bones of her. Lily had a sudden urge to wrench open the door and jump out, plunge back into the streets of London with all their rough comfort and make her way home. Keeping herself on the seat by an effort of will, she gripped the strap hanging by the window and disobeyed one of her mother's cardinal rules: a woman should never ask questions.

'Where are we going?'

'Coast,' the man replied, his eyes flickering away. 'Ramsgate.'

'And might I know the name of the theatre where I shall appear?'

'You will appear. And you will disappear.'

'What do you mean, Professor?'

'Soon see, Miss Bell. All in good time.'

He got a mechanical pencil from inside his jacket, opened a notebook and began making notes in the margins of a page filled with diagrams and what looked like mathematical formulae. His sister was equally engrossed, hunched over a length of black fabric with the distinctive twisted weave of mourning crape, hemming it with careful stitches.

The whip's shout rang on the air, hooves clattering on the metalled road. Lily was sure she'd never in her life travelled at such speed. Rows of terraces gave way to copses of bare-branched trees, a common where a white horse grazed, a grand grey old house standing alone behind its walls. As the two pairs galloped past orchards and hop fields, the carriage rocking and swaying like a giant, battered cradle, it began to rain. Water pelted the windows and seeped round the door, dampening the straw on the floor. The mirror above the seat opposite Lily misted over and her reflection blurred then vanished. She could no longer snatch glimpses of the feathers waving on her hat, check that it was really her that sat in this coach on this spring day, racing towards her future.

The spinster started as Lily entered the room, springing to her feet, her thimble rolling from her lap.

'I didn't hear you on the stairs.'

'Mother says I have a light step,' Lily said, retrieving the thimble, handing it back. 'Good morning, Miss Salt.' The parlour was square, bow-windowed, the mantel cluttered with sepia-tinted photographs in sharp shell frames. A red velvet chaise was pushed up against one wall, next to a stand of ferns and aspidistra that contrasted oddly with the watercolours of sea and sky that filled the walls. Lily had put on her summer muslin and embroidered mules, dressed her hair with care, pinning the front sections in coils, leaving the rest hanging loose down her back.

'Are there no other guests?'

'My brother has reserved this room for our private use.'

Lily felt disappointed by the idea that she wouldn't see any of the other guests. Or be seen by them. She picked up a photograph from the mantelpiece of a little curly-haired child, looked at the innocent gaze of the eyes, the dimpled chin.

'Did you sleep well, Miss Salt?'

'Yes, thank you.'

'Only, I thought I heard you cry out. Perhaps you dreamed.'

'Perhaps you imagine things,' the woman said, peering at the crape, her face taking on a faint tinge of colour.

Faye Salt was thirty or more years of age, her auburn hair less faded than her older brother's, her clothes of once-fine quality. In her long-cuffed challis dress, a silver locket at her throat, she might have stepped out from an old oil painting hung high on the wall in some forgotten country manor house. Lily imagined herself playing the role of the spinster, the dutiful sister assisting her brother in his endeavours while her own life dwindled away.

'Where's the professor?' she said, more gently, putting down the photograph.

'He went out early. He said he had arrangements to make.'

'In that case, shall we go for a walk? I long to see the sea.'

The spinster held up the length of black silk. 'Before we go anywhere, miss, I'm to attach this to your bonnet.'

Lily looked at the dark rectangle. She pictured her shallow-brimmed straw, the grey satin ribbons that matched her eyes, and laughed.

'I'm not in mourning. I don't need a veil, Miss Salt. I've never worn one in my life.'

The woman gestured at an antiquated black bonnet and cloak laid over a chair by the door. 'These are for you,' she said.

Sitting down on the chaise, Lily felt winded. 'An actress must be versatile,' she said. 'But I didn't expect to play a crone.'

'Not on stage, Miss Bell. You're to wear them when you leave the house.'

'But... why?'

'Those were his instructions.'

Miss Salt began stitching the veil to the brim of the bonnet with quick, purposeful movements of her needle. Lily ran her hands over the worn, soft pile of the velvet chaise, smoothed her skirt over her knees. She was about to begin her stage career; had a chance she had longed for since childhood. When he wasn't at the card tables, her stepfather was a scene painter. For as long as Lily could remember, their cramped house in Stepney had been magically expanded by the worlds that took shape under his hands. He worked standing or from a set of wooden steps, making daubs that from close by couldn't be interpreted but from a distance translated into English country gardens ablaze with flowers, blood-soaked Belgian fields, moonlit groves where nymphs disported.

Lily acted as his model. Before ruined castles, desert sands and plush drawing rooms, in costumes fashioned from old curtains, scraps of satin and lace left over from the trimming of hats, she'd played Cleopatra, Medea,

Joan of Arc, posing for Mr Bell's clients in the freezing studio, bringing his backdrops to life. 'It gave you ideas,' her mother complained, but the truth was that it had given her only one idea. She was an actress. That was her vocation, the reason for her existence, and she would succeed not because she was a great beauty – she wasn't – but because of all that she felt inside and longed to express.

She stood up, looking into the convex mirror over the mantel that turned the room behind her into a strange distorted world, curving the windows and the walls, shrinking the spinster on the sewing chair to a tiny figure.

'No doubt your brother has his reasons,' she said, turning round. 'He's a professor of the theatrical arts, is he not?'

'No,' Miss Salt said stiffly, restored to life size, holding out the bonnet. 'He is a professor of ghosts.'

Two

Gulls swooped over the roof of the long, low building. Inside, the workshop was dry and dusty, the air charged with a fine, white haze as if schoolboys had been pelting each other with flour. The mason was at his bench, bent over a slab of stone, delivering sharp taps to a chisel with a hammer. Erasmus Salt rapped his stick on the floor and the fellow laid down his tools, removed a pair of protective spectacles and untied the bandanna that covered his nose and mouth.

'Morning to you,' he said.

'White marble,' Erasmus said, raising his voice against the mournful cries of the birds outside, the bluster of the March wind. 'Plain lettering. Wording in simple form.'

'My condolences.' The mason reached for a dusty pencil. 'Who is the late?'

'Young lady,' Erasmus said, taking off his hat, casting down his eyes. 'Not twenty years of age.'

The mason nodded and for a moment stood in silence. 'Will you be wanting an angel?'

'Angel?'

'It makes a seemly tribute.'

Erasmus affected consideration of the idea. It was a good one. Would pay for itself, in time. 'I believe she would have liked that,' he said, piously, selecting from the drawings the mason brought out one that depicted an angel seated, her chin resting on her hands, her wings poised as if for flight. Locks of white marble hair curled over her narrow shoulders and down towards her waist.

'This will do very well,' he said.

'Date of birth?'

Erasmus felt for the note in his pocket. 'Eighteen thirty-one. September first.'

'And when did the young lady pass away?'

'Just yesterday,' Erasmus said. 'Slipped from a cliff. Quite tragic.'

Reaching into his pocket again, bringing out his handkerchief, he dabbed at his dry eyes.

Three

The veil hung in front of Lily's face, grazing her cheeks, her lips. Through the twisted weave, everything looked soft-edged and flat, as if the street, the little bow-fronted houses painted pink and white and blue, the higgledy-piggledy chimney pots and the great, watchful birds perched on the ridges of the roofs, were no more than a painted canvas. She was in character, she decided, playing the part of a reclusive actress just arrived from London.

As they reached the end of the crescent, a gust of wind nearly blew her off her feet. Silver glinted through the crape and letting go of Miss Salt's wrist, Lily threw back the veil. The light was blinding, brighter than she'd known light could be. 'I must at least see the sea,' she called over her shoulder, hurrying across the road and over a grassy cliff top. At the edge, she stopped. Far down below, two hundred feet or more, the sea stretched out – vast and shining, a great silver mirror dotted with elegant, tall-masted ships. On the horizon, shimmering against a deep blue sky, was the white, crinkled edge of the Continent. Lily had lived all her life in London, was used to slices of sky carved up by steep-sided buildings, the atmosphere fogged with smoke and steam, the horizon punctured by chimneys and spires. Seeing so much of the world in a single panorama made her feel intoxicated.

Ignoring the spinster's calls, she set off down a set of wooden steps that zigzagged down the side of the cliff. She reached the bottom and walked towards the water, the heels of her mules sinking into the sand, the hem of the cloak dragging. The wind was less down on the beach and the sea sounded soft, as if the waves whispered a message. A fringe of lacy foam sallied forward and almost flooded the toes of her shoes. Jumping back, bending to dip her fingers in the water, Lily felt its cold greeting. Her life lay before her, vast and shining as the sea itself, and she felt a terrible kind of happiness, terrible because it was so intense and because she felt, for the first time in her nineteen years, alone.

In the distance, further along the beach, a figure seemed to dance. His shirt billowed in the wind, and his hair; he looked up at the sky, moving his arms and his feet. The man was juggling – tossing balls into the air and catching them, moving on the spot, the cliff at his back. A ball fell and he let the others drop, gathered them up and then stripped off his clothes and waded into the water. Lily caught a glimpse of broad shoulders, a torso narrowing to the hips, before the man plunged into the sea.

A shout went up behind her. A man was hurrying over the beach towards her, one hand clamping his hat on his head, the other using his stick to hasten his progress. In the instant before she recognised him, a shiver ran through Lily.

'Surely,' she said, tugging the crape back over her face, straightening the bonnet as the professor arrived in front of her, 'no one need be veiled at the seaside.'

Professor Salt scowled down at her. 'Vital,' he barked, gripping her shoulder with strong fingers, 'that you are concealed. Do I make myself understood?'

For a moment, Lily felt glad of the veil. She could hide her sense of shock that he should dare to touch her, avoid meeting the man's oddly bright eyes. 'But why, Professor?' she said, shaking herself free.

When he spoke again, his voice was returned to its customary silkiness. 'For the performance. You wouldn't wish to jeopardise it, I trust?'

'No,' Lily stammered. 'That is the last thing I would wish. I will do everything in my power to make the play a success. I'm ready to begin rehearsals immediately.'

'In that case, we'll waste no more time.'

They walked back over the beach, past a couple of dilapidated bathing machines, their ragged canvas hoods flapping in the wind, to the steps. She wouldn't allow herself to be cowed – an actress must always retain independence of mind – but she would ask no more questions, for now. On the last landing, Lily stopped and glanced back. Far out from the shore, the dark shape of a head was moving through the water.

The professor waited at the top, next to his sister. Brushing white dust from the shoulders and arms of his coat, he removed his hat and blew a drift of it from the rim.

'Come, ladies.' He smiled, returning the hat to his head, gesturing for them to proceed. 'Let us go to the theatre.'

The New Tivoli occupied one side of a small, cobbled square in the old town. The elegant columns at the front were chipped and splashed with birdlime, the great double doors padlocked. Salt led his sister and Lily down an alley by the side of the theatre, past an overturned rowing boat, to a stage door. Lily had long dreamed of entering a theatre through the stage door and on crossing the threshold she felt a frisson of excitement, as if she were a bride entering her new home.

A barred window let in a dull gleam of daylight that illuminated rows of steeply raked bench seats, a gallery above and, on the walls to the sides, raised boxes draped with swags of lace. The ceiling was painted with twin golden masks of Comedy and Tragedy, one face laughing and the other grimacing. A thick, seaside dampness pervaded the air.

'A fine establishment,' Erasmus Salt said. 'I'm sure you will agree, Miss Bell.'

Discarding the bonnet and cloak on the front row

seats, Lily went up the stairs on the side of the stage and with small, reverent steps, walked out onto it. The stage was larger than it appeared from the auditorium, the green baize worn thin, a huge chandelier hanging overhead. Standing beneath it, looking out at the auditorium, Lily thought of all the actors who had trod these boards before her, imagined the theatre full, every seat taken and the people lost in rapture, or grief, or pity. The New Tivoli was shabbier than the theatres in the West End of London, with polished brass and glass, mahogany doors, seats upholstered in red plush, that her mother had on occasion taken her to. It didn't matter. What mattered was the play. Elated to be there, in the place where she would make her debut, she began to turn in a circle, her skirts swinging out around her, spinning until she staggered and almost fell, then stopped, steadied herself and curtseyed. Only Miss Salt sat in the pit. The professor was crouching by a gas lamp at the side.

'What is the play, Professor?' Lily said, walking over to him.

'Not a play, Miss Bell,' he said. 'A marvel. Miracle. Wonder of natural science.'

She felt off balance again. 'But what is my role? My character?'

'Not a *character*. A ghost. Here. I shall acquaint you with the ghost machine.' Standing up, getting out the notebook that he'd had in the coach, the professor began turning the pages, pointing at a series of diagrams. 'So this is the angle of reflection – and this represents...'

Watching the words stream through his crooked bottom teeth, turning the ring on the middle finger of her right hand, Lily found herself thinking of her mother. As Lily's trunk had been bumped down the stairs, Ruth Bell had emerged red-eyed from her bedroom at the end of the landing. She'd pulled the opal ring that she'd had from her own mother from her finger, twisted it over the knuckle and held it out. Lily had loved the ring since she was a child; the stone was iridescent, turquoise and blue and green, the colours shifting in the changing light. For her it had represented beauty, a promise of a life she might aspire to.

'This is for you,' Mother had said, her eyes streaming again, her face contorted with some awful emotion that Lily couldn't recognise. 'If you ever want for money to come home, sell it.'

'Keep it, Mother. There are wages and in any case, I won't want to come—'

'Take it, Liza.'

Only her mother called her Liza. It was her pet name for her, taken from her middle name, Elizabeth. 'Follow your dreams, Liza,' Ruth Bell had said to her, from when Lily was little. Then she would add under her breath, 'Don't make my mistakes.'

Lily felt a sudden longing to see her mother, standing in front of her in her Sunday best, her hair brushed, her hands soft with cold cream and her face, if not happy, then composed, at rest in a way it never was during weekdays. She hoped her mother's nerves had calmed, with the debt settled, and that she could now hold up her head in the street again instead of running out to the grocer's in the twilight, avoiding the stares and whispers. Professor Salt couldn't have known the torment his bailiffs had inflicted. He would never have allowed it.

He had finished his explanation. Moving across the stage, he disappeared into the wings. Minutes later, towards the front of the stage, a large rectangular trapdoor opened downwards. The professor's head and shoulders emerged through it.

'This way,' he said, ducking back down again. Squashing her skirts through the aperture, Lily climbed down a ladder into a hidden chamber. It was small, no more than twelve feet by ten feet, and dark, the walls lined with heavy black velvet. A low ceiling, also covered with black cloth, sloped forward; at the front of the little room was a great mirror, placed at an angle so that it leaned backwards.

'What is this place?' Lily said, uncertainly.

'This, Miss Bell, is the blue room.' Salt held up a lit candle. 'Where you will rehearse your return from the next world.'

His sister arrived down the steps, climbing awkwardly, and Lily felt her way around the perimeter, trailing her fingers over the soft, enclosing walls. Outside the bright halo cast by the flame, the darkness was stifling, so thick it seemed like solid matter. She tried to imagine performing here, concealed from the audience, invisible to them. From what she'd gathered of Erasmus Salt's explanation, she was to provide nothing more than a disembodied voice, some transient reflection of herself.

'No doubt your machine is a marvel,' she said, trying to hide her growing sense of dismay. 'But how may I play a ghost in a place where I cannot be seen?'

'Told you,' Professor Salt said, leaning towards her, his eyes gleaming. 'You will not play the ghost. You will become her.'

He left, climbing the steps out of the room, taking the light with him. The darkness deepened, and from a corner the spinster moaned. Pushing past Lily, she grasped the sides of the ladder and dragged herself up towards the glimmer of light coming from the stage. Seconds later, there was a thud overhead as if someone had dropped a sack of potatoes. Lily scrambled up the wooden ladder and saw Miss Salt in a heap on the baize, her skirts ridden up over her boots. Her face was grey and her eyes half closed, rolled back in her head. For a terrible instant, Lily thought she was dead.

'Miss Salt! Miss Salt?' She squeezed her clammy hand, patted her icy cheek, and the woman's eyes flickered. She sat up and after a minute allowed Lily to help her to her feet. Pulling her mantle around her shoulders, the professor's sister looked out at the shadowy auditorium.

'It's the dark,' she said, in a tremulous voice. 'The dark.'

Four

A hand grips his shoulder. He is deep down under the surface but the hand jerks him upwards. 'Erasmus!' That is his name. He is Erasmus. He opens one eye. At first, there's only darkness, and then he makes out his father, bent over him. Father's whiskers meet under his chin in two broad stripes; his breath is sharp and sour.

'Get up,' he says, his voice slurred. 'Come and see your mother.'

'Yes, Father.'

Scrambling out of bed, Erasmus pulls on his nightcap. He closes his mouth so he is not *gawping like an idiot*. He needs to piss but doesn't dare to use the pot.

'Hurry up.'

'Yes, Father.'

Father is in the doorway, waiting for him. He is dressed in a black jacket and a white shirt and where his bow tie should be, the collar is open, the studs unfastened.

'Hurry up, damn you,' Father says. Erasmus rubs his

eyes. He must do as he is told or Father will hurt him, hurt him in a way that Father pretends doesn't hurt, twisting his ear or tickling him too hard so he has no breath left to scream with or holding him out over the parapet of the bridge over the river as a joke. Father is like the puzzle jug in the kitchen that has three spouts and Erasmus never knows where the water will pour from; his father pours funny then serious then angry.

Father reaches out and grabs him by the wrist, pulls him along the corridor. Erasmus has to run to keep up, the boards creaking underfoot. He stumbles on a rug and Father yanks him to his bare feet, pulls him through the long drawing room at the front of the house, under the dark-browed men on the walls who could never have been boys. They pass along a hallway and through the concealed door to the servants' staircase. Up one uncarpeted flight of stairs, then another. At the very top, Father stops. Holds the lamp aloft.

The trapdoor to the roof is open. A cold wind gusts down through it and Erasmus starts to shiver, his teeth chattering. Night has entered the house; it is not held at bay by glass and curtains, walls and ceilings, it is stalking the passageway and he's breathing it in.

'Go and see your mother,' Father says, lurching on his feet, shoving Erasmus towards the iron ladder that leads to the trapdoor.

Erasmus bites his lip. He has a stitch and he's struggling not to cry. Mother's room isn't up here. He's been tricked again. He is *a little fool.*

'Go on,' Father roars. 'Get up there.'

Erasmus shrinks inside, his being turning hard and secret as an acorn. Grasping the sides of the ladder, gripping the cold bars, he gets one foot up onto the bottom rung, and begins to climb. The ladder is vertical and if he lets go he will fall off it and die, like the stable boy who fell from the hayloft. He can see nothing, can only feel the iron rods, narrow and hard on the soles of his feet. He reaches the top and crawls out on his hands and knees onto the cold, smooth lead. The moon is big and round and the slates are silver grey and silent, a city of steep-sided slopes and narrow troughs, the four great stone lions on each corner of the tower keeping watch over the kingdom of the roof. Each lion has the family motto inscribed on its plinth. *Non Omnis Moriar.* I Shall Not Wholly Die.

Father arrives, coming up the ladder and onto the roof, tearing the knee of his trousers, cursing as he gets to his feet. Grabbing Erasmus's arm, he pulls him again along a walkway. The two of them are moving fast but Erasmus sees everything clearly. The moon is hidden now behind high soft clouds that spread the light evenly, illuminating on one side the stone parapet topped with lichen, on the other the slope of a roof like a smooth, even mountain. The big, rough-edged, grey tiles are still and patient.

They cross a square section of lead to where the tower is. Look, Father says, stopping, jerking back Erasmus's head with his hands. Erasmus is looking up at the tower where the lions are but he doesn't see the lions. He sees Mother, standing on the flat roof. She's wearing a white dress, the one in the painting. Silver feathers wind around her neck and the eerie light glimmers off her dress, her shoulders and the cascade of her white-blonde ringlets, as if every part of her is made of moonlight. She is the most beautiful vision Erasmus has ever seen and he forgets to breathe.

'Here's your firstborn come to say goodbye,' Father shouts. 'Say goodbye to Mama,' he says, more quietly. Erasmus gulps cold air. It is a joke, after all. He must find it funny, mustn't be a *bloody brat*. He forces a laugh.

'Goodbye!' he calls, his voice high and shrill in his ears.

'Wave to Mama.' Father jerks his arm up into the air, gripping it too tight. Erasmus waves his arm, madly, back and forwards.

'Goodbye,' he screams. 'Goodbye, Mama.'

At the same time, Father shouts, 'Go on. If you're going to.'

Mother turns and looks down at where Erasmus is, straight at him. He stops waving. It is her turn, he is waiting for her to wave back but she takes three steps towards the very edge of the tower, slowly, one, two, up onto the parapet, and then she is flying, a silver bird with silver feathers, her wings spread, her hair streaming behind her. She plummets, downwards. Disappears. There is nothing – only the empty tower. The empty air. The roof, lit like a stage.

Erasmus woke up, his limbs rigid, jaw clenched. He lay in the darkness as the outline of a tallboy emerged, the shape of his own hat on top of it. Outside, an invisible pack of gulls screamed and scrapped and flapped. As the minutes passed, the pain in his jaw, the ache in his molars, began to ease. He was here, now. Not there, then. He would never be there, then, again. And, if his great work succeeded – not if, he reminded himself, but when – he would see his mother restored to life. *Non Omnis Moriar.*

Five

At dinner, Faye found herself sitting opposite Lily. The girl was dressed in pink taffeta, the white satin bow at the neck accentuating her unusual hair. It was white-blonde, so pale it appeared in the light of the lamp suspended over the table as if bleached by peroxide. Her eyebrows and lashes were the same.

'How does one become a ghost professor?' she said, propping her elbows on the table.

'Through years of investigation, Miss Bell. Patient study and experimentation. And consultations with others working in the field, of course.'

Faye broke a water biscuit into pieces, pressing the sharp crumbs against the damask with the tips of her fingers. It was new, this title that Ras had given himself. She wished that when he'd finished university he'd taken orders, as their father and mother would surely have wished. Become a Reverend rather than a self-appointed ghost professor. Although if anyone deserved the title, Faye supposed it was Erasmus.

'You can call me professor in that case,' said one of the other guests. 'Professor of the Racehorses.'

The man's wife and daughter laughed and Erasmus's features stiffened. Putting a glass of wine to his lips, he drank, setting it down half empty. From the side of her spoon, Faye took a sip of pea soup. Erasmus had instructed her to keep the girl away from every living soul but they'd both failed to anticipate other guests at Mrs Webb's drop-leaf dining table.

'What form of study?' Miss Bell persisted. 'How can you study ghosts?'

'Shall explain all you need to know in due course,' Erasmus said, his smile not reaching his eyes. 'Rest assured of that.'

Faye put down her spoon. 'Are you fond of the seaside, Miss Bell? Did you visit as a child?'

'Yes, Miss Salt,' Lily said, distractedly. 'When we were able.'

'I have never in my life been in a bathing machine,' volunteered the other young lady present at the table. 'I'm dying to try sea-bathing, when the weather improves.' The aspiration proved to be shared by Lily, and to Faye's relief subsequent courses of fried plaice, curried mutton and apple tarts passed in discussion of the health bene-fits of salt water and tonic air, and the risks for ladies of being observed through gentlemen's binocular glasses. Later – after Turkish coffee, cordial goodnights to the other guests, an invitation from the wife to Lily to join them for a walk the next day, which Erasmus on her behalf refused – Faye, Erasmus and Miss Bell retired to their own parlour.

A driftwood fire hissed damply in the grate and, pushing the red velvet chaise closer to the hearth, Miss Bell stared into the curls of smoke, sucking on the end of a strand of hair. Erasmus paced up and down, rattling the china in a corner cabinet. He hadn't rid himself entirely of the white dust, Faye noticed. Some remained in his hair, on the cuff of his jacket. She wondered what it was.

'We shall dine in here from now on,' he said, making a bow from the doorway. 'Your forgiveness, ladies. Work to do.'

Faye got out one of the skeins of fine white lambswool she'd bought before leaving London and enlisted Miss Bell's help to wind a ball. The actress opened a book of plays and by the light of some ill-smelling candles – piped gas had yet to reach the crescent, the landlady had complained as she ladled out the soup – Faye got out her crochet hook and with no clear purpose in mind, began to cast on.

She had returned to her childhood home only recently. Neither of the carters waiting outside the station had been willing to take her up and she'd walked from the station, struggling with the weight of her valise, barely noticing the tunnel of tall oaks through which she passed, their gnarled arms linked over her head. Beyond the deserted smithy at the crossroads, stopping for a minute to rest, she'd felt the temperature plummet, as if she'd stepped into an icehouse. As she put down her bag, she heard a cry – a choked, strangled cry that sounded like a woman's. With a sense of dread, her skin prickling, Faye looked around her.

'Who is it? Is anyone there?'

No answer came. The lane was empty ahead and behind and she heard nothing more, only birdsong, the seething quiet of grass and moss and trees, the musical trickle of an unseen stream.

It was dusk by the time she arrived at the old house. Nether Hall stood in a hollow and only the top of the tower on the east wing emerged from the low-lying mist, the lions standing proud. Passing the iron gates, continuing on down the lane, she climbed the stile and entered the grounds beyond the kitchen garden. The chalybeate spring still flowed. Cupping the rusty brown water in her palms, she drank, then made her way past the stables and towards the house, her feet silent on the sandy ground. As she approached the great studded front door, it opened. Her brother emerged and stood on the threshold, pulling on his gloves. His head was bowed, his shoulders set like a bullmastiff's.

'Erasmus!' she said, from the shadows. 'Good evening.'

'Expected you sooner,' he said, without surprise. 'Didn't you get my letter?'

Faye looked down at the boot scraper, the familiar stone threshold. 'I came as soon as I could. Why did you send for me?'

'Got a use for you. You'll help me out, I trust?'

She'd nodded, her mouth dry again. 'Of course I will.'

Her bedroom was as she'd left it but musty-smelling and cold with the particular chill of a room long un-occupied. Shaking dust from the bed curtains, prising open the window, she sat down at her old writing desk. The blotter bore traces of her own handwriting – faint, reversed, illegible. Opening the roll top, twisting the lid from an inkbottle and breathing in the familiar smell of iron and clove, Faye thought for a moment about taking up her diary-writing again. The page wouldn't condemn her and to it she could relate those things that couldn't be uttered to a living being. Getting to her feet, she screwed the lid on the bottle, flung the pen and notebooks back inside the desk and shut it with a clatter of slats.

'Forget,' she instructed herself, speaking aloud. 'Forget. Forget. Forget.'

Later that evening, Faye found Erasmus sitting alone at the dining-room table. He was hacking slices from a side of bacon, dipping his knife into a pot of yellow mustard, sandwiching the meat between doorsteps of bread. She was about to try to speak with him, find out what his purpose for her was, when the door opened and a man came in with a tray.

'Balthazar!' Faye said. 'How are you keeping?'

The man set down the tray and saluted, making a deep, groaning noise.

'Enough!' Erasmus banged his knife on the table and Balthazar left the room. Faye took two cups and saucers from the sideboard. She poured the coffee, set one down in front of her brother. The cups were the old ones, their childhood favourites, with painted pictures of grasshoppers and ladybirds around the rims. Insects they had once believed might take flight.

'Why did you send for me?' she said.

'Because I need you.'

Faye felt a rippling shudder inside of loyalty and pity and fear. Erasmus wasn't a bad man, whatever the world believed. No case against him had ever been proved. Maria Hedges had simply disappeared and Erasmus had been more concerned than anyone, leading the search party that went out scouring the woods and fields, helping to drag the lake. Nothing had been found, not even a stitch of clothing, a single shoe. It was shameful, the way the villagers had turned on him, the servants fled. All apart from poor Balthazar, who wouldn't be able to find another position.

'I can see that you need me, Ras,' she said. 'I'm back now. I will keep house for you.'

'Travelling to London,' he said, shaking his head.

'London? How long will you be away?'

'You too.'

'Me? But I have no wish to go to London.'

Erasmus put down his sandwich and stared up from his plate, not at Faye but at someone behind her. Faye knew that he surveyed the large painting on the wall

– their mother at the time of her wedding, her round breasts lifting out of her ivory gown, her face and shoulders alabaster, her distinctive white-blonde hair a mass of ringlets on each side of her face.

Throwing his napkin on the floor, her brother got up from his chair. 'We shall leave as soon as it can be arranged. Goodnight, Faye.'

Six days later, they were in the snug of the George Inn at Southwark, the small room vibrating with the roar from the public bar below. Erasmus paced three steps in either direction, glancing out of the window, checking his watch and holding it to his ear. Faye perched on a settle in the corner, underneath a poor bald canary in a cage. It was early evening and they'd left Nether Hall at dawn, Erasmus still refusing to explain where they were going or why. She'd put on her stockings inside out, she realised on the train to London; she felt inside out herself.

A man arrived in the doorway, breathing heavily, his trousers spattered with paint. The canary shrilled and fluttered its wings against the bars and Erasmus emptied his wine glass. 'Brought the money, have you? In cash?'

'For the love of God, Salt. I—'

'Professor,' Erasmus said. 'It's Professor Salt.'

The man sat down on a stool. 'Call off your thugs, will you? Been again last night, knocking the door at midnight. Neighbours all at their windows. The wife's losing her wits.'

'A debt's a debt.'

'I cannot pay,' the man said, with a flash of anger. 'You know damn well I cannot. You've had everything I've earned these last weeks. Everything I've got. What more d'you want from me?'

Erasmus drew out a leather pouch from his pocket and thudded it on the table.

'Ghost,' he said, directing his eyes to the smoke-blackened ceiling. 'Dead and buried. Brought back to life. That's what I want, Bell.'

Under her travelling dress, Faye's skin crawled.

'I don't hold with your ghosts,' Bell said. 'Never have. Keep me out of it.'

'Not you. Your daughter.'

'Daughter?'

'Got a daughter, haven't you?'

'The wife has.'

'I saw her when I had the honour of visiting your workshop last time. Unusual colouring. It was her innocent appeal that persuaded me of the necessity of making that first loan.'

Bell slumped and shook his head. 'Not a chance. The missus dotes on her.'

'I daresay you can persuade her. Inform Mrs Bell that the girl will appear on the stage. This lady –' Erasmus gestured in Faye's direction '– will act as her chaperone.'

The man shifted his gaze.

'Sorry, miss. Didn't see you sat there.'

Faye returned his nod, her face expressionless, her mind churning.

Erasmus held up the pouch and clinked the coins inside.

'Debt forgotten. Including the interest. Bailiffs called off. Twenty guineas a year in wages, paid to her father for safekeeping.'

Pulling out a furled, black-edged document, Erasmus untied a black ribbon, flattened out the paper on the table next to the purse and presented Bell with a quill. Mr Bell peered at the document.

'Forgotten?'

'Said so, didn't I?'

'Wages paid to me? In advance?'

'Deliver her here tomorrow and twenty guineas is yours.'

'All I ever wanted was opportunities for her,' Bell said, unconvincingly, scratching a signature.

In the attic room Erasmus had taken for her, Faye pushed a chair against the door. She drew the curtains mechanically, barely noticing the cries of the drunks in the street below, the thumps on the wall from the room next door. Getting into a damp bed, watching the trembling, distorted shadows cast by the nightlight, she felt a sense of dread about what new stage of his morbid preoccupations her brother was pulling her into.

Six

❧

The dolls house was three storeys tall, double-fronted, with a Mansard roof. Her father had given it to her as a birthday present, half a century ago. Inside, rich-hued Turkey carpets lay flat upon the floor, an aproned cook presided over a kitchen where an undiminishing ham dangled above the range. Milk never turned and potatoes didn't sprout; none of the inhabitants had grown old or estranged, although Cook missed an eye and Baby's rosy cheeks were chipped.

Ruth Bell removed the provisions – baskets of eggs, onions and varnished bread rolls – from the dresser and by the light of her own oil lamp, with a scrap of silk, began dusting a roasted duck. Liza used to love to play with the house. It was she who'd made the cradle from a matchbox draped with flannel, she who'd painted Baby's plaster cheeks. Putting the peaches back in the fruit bowl, Ruth stood the maid by the door with a tray in her hands and ranged the family around the dining table,

Father at one end in his carver chair, and Baby at the other in the high chair.

She missed her youngest like a limb. Born ten years after the others, the unexpected child of her later years and her only daughter, Liza was part of herself. The best part. Liza had been her baby till long after she was walking and talking, wanting to do up her own buttons. Was still her baby when at fourteen years old she began to menstruate, grew moody and insolent and declared that she should have been born to the theatre manager Madame Lucia Vestris, not Mrs Ruth Bell, then she would have had a chance of a life in the world instead of a living death between the parlour and the kitchen, running errands for her brothers. Ruth had feared for her unruly child, wanting more than it was fit for a girl to want, not understanding that she couldn't follow the paths the boys had taken that led out into the wide world. At the same time, she'd wanted to see Liza live her dreams. Walk the boards perhaps, in tasteful artistic productions. Earn her own money.

This was Liza's taste of adventure, Ruth told herself. Her hour of freedom. Salt was a cad but there was a sister to look out for her. The season would end and Liza would come home. A suitable husband would be found, grandchildren born. Liza would start to understand life differently, see things as a woman and not through the eyes of a girl. At the thought of her daughter's return, Ruth felt contentment spread through her, expanding her heart and straightening her spine.

'Life will go on,' she informed the dolls. 'She'll be back before you know it, Cook.'

Beyond the bedroom, feet pounded on the stairs, the sound followed by an urgent knocking. Jen flung open the door and almost fell through it. Latching the front of the dolls house, Ruth issued a rare reprimand.

'No need for haste, Jennifer dear.'

'Letter, missus,' Jen croaked. 'By the evening post.'

'It's from Miss Lily, I daresay. To let me know she's begun her play.' Ruth replaced the miniature boot scraper, rubbed the brass letterbox with a scrap of chamois. 'Or perhaps she's changed her mind. She's written to say she's coming home. Give me the letter!'

Jen made a strangled noise and, turning, Ruth saw the envelope edged with a thick black border, sealed with black wax. She was aware as she reached for it that she inhabited one of those moments that occur only rarely but that change everything, turn day to night, like an eclipse of the sun. Taking her paper knife from the drawer, with a shaking hand she slit open the envelope and withdrew a single sheet of notepaper also edged with black.

In his workshop at the end of the garden, Alfred Bell looked up, disturbed by the sound of an animal howling. He returned to his palette, shaking his head, troubled by the thought that some wretch was beating his dog.

Seven

The counter was strewn with half empty pots of grease-paint, rags screwed into balls, pads of dirty cotton wool and a jar of faded flowers, their petals light and dry as tissue paper. A brush, the bristles tangled with coarse dark hair, lay on the floor in one corner; by the mirror, the single gas mantle spluttered.

Balancing on the only chair, peering at herself in a spotted glass, Lily thought of the dressing room she'd imagined – a bower of violets and freesias, the walls decorated with cards from admirers, and a rosewood dressing table with separate compartments for combs, rouge and kohl, jewels, a large bottle of an exotic, musky perfume of which Ruth Bell would strictly disapprove. Her mother only permitted florals. A crash came from somewhere nearby. In the labyrinth of spaces under-neath and behind the stage, sceneshifters were cursing, hammering, calling to each other. The professor had instructed Lily to stay in the dressing room until his sister came for her, had seemed on the verge of locking her in. She had no costume yet to change into. Grabbing an old broom from the corner of the room, Lily began to sweep the floor, raising clouds of dust, sending balls of hair and fluff scurrying across the floor.

Before long, Miss Salt put her head around the door, saying the limelight was prepared. Lily dropped the broom and went with her the few yards to the blue room, entering through a curtain that concealed a gap in the wall of the velvet-lined chamber. The cramped room was as claustrophobic as it had been the first time she set foot in it, the ceiling barely clearing her head, the darkness relieved only by a couple of rush lights. She nodded at the gasman and he gurned and grunted. The gasman was the only member of the theatre crew that the professor couldn't prevent her seeing, since he oper-ated the limelight in the hidden room. Balthazar was a mute. He couldn't speak but took instructions from the professor and made himself understood through groans and gestures. He was a curious creature, his close-cut salt and pepper hair, protruding ears and low forehead rendered him both ugly and oddly compelling to look at, like a gargoyle.

The professor had at last explained to her what form the play was to take. Lily played the ghost of a bride who, to avoid a union forced on her by her family, had jumped from a high tower on the eve of her wedding day. In the cameo, she was three times summoned from beyond the grave by the ghost professor. She first appeared in the garret of her secret lover, a poet, who mourned her. The poet took her for a trickster, tried to run a dagger through her heart, but found that it left her unharmed. In the second scene, at a ball, he danced with her although his arms could not hold her. When she appeared to him by the side of her own grave, the poet was forced to recognise her as the living ghost of his own sweet love. She had not more than two dozen lines to speak, all of them addressed to her lover.

Professor Salt's ghost machine depended on reflections. In order to be seen on stage, Lily had to remain within the brilliant circle of light cast by the lime, able to move three steps forward, three back, pass a posy of flowers, receive a poem, engage in a dance, while being reflected in the tilted mirror.

In the hours of rehearsal that took place every afternoon, Lily remained in the hidden room while Professor Salt moved between the blue room, the stage and the auditorium, adjusting the angle of the mirror and the sheet of glass that was raised up invisibly at the front of the stage in order to carry her reflection. By means of coded taps on the partition, he signalled for the gasman to ignite the limelight or extinguish it. The room under the stage was alternately almost dark, or blazing with light as the lime in the corner glowed white-hot in the heat from the lit gas jets. Lily was training herself not to blink while the lime flared; when the gas was extinguished and the lime cooled, her eyes streamed in the chemical fug.

*

After a week, a male actor joined the rehearsals. From then on, while she remained in the blue room, the man rehearsed his role above her head. Occasionally, during lulls in proceedings, Lily heard footsteps moving rhythmically, light thuds on the baize, a muttered exclamation. The actor was juggling, she realised, and she felt a dart of happiness as she remembered the man on the beach, the way he'd seemed to dance all alone, the feeling he had communicated of youth and freedom. There was no call for her to meet the man who was to play her stage lover, the professor informed her; in fact, the secrecy of his technique prohibited it.

While the professor adjusted the great mirror, the sheet of glass, and called her back from the next world – in portentous tones that made her spine tingle – Lily passed the time by reciting lines of Juliet's. *My ears have not yet drunk a hundred words, of that tongue's utterance, yet I know the sound.* She had the impression that sometimes the actor ceased his juggling, and listened. Once, she was sure that she heard him lie down as if to put his ear to the baize. She spoke a little louder – *How cam'st thou hither, tell me, and wherefore?* – and heard a chuckle, a muffled knock on the boards.

'What's the name of the actor, Miss Salt?' she said that evening as they made their way back from the town to the lodgings.

'A Mr Ames.'

'Is his hair of longer than average length?'

'I suppose it is.'

'And does he pass the time juggling balls?'

'He does,' Miss Salt said, distractedly. 'And in conjuring, I believe.'

They continued, past a long low building that by the strong smell of kipper announced itself as a fish smokery, past the dim outline of a bazaar lit by a line of flaring gas lamps, the indistinct brickwork of an assembly rooms. Strains of piano music floated out and, hearing the tender notes, Lily felt a sudden wave of homesickness, not only for her mother but for life itself. Rehearsals had been going on for a fortnight, perhaps longer; she was losing track of time. Hidden away under the veil and cloak, denied any form of society, she was starting to feel like a prisoner.

'I ought at least to be allowed to meet my fellow actor,' she said. 'Don't you agree, Miss Salt?'

Taking Lily's wrist, the spinster steered her across the tramlines and they began walking up the steep hill to the west cliff, heading into the wind.

'My brother forbids your acquaintance with anybody, Miss Bell,' she said.

'Yes but why? On what grounds?'

'On the grounds that you are a ghost.'

Behind the twisted weave of the mourning crape, in the dim and lonely atmosphere it created, Lily laughed. 'I play a ghost, Miss Salt,' she said, her words half carried away by the wind. 'That is all.'

Eight

The rain was growing heavier, spattering his nose and shoulders, the backs of his hands. Tom Ames moved into the mouth of his cave in the chalk cliff. It would be illogical not to go into the sea because it was raining. He swam every day and this one would be no different. Sliding his knapsack off his shoulders, he dumped it down on the sand. His tongue was thick and his head felt stuffed with wool; he'd stayed too long in the tavern by the harbour the previous night, pouring pints of the local bitter down his throat, unaccountably moved by the sea shanties the men sang. 'Crossing the Bar' still rang in his ears.

Pulling off his shirt and trousers, leaving them on a rock, he walked naked out of the cave and into the sea, grimacing as the soles of his feet encountered stones half buried in the sand. At waist height, he launched himself face down into the water then surfaced, gulping air, and began swimming strongly and cleanly, diving through the waves, the town shrinking behind him. As the first shocking chill subsided, he turned on his back and bobbed on the salty swell, looking up at the sky, opening his mouth to catch drops of fresh rain.

He was in the town for the summer, intended to spend his time practising magic tricks, preparing himself to set off for the Continent when winter came. Tom wanted to see other countries, not from the windows of trains or stagecoaches but from the streets, performing as he went, travelling south to the warm blue Mediterranean and swimming there. He'd taken the role at the Tivoli for the ten bob a week it offered, just enough to pay his rent, keep body and soul together. In his lodgings in the street named Plains of Waterloo, he had been working his way through the magician's bible, *Hoffmann's Magic*, practising the tricks with the accompanying patter. It was necessary to be able to say one thing with the lips while doing another with the fingers. That was the conjuror's art. Alone in his room, he practised whisking handkerchiefs and coins out of his sleeves while saying aloud: 'I am on my knees, praying to God. I am eating fried plaice with salt and vinegar. I am kissing a girl.'

Tom's mind returned to the actress. He wondered again who she was. What she was. Not a ghost. He knew enough of sorcery to be sure of that. No ghost ever attended rehearsals, fancied herself to be Juliet in the lulls between repeatedly going through the words and movements, grew impatient with uttering her few lines again and again. Hearing her express undying love for him, declaring his love for her as they played their respective parts, was having a curious effect on Tom.

The previous evening, he'd accosted Salt after the rehearsal, humouring him in his mode of address.

'Professor! I should like to meet the actress.'

'Actress?' the bloke had growled, his supercilious manner momentarily forgotten. 'What actress?'

'The one that plays my dead mistress,' Tom said, coolly. 'I would like to pay my respects to her.'

'The ghost arrives from the ether,' said Salt. 'From the next world. She does not consort with humankind.'

The older man's voice was terse, his eyes bright with some strange fervour, and for a moment Tom felt his scepticism wavering. It was true that he'd never actually laid eyes on the ghost. Had only heard her voice; her laugh. He remembered the art to which he had consecrated himself, his own growing capacity to deceive with magic tricks. The thing was to fool others but not yourself. Never to pretend to yourself that sorcery was anything more than sleight of hand. If you started to believe that you could work magic, undo the natural order of things, that was the work of the devil.

'Mr Salt,' he had said, more lightly than he felt. 'You take your artifice too far.'

His toes and fingers were losing sensation. He turned and swam back towards the shore, against the ebbing tide, every stroke an effort. Putting his feet down, finding the seabed, he staggered from the water and shook himself like a wet dog, his head and heart cleared, his intention strengthened. With or without Salt's permission, he would get acquainted with the ghost.

Nine

The pungent, preservative reek of patchouli pervaded the parlour. The chest – made of dark wood inlaid with yellowed ivory, with a small silver key in the lock – stood under the bow window. Sitting by an untouched cup of tea, Faye wished she had thrown away the key. She ought to have hurled it into the lake at Nether Hall. The chest had arrived early that morning, along with the box of stage paints, and so far she had not been able to bring herself to open either.

'What's that smell?' Lily said, coming into the room, sniffing the air. She was in her wrapper still, her hair tousled, her narrow feet bare. Despite her nineteen years, she looked to Faye like a child, a tall and beautiful child, untouched by life. 'And what's this?'

Faye took a sip of her tea. 'Your costume, I believe.'

'Really?' Kneeling in front of the chest, Lily turned the key and began pulling out the contents, running the white feather boa through her fingers, exclaiming over the ivory kid gloves, the wax circlet of orange blossom.

She shook out the long swathe of veil and held it up, with a cry. A jagged rip gaped in the finely worked silk lace; red stains discoloured the border.

'It's been torn. And marked. I wonder how...'

Rising from the sewing chair, Faye snatched the veil out of her hands, stuffing it into her sewing bag. 'I will mend it, Miss Bell,' she said.

The dress was at the bottom of the chest. Lily gasped again as she unwrapped the brown paper, shook out the skirts and held the garment against her body. It was ivory silk, dainty and exquisite, the bodice narrowing to a point, the skirt full, the hem heavy with frills.

'It's beautiful,' she whispered. 'It doesn't look like a stage costume. It must have been a wedding dress. Or a ball gown. I wonder who it can have belonged to.'

The smell intruded more powerfully into the room and Faye went to the window and opened the casement, letting in a blast of cold air. 'My brother has requested I prepare you for your photograph. We have no time to waste.'

'I will go and wash.'

Once the actress had left the room, Faye pulled out the veil and examined it. A ragged, right-angled tear distorted the fine silk; vivid streaks of carmine were smeared along one border. Ringing the bell for the skivvy, Faye dispatched her to the chemists. She mended the tear as best she could and when the child returned, mixed a solution of salts of tartar and began sponging the gossamer mesh, forcing herself as she worked not to think and not to feel. Above all, not to remember. Only to concentrate on cleaning off the marks, dabbing the lace dry with a clean muslin rag, dipping it in dilute China tea to restore the ivory shade that flattered pale hair and skin better than pure white ever could.

Upstairs in the bedroom, while Faye dampened Lily's fine, silky hair and rolled it in papers, Lily explored the box of stage paints. On top was a wooden tray, divided into compartments, each holding little pots. Underneath, neatly arranged, lay a bundle of camelhair brushes; cold cream and cotton balls; a hank of coarse brown hair; a well-thumbed instruction manual with the face of a Pierrot on the cover. In silence, Lily lifted out rouge and whiting and burnt umber, twisting lids from jars and sniffing the contents, smearing powders of pearl and violet on the back of her hand.

'They've been used,' she said, after a little while, from under the stiff mass of papers. 'They've all been used before.'

Faye felt unprepared. Erasmus hadn't warned her that the costume and greasepaint were being delivered, had not instructed her as to what she should tell the girl. In the dressing-table mirror, she saw her own uneasy expression, met Lily's enquiring eyes. The two women looked at each other in the glass with a directness that Faye had tried to avoid.

'Was there was another ghost?' Lily said, suddenly. 'Before me?'

Taken by surprise, Faye for a moment could find no response.

'There was, wasn't there!' Lily cried, her face bright with curiosity. 'Who was she, Miss Salt? Where did she appear?'

Faye stared at the top of the girl's head, unrolling a paper, pretending to test whether the hair was dry. 'Nowhere. She assisted the professor with his experiments. That is all.'

'What is her name? Why didn't she take on the role? I must know all about her.'

In the mirror, two bright spots flared on Faye's cheeks. 'You ask too many questions, miss,' she said, sharply, repinning the curl. 'Close your eyes. I will apply the paint.'

Smoothing a base of white greasepaint over Lily's face and neck, Faye tried to steady her hands. She traced fine lines of black kohl along Lily's inner eyelids, adding red dots in the corners for extra emphasis and dabbed the girl's pale eyebrows with crushed pearl; she dusted her shoulders and arms with rice powder, smoothing it over her skin with a hare's foot, sending up plumes of fine, sweet-smelling powder that made Lily sneeze. Later, after pulling out the curling papers, Faye helped the actress into the gown, feeling in the bottom of the trunk for the old whalebone hook and using it to fasten the buttons that ran up the side of the close-fitting bodice.

'You are ready, Miss Bell.'

Lily went to the mirror-fronted wardrobe and stared at herself.

'Well,' she said, turning. 'Will I pass as a ghost? Do you recognise me?'

The greasepaint accentuated the girl's unusually pale skin. The dress hugged her waist, left her whitened shoulders bare, the boned bodice cupping her breasts. Her fine hair cascaded in ringlets about her shoulders. For a moment, Faye had the impression that Clara Grace had stepped down from her ornate, imprisoning frame and stood before her, warm and alive and young, her eyes shining. Involuntarily, she stepped back, knocking into the dressing table. The box of paints crashed to the floor, pots rolling over the boards, bronze and crimson and ochre spilling out. Faye knelt down, pinching them up, sweeping the floor with her bare hands, securing the lids.

'It's time to go, Miss Bell,' she said, standing up and rinsing her fingers in the ewer, the water turning a dark, rusty red. 'My brother will be waiting.'

Faye led Lily through the maze of narrow streets that formed the old town, past groups of men drinking outside taverns in the late afternoon sun, shopkeepers calling out reduced prices for cabbages, a boat builder patching a hull from a cauldron of pitch. Lily was silent, but from underneath the cloak the dress made an insistent, rustling whisper, emitted a musky, wafting cloud. Passersby dipped their heads in condolence, wrinkled their noses at the drifting odour.

A closed sign dangled in the window of the photography studio but Erasmus was inside, waiting for them. He unlatched the door and let them in, glancing at Lily's shrouded figure, addressing Faye.

'In costume?' he said.

'Yes.'

'Face painted?'

Faye nodded, mutely, and they followed him to a studio at the back of the premises, a long, empty room with one glass wall shaded by canvas blinds. At the far end of the studio, under a section of glass roof, was a backcloth of painted ferns sprouting from a painted stone wall, ivy clambering around crumbling pillars. A man in shirtsleeves stepped out from a wooden cabin, wiping his hands on an apron.

'Good evening...' he began.

'As we agreed,' said Erasmus. 'No assistants. No display in your window or signature on the print. No discussion with anybody.'

'Understood, sir,' said the photographer, adjusting one leg of a tripod that supported a large wooden camera. 'It won't be the first picture my clients have not wished to make public.'

He gave a wolfish wink and Erasmus gave in return a humourless stare.

'It'll be made public all right,' he said. 'It'll be all over. But if anyone asks, you will know nothing of where it came from.'

At the other end of the room, next to a display of

photographs of the dead entombed in flowers, Faye helped Lily out of the cloak and bonnet. Unbuttoning her boots, she laced the narrow silk slippers onto the girl's feet, eased the ivory kid gloves up past Lily's elbows and arranged a pearl choker at her throat. Miss Bell shook her head of newly curled hair, lifting the crinkled platinum mass and allowing it to fall on her bare shoulders.

'Well, Professor,' she called, sending her voice down the length of the studio, stretching her arms out before her as she walked towards him. 'Do I look the part? Your sister seems to believe I do.'

Erasmus turned. He opened his mouth, and closed it. Nodded. Raised his hands and let them fall. Then, stiffly, he bowed.

'Most effective,' he said, his voice a croak.

Lily made a mock curtsey. Glancing at the painted raven perched on top of the painted wall, she glided over to it in the careful steps demanded by the soft, flat slippers and positioned herself in front of the canvas. Erasmus stared at her, as if transfixed.

'Am I broken-hearted, Professor, because I am no longer of this world?' Miss Bell was saying. 'Ecstatic, because I'm returned? What mood shall I portray?'

The photographer ducked out from under his black cloth.

'The plate will spoil. We must proceed.'

Erasmus indicated a spot slightly further along the backcloth but gave no further instructions. Lily Bell didn't appear to need them. The actress faced the camera, her body half turned from it, her face beatific, her expression neither sad nor joyous but wistful, the eyes not those of a young woman but of an eternal soul. Faye leaned on the wall, unable suddenly to support herself, experiencing a sickening sense of *déjà-vu*.

'Yes,' came the muffled voice of the photographer. 'That's it. Hold still, miss.'

Ten

The auditorium was in near darkness. For the dress rehearsal, Erasmus had positioned himself where he could both see the ghost and signal to the gasman, in the centre of the front row seats at the New Tivoli. At his cue, the red plush curtain was winched up, the house lights dimmed further and the stage lights – a row of footlights on each side and a gas chandelier over the centre of it – went up, revealing a young man attired in black breeches and an old-fashioned, bell-sleeved white shirt. His feet were bare, his expression sombre.

Tom Ames walked forward so that he stood upstage, facing the empty seats. He played a man in mourning, a wide black band tied around his upper left arm, his forehead lined with charcoal, his cheeks made hollow with blue shading, long hair powdered grey. No powder or paint could disguise his upright bearing and air of strength, the frankness of his face.

'I love a maiden,' Tom pronounced. 'A maiden lost to me.' He looked around, as if searching for her in the stalls, the gallery, the private boxes, and crossed his hands over his heart. 'I would give my very life to see her. I will pen a poem to her beauty.'

Moving to the back of the stage, the actor sat at a desk in front of a backcloth depicting a garret, patches of plaster falling off to reveal the lathes beneath, the grate empty and the glass in the dormer window cracked from side to side. Through the window, a silvery half moon hung in a star-stained sky. Writing at speed, sighing all the while, the man threw down his quill and tore up the paper, throwing the scraps in the air. He dashed his hand against his brow.

'Words are not enough. There is no comfort in this world for me and I must go, this very night, to that bourne from which no traveller returns.'

For a conjuror, his acting was adequate, Erasmus thought again. The fellow gave every impression of anguish. Opening a drawer in the desk, Tom pulled out a dagger. 'I cannot live,' he called, raising his arm to its furthest extent. 'Without her.'

As the stricken poet was about to dash the knife into his heart, Erasmus rose to his feet and gave a light tap with his cane. 'I summon the ghost,' he intoned, slowly, his voice grave and respectful, his concentration absolute. 'To return from the next world. To make herself apparent.' The stage lights dimmed and a moment later, in a blaze of light, a woman appeared in the garret. She was a slim, straight figure in a low ivory gown, her head bowed, face concealed behind a fall of lace. Every hair on Erasmus's body bristled and rose. He neglected to check the plane of her feet, her position in relation to the actor, their relative levels of illumination. All he could do was absorb the vision, his flesh tingling, his senses confused.

'Who is this that would have sport with my grief?' cried the actor. Raising his arm, he plunged the dagger into the woman. The blade passed through her without resistance and the ghost took a step forward, lifting the veil from her face. The poet dropped to his knees, the knife slipping from his hand. 'Have I died?' he cried. 'Or do I dream? Is it I who have come to you? Or have you returned to me? Whichever it is, I thank God for it. We shall never be parted again.'

The swain got to his feet and as he moved to take the ghost into his arms, Erasmus gave another tap on the partition under the stage. The footlights on the stage brightened and, as mysteriously as she had appeared, the beautiful creature vanished. She did not walk into the wings, was not lifted aloft by means of imperfectly concealed wires nor lowered by a trapdoor. She simply was present, and then not present.

The young man looked around in bewilderment. 'Where are you? Must you play tricks with me? Come back.'

He rubbed his eyes. Slapped his face with both hands and dashed a glass of water on his head. Despite the impression he gave, from where he stood at the back of the stage, Tom Ames couldn't see the ghost. Neither of the two could see the other. Only the audience could see both of them, the actor on the stage and the ghost perfectly reflected in the tilted sheet of polished glass, the glass concealed by its cleanliness, the dim stage lighting. The youth would never see his supposed love. Nor would Miss Bell see the actor. Erasmus had prohibited their meeting. The ghost was his and his alone.

Ames kneeled in prayer and at a further signal from Erasmus, the curtain fell. In minutes, the sceneshifters hauled in a different backcloth, altered the props on stage to represent a ballroom. The poet in the second act was at a dance, spurning the living, and drinking alone in a secluded alcove when at Erasmus's call the ghost appeared for a second time, unveiled, her slender neck roped in pearls, her hair gleaming white. Her face was oval and her lips reddened, her eyes dark pools; she was pure radiant spirit, sharply beautiful, a woman made of light, the gown draped gracefully against her slender body. Now, she held in her hands a bunch of white roses. Lifting them, she appeared to drink in their fragrance. Her satin-shod feet took three light steps towards her lover and she held out the bouquet. 'Accept these as a token of my love.'

Erasmus watched as the youth raised his head, reached out his hand and gave every impression of taking the flowers directly from the ghost's fingers. He handled the trickery adroitly, had the ability to conjure flowers given to him by the ghost from his baggy sleeves, return confetti into whole sheets of paper. The co-ordination between the two was remarkable, appeared effortless. Tom raised the blooms to his nose and looked up again, seeming to see the ghostly bride. 'These flowers are proof that you live.' He sprang to his feet, speaking in an intimate, unaffected tone. 'Touch me, beloved. If you are alive, let me feel your warmth.' The ghost's face softened in tenderness; the impression of thwarted lovers was utterly convincing.

Erasmus tightened his fists, bent forward in his seat as the poet reached for his lover's hand and found himself again unable to touch her. The ghost smiled sadly. 'I do not live,' she said. 'Not as you mortals live. When I am gone, forget me not.'

Erasmus tapped on the board. Her radiance softened and dimmed, her entire and perfect being seemed to fade and she vanished into the ether. Dropping the flowers, Tom Ames reached into the space where she had been, examined his empty hands. He picked up the posy and cradled it. 'She came to me. She gave me these roses.' He turned to the stalls, to the imagined occupants of the boxes. 'You saw her, didn't you?'

In the third act, the curtain rose to display a lonely churchyard where the poet mourned beside a newly dug grave, against a backdrop of stark, leafless trees, their branches black veins against a violet sky. Rising to his feet, tapping his stick on the partition that comprised the front of the hidden room, Erasmus commanded the spirit to return. 'Come to us if you will, o fair one,' he chanted, in the rhythms of prayer. 'Pull aside the veil and pass from that world to this.' Within seconds, the figure took shape again – fainter now, standing at a distance from the mortal, holding out her hands as if her sorrow was greater than any human grief. Erasmus felt a charge run through his heart and his groin; he saw her afresh, with a renewed shock, this otherworldly female, this vision of womanhood.

The youth groaned. 'Never leave me again. By all the saints, I implore you.'

'I must leave you.'

'I wrote you this poem,' said Tom Ames. 'That you will never read.'

He gestured towards the litter of torn scraps on the ground and a sheet of white paper appeared whole in the ghost's hand.

'Goodbye, my love! Farewell. We will meet again in a better place.' Her voice was high, sweet, and it was impossible to say quite where it came from although it synchronised perfectly with the movement of her lips. She lifted her hand in a half-wave and was gone. Moments later, her despairing lover picked up the knife and dashed it into his chest. With blood spurting from a sausage skin pinned inside his shirt, he fell lifeless on her grave. The stage lights dimmed, the curtain fell and the house lights went up, revealing the dingy walls of the auditorium, the scuffed matting along the gangway.

Erasmus couldn't move. He stood motionless, con-sumed by a sharp excitement, the ghost imprinted on his retinas, on every sinew of his body, and somewhere deeper that felt like his soul.

'Everything satisfactory, Prof?' said the actor, emerging from the wings, shaking flour from his hair, untying the black band from his arm, his breast glistening scarlet.

Breathing in the pall of spent gasses, Erasmus could only nod.

He'd been standing at the library window in the gloom of a November afternoon when he first noticed Maria Hedges. She was walking away from the house, a little black hat on her head, her hair a pale river flowing down the back of her shawl. The image fixed itself in his mind like a photographic negative and refused to fade.

Erasmus had seen the girl knocking around the village since she was a kid. She was one of the Hedges tribe, had a dozen or more brothers and sisters, was distinguished from the rest only by her colouring. Like a white rabbit, Birdie had sniffed, when she took her on as a scullery maid. And as for her manners... A week or two afterwards, unable to rid himself of the image, he sent for her. She'd stood in front of him in the library, clasping raw hands too large for her wrists, her hair bundled up in a mobcap. She hadn't looked down at the wide oak floorboards, or even at him. She'd stared around her, at the gallery filled with shelves of leather-bound books, the apparatus at the far end of the long room, the desk piled with instruments and papers. The great mirror.

'Mrs Bird said you worked in here,' she said. 'Is this what you call work?'

'Yes. It is.'

He must have her for the ghost, he understood in that moment when he realised that she might refuse. Only she would be right. Look right. 'I need a woman,' he had said. 'I'm conducting an experiment.'

'I'll think about it. What do you want me to do?'

'Dress in costume. And appear in the ghost machine. I'll pay you, of course.'

'Like I said, sir. I'll think about it.'

And before he had a chance to dismiss her, she'd walked out of the room, leaving the door open.

Faye didn't come down for dinner that evening. He'd dined alone, under the gaze of the portrait of Clara Grace Pepper that hung still, would always hang while he lived, on the wall at the far end of the dining room. Till the day he died, Erasmus's father had maintained the pretence that their mother might one day walk through the door. Erasmus had maintained it too. He'd intended after Father died to tell Faye the truth. But the moment had passed – from being too soon to too late. He had missed it.

Erasmus escorted the women back to the lodgings and went out again. It was high water, the ships risen up with the tide, the air filled with the eerie and discordant sounds of a ghostly orchestra. Riggings thrummed and snapped in the wind; masts creaked; ropes strained at their moorings. A gang of smack boys roamed around, half drowned by oversized ragged jackets, calling after him for farthings. Erasmus ignored them, passing the locked door of the sailors' church and walking swiftly along the quayside.

A little way inland, in an alley too narrow for coaches, he found what he knew he would find: a dwelling with its porch illuminated by a lamp with a red shade, its door standing open. Entering the hallway, he passed a pair of sailors, one still buttoning his bellbottoms. The air was still and thick, scented with penny whiffs. A bawd clad in a violent shade of green emerged from a back room.

'Evening, sir,' she said. 'I don't believe we've—'

'Pale hair,' he said. 'Pale skin.'

'I've got just the girl. Came in from the country just a couple of days ago—'

'What price?'

'Three bob,' she said, her tone markedly rougher.

Erasmus dug in his pocket, found a half crown and a sixpence, and handed them over. The woman led him along a passageway lit by candles guttering in their sconces, up a flight of greasy stairs. Stumbling on a rotten floorboard, he almost fell through the door she pushed open. Inside, surrounded by flowered paper peeling from the walls, a girl sat on a low bed. Her hair was bleached, her complexion green. She wore a pink dress, her neck and the tops of her little breasts exposed.

'Name of Abigail,' the woman said as the girl crossed her hands over her chest. 'Only sixteen and just arrived—'

'That's enough,' said Erasmus.

'Half an hour.'

The bawd banged the door behind her. Erasmus fumbled to get off his coat. Now he was here, he wished he was not. Wanted only to get it over with. 'Lie down.'

He extinguished the lamp and saw only the vision in his own mind as, pushing the girl onto her back on the bed, he raised her short skirts, parted her thighs and, dragging his lazy member from inside his trousers, thrust into her. He climaxed quickly and unsatisfactorily, sickened in equal measure by the stench of cheap scent, his own abnormal compulsions.

Eleven

There were half a dozen in a row, newly appeared on the wall of the assembly rooms, glue still dribbling down the brickwork. Lily crossed the road to look at the posters. Each bore the same engraving in black and white – a woman's face, her eyes and lips accentuated, ivy leaves curling over stones behind her head. It was Lily but not Lily. Like her but not her. 'Look, Miss Salt!' Throwing back the veil, she began to read the Gothic type printed underneath.

A maiden lately of this world who returns at the
summons of the ghost professor
Lily Elizabeth Bell
September 1831–March 1851
Slipped from a Cliff
RIP

The spinster had arrived beside her.

'It says I'm dead,' Lily said, slowly. 'That I fell from a cliff. He's used my name.'

Faye Salt peered at the poster. Grasped the locket at her neck.

'It must be necessary for the illusion,' she said, after a while. 'He would not have done it otherwise. We shall miss supper.'

Lily pulled the veil back over her face and they returned to the crescent in silence, Lily stumbling on kerbs, refusing to take the spinster's arm.

'I saw the poster,' she blurted out at dinner, over the soup. She had meant to wait till later, meant to make a measured and professional complaint, request that Salt remove her name from the advertisements. Instead, she felt on the verge of weeping with rage and shock.

'It would be difficult not to see them,' the professor said, pleasantly. 'Since they are all over the town.'

'It says I'm dead.'

'All ghosts are dead, Miss Bell. Are they not?'

'Yes, but you've used my name. My real name.'

'Whose else could I use?'

He looked at her fixedly and Lily felt as she had in the hired coach when they left London, suddenly afraid, as if she ought to flee. Mrs Webb came in with a pie and the professor's sister began remarking on the warm weather. Lily got through a few spoons of sorrel soup, its bitter taste catching in her throat. Everyone must die. She knew that she too must die, but her future, its unknown contours and trajectory, had always felt limitless, as if time had begun with her, had slowed for her, and for her would stand still in a way that it had failed to do for others. At the sight of the two dates, the measure of her life taken, some innocence had perished.

Later, sitting on the high bed, swinging her legs, the soles of her feet brushing the flattened scrap of sheepskin on the floor, Lily wondered if she had overreacted. This was an experience, of the kind that people who had been much in the world had many to recount, and she until now had had none. The show opened to the public the following night. If it proved popular, it might run for the season. In the future, when she was established in her career, she would give interviews in which she recalled playing the part of a ghost, in a fashionable resort by the name of Ramsgate, and how the advertisements had described her as *lately of this world*. The journalist would ask if she had felt perfectly comfortable with that description. 'Oh no,' she would smile. 'It was a dreadful thing to see my life cut short in that way. But an actress must sacrifice for her craft.' She had a sudden odd feeling of wanting to discuss the poster with Mr Ames, to let him know that she was not dead but alive and young and warm-blooded. That she would like to dance on the beach with him, to take her bow next to him on the stage. To live, freely and fully, as she might have done if she'd been born a man.

Moving to the washstand, she began brushing her teeth. After supper, the professor had offered her a guinea, remarking that since her father – stepfather, Lily had corrected him – was taking her wages for safekeeping, she was doubtless in need of pin money. Reaching out her hand for the coin, she'd felt humiliated. She had expected wages, and the power that went with them; had planned to send the money direct to her mother. If Mr Bell got his hands on it, it would disappear into the pockets of the cardsharps.

Rinsing out her mouth, she spat into the ewer. Her life hadn't ended, she reminded herself. It was only just beginning. Kneeling by the bed, she prayed briefly and fiercely that the cameo would be well received, that she wouldn't disgrace herself by forgetting her lines or confusing the actions. That one day Ruth Bell would sit in a box in a West End theatre, in a bracelet bought for her by Lily to match her opal ring, watch her playing Juliet under the direction of Madame Vestris, and be proud of her daughter. *Amen.*

She got into bed and, curled up under the weight of blankets, felt a tear slide down her cheek onto the pillow. Her mother hadn't written. Lily missed her more than she'd expected. Missed talking to her at the kitchen table about her hopes, her fears, almost anything that came into her head, while Ruth Bell shelled peas or kneaded dough, nodding and murmuring, saying little. Missed the touch of her hands; the scent that hung about her of lye and lavender; the sound of her tuneless singing. Most of all, she missed some deep, wordless familiarity, a comfort that she hadn't even known that her mother provided until it was lacking.

The spinster was brushing her hair for bed. She'd seemed uneasy all through supper but had kept quiet on the subject of the poster. It was obvious that she cared only for obeying her brother's orders. Almost as if she feared him.

'Was the professor's first ghost ever described as dead?' Lily said, sitting up.

Faye put down her brush. 'Why do you ask?'

'I wondered, that's all.'

Faye moved her head in an inconclusive gesture then, as every night, opened the locket she wore around her neck on a silver chain and kissed the picture inside it. 'She disappeared,' she said, quietly, fastening the catch again. 'No trace was ever found but they never said she was dead. Goodnight, Miss Bell.' She put out the oil lamp, leaving only the smell of the smoking wick, the glow of the nightlight she insisted on.

Lily lay on her back with her eyes open, wondering what could have befallen the woman, where she had gone, and why. She felt oddly close to her, as if even though she knew nothing about her, not even her name, they were in some way intimate. She wondered if the first ghost had been shut away from the world, and if she had had to get used to it, as Lily had. It was a terrible failing in human beings, that they could grow accustomed to even the most unsatisfactory of circumstances. But perhaps the first ghost had refused to wear the cloak and veil. Had rebelled and run away.

Throwing back the candlewick bedspread, silently

opening the catch of the French windows, Lily stepped out onto the balcony. It was made of wrought iron, had a curved awning over the top of it, and was just deep enough to hold two little chairs, a small table. She'd wanted since they first arrived to sit out there, feel the spring sunshine on her skin, crane her neck for a glimpse of the sea beyond the chimney pots, but Miss Salt always refused. 'You might be seen … The professor insists …'

She wouldn't be seen now. Apart from a tomcat yowling somewhere nearby, the crescent was deserted. Resting her hands on the balustrade, she breathed in the rank, honest smell of salt and seaweed, her loose hair moving in the breeze. Between drifts of charcoal clouds, the moon shone, almost full, the face in it clearly visible in three-quarter view, the expression benign and wise. Since she was small, Lily had thought it looked more like a woman than a man, a kind and ancient woman observing the follies of the world. In the distance, the sea roared and murmured in its ceaseless monologue.

The following night would be the first public performance for Mr Ames as well as herself. She wondered if he too felt nervous. They'd still never met but they had begun exchanging a few words through the trapdoor, in those rare moments when both the professor and his sister were out of earshot. Mr Ames made Lily laugh; he was irreverent about Salt who he said would surely dissolve in a shower of rain, if he went out without his cloth umbrella. Even ghosts needed a breath of sea air, he said. A scoop of ice cream. Did she have any ghost friends to take a walk with on a Sunday afternoon? If not, a mere mortal by the name of Tom Ames was at her service. Lily had wanted to explain that she was virtually a prisoner, but her pride had prevented it. She had a whole host of spirit friends, she'd said, thanking him kindly. Couldn't he hear them chattering?

A dustbin lid clattered to the cobbles in the street below. Glancing down, Lily saw a figure on the other side of the crescent, caught a glimpse of a face, a white shirt. It must be Mr Ames, come to wish her luck. A rush of pleasure ran through her and she leaned forward, raised her hand in a wave – and realised that it was Professor Salt that stood below, looking up at her on the balcony. For a long moment, neither of them moved. Lily turned and stepped back into the room, closing the window behind her.

Twelve

The musicians began tuning their fiddles, discordant sounds rending the air, and Miss Salt left the blue room, slipping out through the place where the dark velvet hangings overlapped. A procession of feet tramped by on the other side of the partition and as the New Tivoli filled up, Lily's legs began to shake. She'd imagined stage fright to be a glamorous, almost pleasant sensation, not this sickening sense of fear. She had a feeling of standing naked, as if not just her body but her most private, hidden self was about to be exposed to strangers. In the near dark, she ran her hands over her breasts and waist and hips, reassured herself that she was clothed, that the gown covered her.

A low groan came from the corner. Balthazar positioned his inflated bags of gas and a minute later extinguished the rush light. Darkness filled the room. The music died away and feet thudded over the boards above Lily's head.

'Ladies and gentlemen! Welcome to an entertainment

that is unique, a spectacle that will fill you with wonder, that you will never forget for as long as you live.' It was Mr Pendragon, manager of the New Tivoli. 'Not to be found anywhere else in the town of Rams-git, in the county of Kent, the country of England.' With each of his hyperbolic claims, the answering roar from the audience grew louder. 'Not to be found anywhere else in this whole, wide world. Tonight, you will witness a ghost, the ghost of Miss Lily Bell, a maiden summoned here from the next world by the extraordinary, unearthly powers of the ghost professor.' The crowd stamped their feet, banged the arms of their seats, and Lily couldn't be sure if they cheered or jeered.

'One fact distinguishes this lady from all others. Any man may for a small consideration look upon her.' The impresario paused as a single violin note pierced the air, built to a crescendo then abruptly ceased. 'But no man may possess her.'

A deep, male roar went up, penetrated by a shrill female voice. 'I'd like to see them try.'

In the dark, Lily's face burned. The footsteps pounded back again towards the wings, a squeaking pulley raised the curtain and the audience quietened. A different pair of feet crossed the stage, the actor's step light and sure. Silently, the gasman inched down the wide trapdoor, glimmers from the footlights spilling down into the blue room. Tom Ames's voice grew more distinct. 'I would give my life to see her face once more.' It was the cue. At a knock from the professor, Balthazar ignited the second gas jet. As the lime began to glow, Salt's sombre voice rang out from the side of the stage. 'Lily Bell,' he said. 'You will now pass from your world to ours. Step through that unbreached veil, we beseech you. Come back to us.' The lime grew bright and hot, and the silence in the auditorium gave way to a great collective gasp, to cries of delight and horror. Standing in the pool of dazzling light, blinded by it, Lily knew that she appeared to the audience, that although she could not see them, they were watching.

At that very moment, for the first time, the ghost seemed to enter her being. Hearing the poet's voice, imagining him in front of her, Lily became his love, separated from him by the cruellest of distances, yearning for him. She wasn't herself but the ghost of Lily Bell, returning to a man she loved. For the count of sixty, she stood without moving, the trembling that had afflicted her from her fingertips to her feet transformed to an unearthly stillness. She remained composed as on stage, her lover ran the dagger through her image, women screaming to see it. Lily lifted her bridal veil and, at another tapped signal, the gasman extinguished the jets. The lime cooled, the light in the blue room faded and as the curtain fell on stage, the violinists resumed.

Faye Salt hurried in with a candle, dabbing at Lily's forehead with a sponge, offering water. Lily looked at her, confused, barely recognising the woman. In the next scene, appearing on the balcony of the ballroom, speaking to the poet of her love for him, she offered him the bouquet that she had been destined never to carry down the aisle. When after the second interval the professor called her back to earth for a third time, Lily danced with her unseen partner by the side of her own grave. She was shaking again, not from fright but from the sorrow of parting from her beloved, so deeply felt that she could barely utter her lines.

'I must leave you now, though I would stay. Farewell.'

'Not farewell,' he cried, his anguish sounding as true and deeply felt as hers. 'I cannot live without you.'

Before she knew it, the performance was over. The gasman extinguished the jets and brought down the light; the sheet of glass that had been at the front of the stage was lowered into the blue room; the trapdoor closed. As the curtain fell for the last time, Lily stood in the darkness absorbing the roars and shouts and sobs that echoed through the theatre. Her back ached, her eyes stung and she perspired in the stifling heat. She felt alive, more alive than she had known was possible. The peculiarity of being described as dead, the constrictions of her life with the professor and his sister, fell away and Lily felt whole and free and true, as if at last she was fulfilling her purpose on this earth.

Beyond the encircling arms of the harbour, the moon cast a broad, silvery path across the sea. Lily and Miss Salt walked along the quayside a few yards behind the professor, their footsteps on the old stones accompanied by the soft lap of water on the hulls of the fishing boats, the rustle of Lily's costume. The newly built lighthouse on the end of the harbour wall was lit, the flashing light signalling to sailors that the harbour was at sufficient depth to be navigable if they had need to take shelter from storms out at sea. Mrs Webb had told them about the area of treacherous, hidden sandbanks known as the ship swallower, where hundreds of men had perished. Told them too about the belief of the local people that the gulls carried the souls of drowned sailors, gave voice to their mournful cries for home.

'*Perfugium Miseris,*' Miss Salt said.

'Pardon?'

'It's the inscription on the lighthouse,' the spinster said. 'Refuge of the Troubled.'

It was after one in the morning. A crowd had gathered outside the Tivoli, demanding to know how the ghost would leave, where she intended to pass the night. Mr Pendragon had tried and failed to disperse them; Professor Salt said they would wait until the ruffians grew tired of their sport. Faye had tried to persuade Lily to change at the theatre – urging her to get out of the costume, remove the stage paint – but Lily had felt overwrought, reluctant to be returned so soon to her normal state.

At the lodgings, in the hallway, Lily threw back the veil and pulled off the bonnet. Shrugging the cloak from her shoulders, she caught sight of herself in the hall mirror – her lips full and red with carmine, brows white with crushed pearl, cheeks blanched. She looked unnatural as a china doll, and had an odd sensation of not recognising herself. She'd used lampblack and flour, in the childish games she used to play. Brick dust for rouge. Ruth Bell disapproved of cosmetics.

In the parlour, Faye lit the lamp. The professor lifted the cover from a plate of cold boiled beef. Rolling up a slice of pink-tinged meat, he put it in his mouth. He'd still made no comment on Lily's performance. Judging from the reaction of the audience, and her own assessment, it had gone well. But perhaps it had flopped. She sat down on the chaise and fanned herself as Erasmus Salt took the stopper from the decanter.

'Glass of wine, Miss Bell?'

'Thank you.' She had never tasted wine until she arrived in Ramsgate. Professor Salt had suggested she take a glass after rehearsals, to relax her, and she'd discovered she liked it. Enjoyed the sour, dry taste on her tongue and in her throat.

'I'll take a glass myself,' Miss Salt said, from the other side of the room.

'Go to bed, Faye.'

'I'll wait until Miss Bell is ready.'

'No need.' The professor handed Lily the wine. Lifted his own glass.

'I must congratulate you. The ghost was—' He cleared his throat. 'A vision. Incomparable.'

'Thank you, Professor.'

Lily took a sip of the wine, trying to hide her pleasure. He drew a chair closer to the chaise where she sat.

'You said you wished to speak to me.'

'Yes.' During rehearsals, Lily had tried to discuss with him ideas she had for how the cameo could be improved but the professor had made it clear that her opinions weren't of interest and after a week or two she'd stopped trying to venture them.

'Now is your chance,' he said, his voice oddly constricted. 'Begin.'

Lily took another mouthful of wine. 'It's only my opinion, Professor Salt, but I think that the cameo is too short. It should be extended, the ghost's role expanded. She might appear first as a living woman, on the stage in the normal way, with her –' she blushed under the paint '– her lover. Acting their times together. Then we could see her take her life, tragically, on the eve of her wedding. In the third act, she would appear as a ghost. She could talk to him, explain to him why she had come back, how she sorrowed to see him in despair. Describe her life in the heavenly realms. The audience would see her both as a living woman and as a spectre.'

Professor Salt said nothing, his eyes bright. On the other side of the room, Faye still stood in the doorway. 'You are fatigued, Miss Bell,' she said, when Lily paused for breath. 'Let us retire.'

'I am not in the least tired, Miss Salt. I couldn't sleep if I tried.'

'Go to bed, Faye,' the professor repeated. 'You were saying…'

He was looking at her, almost hungrily, as if at last he began to recognise her worth and respect her art.

'Goodnight, Erasmus. Goodnight, Miss Bell.'

Her glass, that she'd thought was empty, was full again. Lily picked it up and drank, put it down unsteadily, spilling a few drops. Feeling her head begin to spin, she leaned back on the chaise and the professor reached out and grasped a handful of her hair, his fingers brushing the skin of her neck. 'Go on,' he said, withdrawing his hand. Lily glanced at the door. She ought not to be alone with a man, even one as old as the professor. She must go upstairs to bed. As soon as she had expressed her views, breaking another of Ruth Bell's rules for female conduct, she would do so.

'You see, Professor, the ghost and her lover –' the word slipped easily now from her tongue '– I thought they could be more like Romeo and—'

Sunlight fell into the room in a broad, harsh stripe. Confused, uncertain of where she was, Lily looked at the golden stars that patterned the walls. Her head was pounding and her mouth dry. She could hear Faye, the crochet hook clicking rhythmically against the buttons of her cuff. The spinster must be dressed.

'What time is it?' Lily said, without looking up.

'Past ten. You must have come up late.'

Lily pulled the sheet over her shoulders. She had

the sense that something was awry. Worse than awry, as if something dreadful had occurred. Her head felt thick and slow. She replayed the events of the previous evening, saw herself returning from the New Tivoli still in costume, accepting a glass of wine from the professor, feeling its emboldening warmth spread into her veins. She had been talking about the play, demonstrating to him what the ghost might do if she appeared on stage in the usual way, suggesting lines she might speak, finding him willing to consider what she had to say. Professor Salt had commended her acting, she remembered. Said her performance was sublime, her appearance perfect and no one but she could ever be his ghost. 'Play her,' she'd corrected him. 'Play your ghost.'

The wine had eased her sore throat. It had made her feel happy. She'd enquired about Mr Ames, longing to know more about him. 'Tom Ames?' he had said. 'A magician with no particular talent.' Actors were two a penny, the professor explained but she, Lily Bell, was destined for greatness. For the history books. She was his ghost, he'd said again. Did she understand what that meant?

'I shall not always play a ghost. In future, I want—'

The sensation returned to her of the press of lips on her lips. The abrasion of whiskers. A tongue searching her mouth. Lily felt her lips with her fingertips. The skin was raised and rough. Sore. Closing her eyes, she saw herself lying down on the chaise, announcing that she couldn't climb the stairs, was too tired to remove the costume, and would sleep there. Accepting another glass of wine and feeling paralysed as the professor undid her hair from its pins, ran his fingers through it. He had kneeled before her, lifted the skirts of the costume and, almost before she'd known what was happening, as if her mind couldn't keep pace with her body – she'd felt an intimate and painful intrusion. Something that could not be happening, that it was impossible should be happening, but that was happening. She'd been in shock, befuddled by wine, pinned down by the weight of his body, silenced by the iron fingers clamped over her mouth.

Chair legs squeaked on the floor. 'I'm going downstairs,' Faye Salt said. 'I'll get a fresh pot of tea made.'

As the spinster closed the door behind her, Lily threw off the bedclothes. She was dreaming. This was a nightmare from which she would wake. Tearing off her chemise, her drawers, she examined her body, running her hands over her skin. It was as usual, her breasts untroubled, stomach flat between jutting hip bones, the dark triangle beneath unaltered. There were no marks. Only a rawness at the centre of her. Stickiness on her thighs and a numbness in her being. Grabbing the flannel, she touched it between her legs and examined the cloth. A red tinge appeared, spreading slowly, turning the white cotton pink.

Lily heard moaning and realised it came from herself. She was alive but might as well not be. Her life was over. Everything, every dream she ever had, all the good in her that had been or that might ever be, was finished. She was ruined. And it was her own fault. Pulling on her petticoats, her summer dress, sticking her own straw hat on her head, she ran down the stairs and out of the house.

Thirteen

The water was populated by small, transparent jellyfish that were making his skin sting and smart. Tom waded out over the sand, into the cave he thought of as his own. He'd made his mark here when he first came to the seaside town, carving his initials into the chalk, aware that it was the most basic mark a man might make in the world – but a mark nonetheless.

Standing in the entrance to the cave, he saw a woman further along the shore. She was at the water's edge, looking out to sea, as if she might walk fully clothed into the waves, might strike out over the limpid surface, heading for the cliffs that shimmered on the horizon. It was irrational but Tom felt sure the lonely figure was Miss Bell. Dragging his breeches over his damp skin, pulling on his shirt, he walked towards her, throwing his wet hair back off his face as he went, wondering why she was out on her own, thinking of a way he could approach her without insulting her. At a distance of five yards, he stopped, raising his voice over the sound of the water and wind.

'Miss Bell? Is it you? Out for a breath of sea air?'

She didn't look round. She was crying, he realised, her breath coming in gulps, her frame heaving.

'Is something the matter?'

She shook her head.

'I've longed to meet you,' Tom said. 'I approached Salt but—'

Hearing the man's name, she shuddered and covered her face with her hands. Tom fought the urge to move closer, put his arms round her, comfort her. Find out who'd hurt her and punch their lights out. 'What's happened to you? Has Salt mistreated you?'

'I'm not meant to be here,' she said, wiping her eyes on her sleeve.

'I'll do anything I can to help you,' Tom said. 'If you wish it, that is.'

From far away, a female voice called. A tiny figure was coming down the zigzagging steps, moving fast. Miss Bell turned to Tom. Her eyes were red, her face bruised-looking, but he thrilled to see the clear gaze, the lovely mouth he had studied in the poster that he had taken down from a display cabinet at the theatre and pinned onto the wall of his room. 'I've longed to meet you,' he repeated, quietly, wondering if after all she was a spirit, a beautiful apparition.

'I beg you, Mr Ames,' she said, 'don't ever think of me.

Or if you do, remember me as a ghost. That's all that I am. I have no life now. My life is finished.'

The professor's sister was getting closer, coming across the sand. Lifting the hem of her summer dress, stepping over rivulets of seawater coursing up the beach, Miss Bell walked away. She joined the spinster and the two women stood talking for a minute then climbed the steps up the side of the cliff and disappeared from view.

Fourteen

On the other side of the blue room wall, two women complained to each other about the price of bread. Standing just feet away, Lily wished she was one of them. She had got everything wrong. It wasn't being on stage, or fame, or even art that was precious; it was ordinary life. She'd taken it for granted, had never realised its infinite worth. And now she was outside it forever.

The bell rang for the audience to take their seats and the wistful notes of the violins began. Listening to the music, pierced by its melancholy as she never had been before, Lily wondered how she could get through the performance. Mr Pendragon concluded his introduction, there was a springy arrival of feet over the boards and overhead, the actor fell to his knees. 'Hers was the truest heart in England,' he said. 'Hers the kindest soul.'

Lily felt as if he spoke directly to her. For a moment on the beach she'd wanted to give Mr Ames some indication of the terrible thing that had happened to her, beg him to help her to escape. But she could not. She'd decided before she even left the lodgings not to tell anybody, ever, what had occurred. Positioning herself on the scuffed marks on the floor, braced for the blinding illumination, she waited for the spirit of the ghost to enter her. The stage lights dimmed, the audience moaned in anticipation and Salt's voice rang out, summoning her. People gasped and cried as the limelight blazed and her image appeared on the stage, but the ghost hadn't come. Her performance felt mechanical and stilted and, addressing her lover, she forgot to lift her veil, only doing so at the spinster's prompt.

The first interval came. 'Are you feeling better, Miss Bell?' said Miss Salt, stepping forward from the side of the chamber with a sponge, beginning to touch up the white greasepaint. Lily had told Faye that she was homesick, that she'd gone down on the beach wanting to be alone for a little while and that she had been crying for her mother. Miss Salt held the candle to Lily's cheek. 'Your face. It looks marked—'

Lily jerked her head away. 'It's suffocating in here. I need a bottle of Seltzer water.'

'I'll fetch one,' Faye Salt said, leaving the chamber.

Lily sat on the low stool that they kept in the corner of the blue room. On her right hand, the opal ring looked dull and colourless. The ring, even her own hands, could have belonged to someone else; she felt removed, as if her real self was somewhere up above the ceiling, looking down on a girl in a frayed silk dress, her head bowed, her hands on her lap.

The mute moaned a warning and a moment later Erasmus Salt entered the blue room, slipping in between the velvet panels.

'Ghost appeared in the wrong place,' he said.

Taking a stick of chalk from his pocket, crouching close to the floor, he began retracing the outlines of her positions. The seams of his coat stretched over his broad back and Lily felt again the sensation of intrusion, of numbing, paralysing shock.

'I'm going home,' she said, as loudly as she could. 'Back to London. You can find yourself another ghost.'

Salt got to his feet. He dropped the chalk into his pocket and held up a candle between them.

'You will not go anywhere,' he said, softly.

'Why not?' Lily said. 'I can do as I choose.'

'Bell's had the money. Had it for the season and beyond.'

'He would have informed me, if that was the case.' Even as the words left her mouth, Lily doubted them. She pictured Salt passing something to Alfred Bell in the yard of the coaching inn, her stepfather's eyes flashing in her direction and sliding away. Lily's mind churned. He thought he had bought her. The professor believed that he had purchased her and could do as he wished with her. Mr Bell had sold her like a parcel of goods. He must have known what kind of man Salt was. Her mother had known it too. They had betrayed her.

The bell rang for the audience to resume their seats; the violinists began to play, conveying a yearning sweetness. Salt left and automatically, as Balthazar lit the first jet of gas, the flame flaring yellow then blue under the cone of lime, Lily moved into her position. In the second act, exchanging words of love and grief with Mr Ames, the spirit returned to her. Later, dancing in the imagined arms of her stage lover, she lost herself in the ghost's passionate longing, experienced her rapture at seeing the face of her beloved again.

At the end of the performance, a storm of applause echoed through the auditorium. Women sobbed, pleading for her return, begging to be allowed to see her again. Lily collapsed back down onto the stool. Trapped in the dark chamber, she felt as if she really was a ghost, as if she had disappeared into the noisy roars and the fug of gas, leaving behind only a shell of herself, her face painted, her body dressed in silk and feathers.

Fifteen

Balthazar mounted the stairs of his lodging house. It was his habit to count the *apples and pears* as he went. There were six from street to front door. Nine from the hall to the first floor, these carpeted with a runner. Eight more from the landing to the second floor – wooden, worn by the tread of feet. And six – narrow, drilled by the worm, leading to the attic room for which he paid one and six a week.

On the top landing, he stopped. Reaching into his pocket, he felt the flimsy envelope, tenderly, as if it were a bank note. Ames had given it to him earlier, had instructed him to pass the note to Miss Lily Bell, then repeated *ghost*, mouthing the word as if he addressed a foreigner or a halfwit. Balthazar chuckled to remember it. Seized by the instinct that there was an opportunity at hand, an opportunity that he mustn't pass up, he'd trousered the note. Patting it again, Balthazar stooped under the doorframe.

A sooty-glassed lamp burned on the mantelpiece,

despite the hour. By means of a screen, the room had been divided into two. The front part contained a table and two chairs, a tin chest, a stand like a gallows on which a few garments hung. The back part accommodated the bed, comfortable enough although the one sleeping nearest the wall – invariably himself – was forced to crawl over it to gain admission. Without pausing to remove his coat, Balthazar rummaged in the chest and retrieved a length of cheese wire. He dragged a chair to the table and took the wire to the seal on the back of the envelope. As he extracted the note, Mary appeared from behind the screen. They'd been living tally for years, off and on. She'd refused to go to Nether Hall, after hearing what had gone on there, but she had joined him in Ramsgate, saying the air would do her good. While he worked the limes inside the theatre, she sat outside with a box of yesterday's fruit pies.

Unfolding the sheet of paper, the gasman held it close to the lamp. He had acquired his ability to read and write on the benches of a Sunday school and with the liberal assistance of a length of swishing bamboo. Certain letters – *n* and *m*, which he'd often confused, *s*, which he'd written backwards, *w*, that he'd been unable to say at all without stammering, were his enemies, indelibly associated with the sharp stinging of his palms or calves, his ear being torn half off his head. Letters *o* and *l* and *r* were his friends, easy to get acquainted with, steadfast types that often turned up in pairs.

The note was scrawled, the ink smudged, but the words discernable.

Dear Miss Bell,
I was on the stage this evening during the interval and couldn't help but overhear some of your conversation with Salt. I didn't like what I heard.
If you wish to leave, I am ready at any time to help you get away to your home. Please send word with Balthazar.
Your Friend,
Tom Ames

Balthazar quashed the impulse he felt towards pity for Lily Bell. The tall fellow had a notion to help her escape and judging by the fate of the other bird, it would be better for her if she did. But sentiment was costly; a luxury he'd long ago understood that the likes of Balthazar Pook couldn't afford.

'What's it say?' asked Mary.

'It says –' he pronounced the word as if rhyming with stays, enjoying the trusty letter y on the sides of his tongue, keeping his tone hushed because walls had ears and, except with Mary, Balthazar played the mute all of the hours God gave '– money. A few bob extra for you 'n I.'

Sixteen

The whole of Ramsgate was talking about the late Lily Bell. Erasmus had posted facsimiles of the death notice at the front of the theatre, next to black-edged instructions as to the whereabouts of the grave. Gaggles of women had begun making pilgrimages to the freshly covered mound he'd arranged in St Laurence's graveyard. They left white silk roses in imitation of the heavenly ones she brought from the other side, laid little wax dolls, single white feathers, pebbles of chalk at the base of the headstone. The angel drew admiration; the delicacy of the figure – her white marble chin resting on her unmoving hand, her wings still but poised as if she settled for but a little while – was quite exquisite, it was agreed.

Outside the New Tivoli, people queued from noon for seats, the crowds contained behind wooden barriers hastily commissioned from a carpenter. They streamed in when the doors opened, equipped with opera glasses and lorgnettes, many dressed in mourning attire, bearing pictures of their own departed loved ones. The appeal of the ghost was universal. All classes of person – quality down from London, eminent townspeople, tradesmen, trippers, fishermen and fishwives – were desperate to see her. Females, and often men too, cried out when she appeared, shouted messages for her to deliver to the dear departed. When she disappeared, they wept and moaned, begging the ghost professor by God's grace to summon their own lost daughters and sisters and husbands.

Erasmus had mixed feelings about the success. The takings were good, would fund further experimentation, but he was frustrated by the gullibility of the punters, their willingness to accept the illusion in place of the real marvel that he was working towards. He lit his pipe then got out of bed, threw up the sash and leaned out of the window, gulping in cold air with the smoke, surveying a pair of gulls wheeling on currents of air, rising and falling with no movement of their outstretched wings. Bringing his head back inside the room, he rang for hot water and when the skivvy arrived, requested coffee, bread rolls on a tray. He'd started taking breakfast in his room. Couldn't endure Miss Bell's pinched face and undressed hair, her suffering eyes. He cursed himself for the hundredth time for his foolish, mortal weakness. It was the girl's soul he wanted to possess, not her slender body.

Washed and dressed, successfully evading all the females in the establishment, he set off for the theatre.

It was wet, the rain driving in off the sea. In the alley that led to the stage door, a man sat on the hull of an upturned boat, paring his nails with a blade. On seeing Erasmus, Balthazar jumped up, the muscles of his face twitching as his mouth formed the low growls and moans that passed for communication. Balthazar had been in his employment for two years now. He'd first hired the mute for his skill in the operation of the limelight; he treated the mechanism with respect – which was advantageous, given the cost of it – and more importantly, would not easily be able to pass on what he knew, about the technique or anything else.

'What is it, Balthazar?'

Balthazar performed a search in the pockets of his galligaskins and came up empty-handed. Erasmus checked the anger that rose in him.

'Enough of this,' he said and as he made to pass him, the man retrieved a folded note from somewhere inside his shirt, waved it in the air. It was sealed with a mess of wax and on the front was written *The Ghost Miss Bell*. Erasmus reached for it and the wretch whipped the paper behind his back with one hand and stretched out the palm of the other.

'Villain,' Erasmus said, indulgently. He dug in his pocket. Held out a shilling. 'Hand it over.'

Balthazar busied himself with secreting the letter inside his shirt. Erasmus felt his irritation rising.

'You want more?' he said, pretending amusement, groping for a florin and, with his thumbnail, sending the heavy coin spinning in the air. As Balthazar reached to catch it, Erasmus snatched the note. With the paper in his own hand, his temper abated.

'If there are any more where that came from, bring 'em to me.'

Balthazar bowed and shuffled away down the alley, his shoulders forward, step crabbed. Erasmus unlocked the stage door, unable to rid himself of the impression that the little fellow mocked him. He sat down in the front row of the stalls and by the dim light of a dim day broke the seal and read the note.

That evening, following Ames off stage into the cubbyhole that served as his dressing room, Erasmus watched as the youth pulled off the bell-sleeved shirt stained with red paint and hung it on a nail. The actor wore his hair long, in tails of matted hair that looked like wool, the face underneath held always at an angle. Ames couldn't be more than twenty-five years old. Strong in body and character, was how Erasmus would describe him. His understudy was a dull fellow, with aptitude for neither acting nor magic. It couldn't be helped. Any living actor could be replaced; only his ghost could not be substituted.

'Evening, Mr Salt,' said Ames, glancing up.

'Professor Salt,' Erasmus replied. 'And it is not a good evening. Not for you. You are sacked.'

Ames smiled. Pushed the hair out of his eyes. Pulled on his own striped shirt over a slim torso, the muscles on either side of his chest and in his upper arms rippling as he moved.

'And why might that be?' he said.

'The ghost spoke to me. She appeared in my private quarters, much distressed.'

'Is that so?' said Tom Ames. Off balance now, Erasmus noted with satisfaction. Less cocksure. 'And what did the ghost say?'

Erasmus moved closer. Eyeballed him. 'That I should be rid of you immediately, Ames. That you're pestering her with your mortal approaches. Writing unsolicited letters. She handed your note to me, unopened. Said she didn't wish to know the contents.'

Reaching into his pocket, he got out the note and brandished it in Ames's face. The fellow could elope with Miss Bell that night, if he wanted. But at the thought of him laying a finger on the ghost, even daring to address his creation, Erasmus felt a cold fury. If he'd had a knife to hand, he would have run it through Ames's heart, seen warm human blood mixing with the congealed stage preparation as the fellow staggered and collapsed, never to rise again.

'Get out,' he said. 'If I see your face again, I cannot be answerable for what may happen.'

Clenching and unclenching his fists, Erasmus watched Ames leave. He felt chilled and dilute, thinned out inside. Once a man had seen the life depart from another human being, understood the hair's breadth be-tween this world and the next, experienced that fractured fraction of time, death became a constant companion, the veil between the worlds rent as easily as a silk scarf. To kill was not a mortal sin, but rather an acceleration of natural science. To take a life in this world was to create one in the next. In the future, these things would be understood more widely. For now, only himself and his associates in the Next World Society were able properly to perceive the shape of things to come.

Seventeen

Tom Ames crouched in the darkness behind an upturned rowing boat, his eyes on the stage door through which he had exited two hours earlier. A church clock struck one and Tom cursed under his breath. The old devil must have smuggled Miss Bell and her chaperone out through the foyer, left by the main entrance. The night had turned cold and he had pins and needles. As he stood up, the door swung open. A figure in a tailcoat and leaning top hat emerged and stood in the pool of gaslight, looking up and down the alley.

Tom ducked back down as the spinster sister came out, a bag on her arm. A third person stepped from the doorway. She wore a black cloak, an ugly bonnet that even he recognised as antiquated, and her face was hidden behind a fall of black cloth. No veiling and draping could disguise the lightness of her step, her graceful bearing, the coil of hair on the nape of her neck. Salt turned to lock the door and Miss Salt said something to her companion. The black-clad figure answered, the words inaudible but the voice that floated on the night air clearly recognisable. Tom forgot his thirst, the cramp in his feet.

He leaned forward for a clearer view and the boat shifted on the cobbles, made a grating sound. Miss Bell glanced in his direction. The party began walking towards the spot where he hid. Crouching behind the hull, Tom heard the drag of a hem, the strike of a match. A whiff of spent sulphur mixed with the dark waft of tobacco smoke and when he raised his head again, they were gone. Tom got out from his hiding place and moved to the end of the alley, peered around the corner. The three figures were heading towards the sea, each at a little distance from the other. Moving from the chapel to the doorway of the shuttered Hovelling Boat Inn and on past the smokehouse, his cap pulled low over his face, Tom followed. They continued to the harbour, walking along the edge of the quay, past a great silent paddle steamer gleaming white in the moonlight, and then ascended the cliff by the zigzagging steps known as Jacob's Ladder.

At the top of the cliff, the silent group crossed over the road and turned into a crescent of bow-fronted houses, making their way towards the only lit fanlight. The door opened for a moment and Miss Bell hesitated, stopping at the bottom of the steps as if reluctant to enter the house. The spinster took her arm; the lit doorway swallowed all three figures and the door closed behind them. Almost immediately, light glimmered around the edge of the curtains in a first-floor room and shortly afterwards was extinguished. Downstairs, a lamp burned on.

Returning to his own lodgings, walking in the middle of the deserted road, Tom felt flat. He'd misread the situation, had thought Lily Bell might have feelings for him, as he did for her. It was wrong to have hunted her, but he'd wanted to see her one more time; to know where she lived. Light still flickered from inside the inn, along with the sound of singing. Tapping on the door, gaining admittance to the public bar, he sought solace in the company of strangers.

Eighteen

'The lime's poisoning me. I feel sick all the time.'

'You exaggerate, Miss Bell. Although the atmosphere's close in the chamber, I agree. May I?'

Faye moved to apply the cotton ball to Lily's face, to remove the greasepaint, but the actress brushed off her hand.

'Leave me alone.'

'Your complexion will suffer.'

'What does it matter? I'm a dead thing already. Haven't you seen the posters?'

Faye screwed the lid back onto the cold cream jar. 'Let me know if you change your mind,' she said.

They'd arrived back late as usual. Lily had ceased to take a glass of wine after the performances. She had gone straight up the stairs, without removing her cloak or so much as a goodnight to Erasmus. Faye had come up shortly afterwards and found the girl curled up on her bed in her underclothes, her face still covered in greasepaint.

Faye sat down at the dressing table, starting to unpin her own hair. It was Whitsun and the resort was packed with visitors, the cafes and restaurants crowded, the public houses noisy. Both performances had been sold out at the Tivoli. As the sound of merry voices floated up from the crescent, Lily got up from the bed and banged the French windows shut. 'I hate happy people,' she said, pulling on her wrapper, flinging herself back down on the mattress.

The young woman seemed angry. She'd grown thin and pale from late nights and lack of fresh air, had begun to neglect her appearance. Her hair was greasy but she refused to let Faye wash it. Pimples had broken out on her chin. Even Erasmus had noticed. He'd asked Faye what ailed Miss Bell. Instructed her to bring her back to health and insinuated that her peakiness was Faye's fault.

'Won't you take a sandwich, Lily? You've barely eaten today.'

The girl's face took on an expression of disgust.

'A cup of cocoa? I'll go down now and warm some milk.'

'How could he?' Lily said, sitting up and staring at Faye, her grey eyes full of trouble. 'He didn't even say goodbye.'

'Who didn't?'

'Mr Ames. He just went.'

'Mr Ames left in disgrace,' Faye said.

'What do you mean?'

'He stole a week's takings from the box office. My brother was forced to dismiss him.'

'I don't believe you,' Lily said, as Faye opened the locket, kissed the image inside, and got into bed.

Nineteen

The summer was the hottest they'd ever known, according to Mrs Webb. All through July and into August, the sun glinted off the sea in dancing diamonds of light. It scorched the grass on the cliff top, bleached the trippers' parasols, blistered the paint on the front doors of the crescents and cottages, melted the pitch on the slipways.

Walking along the cliff top to the theatre each afternoon, Faye Salt's wrist under her fingers, Lily looked through the black crape at the crowds down on the beach. In another world, silhouetted children raced silhouetted donkeys along the sands, girls her own age crowded into bathing machines and were pulled by horses into the sea, emerging to frolic in the waves, their hair growing damp, their shrieks carrying on the air. Her back prickling with sweat under the heavy cloak, she passed the artist selling his shell camellias, country-women hawking cherries and roses, Ethiopian minstrels making their strangely affecting music.

Lily had kept to her vow never to tell anyone,

including the professor's sister, what had happened. She would never marry, she had decided, so would not be forced to explain herself to any man. She would devote her life to acting. As soon as she could, she intended to escape back to London and search for a role in a theatre. Any role, however humble, would satisfy her as long as it enabled her to rent a room and develop her craft. She couldn't go home; what would she tell her mother? How would she face her? Ruth Bell would only need to take one look at her to know what had happened. She'd never in her life kept a secret from her mother.

Lily planned to give Faye Salt the slip, pawn the opal ring in one of the many establishments in the old town where the three golden balls were visible, and buy a steamer ticket. Before she could make a move, she needed a sign. Week by week, then day by day, and finally hour by hour, Lily waited.

Her twentieth birthday came and went. The sun began to cool; the long days shortened; the sea grew surly and brown. Nothing. The sense of creeping fear she lived with grew more insistent. Since she was small, Lily had overheard the talk of women in her mother's kitchen. On the first Sunday of September, after the cold beef that Mrs Webb invariably provided – the landlady was a Sabbatarian – after the plates and vegetable dishes had been cleared away, and the others had repaired to their rooms, Lily closed the door of the little parlour, lit all five candles and blew them out, lowering her face to the wicks, sucking the smoke deep into her chest, holding it there until she thought she would suffocate. Beyond making her cough and choke, giving her a sore throat, it had no effect. The following Sunday, she emptied the remains of a decanter of gin from the sideboard down her throat; swallowing the last of it, she climbed the stairs and threw herself from the first floor landing to the hall, bumping down the coconut matting, grazing her palms and her elbows, ripping her blouse. Nothing changed apart from the bruises that blossomed on her knees and hips.

On the third Sunday of the month, Lily asked if she could go with Faye to church. St Laurence's was ancient, the walls knapped with flint, the graveyard lushly green; the rain had returned. Inside, muted white light fell in shafts from deep, arched windows. Next to the pulpit was a carved figure of the Virgin, cloaked in vibrant blue, her infant on her lap. Kneeling in one of the public pews at the back, closing her eyes, Lily prayed as she had never prayed in her life. With all her heart, all her soul, she begged for the return of her courses.

The voices of the choir rose sweet and pure; the stink of fish and sweat and ale from the free pews mingled with the scent of perfumed hair oil and cologne wafting from the high box pews. Rising from the hassock, bathed in the weighty boom of organ music, Lily felt a sense of absolution. God knew her remorse. He would not punish her further. As the congregation began the hymn, a faint but unmistakeable twinge rippled through her belly. It was unlike any sensation she had ever experienced. Lily opened her mouth but could not sing. The feeling came again, so slight she could not be sure she hadn't imagined it. Her prayer had been answered. Laying down her hymnbook, whispering to Faye Salt that she would wait outside, she edged her way along the pew and left the church.

It was sunny, the breeze lifting the veil from her face. The churchyard was empty and Lily wandered past the great stone tombs of the town's important dead. For the first time for weeks, she felt happy, glad to be alive, almost light-headed with relief. Soon, she found herself among small, lichen-covered stones, in the part of the graveyard where the humble people lay. It was peaceful to be surrounded by the dead. They wanted nothing from her except that she should tread lightly, read their names. *Charlotte, Eliza, Adela*; all late of this parish. Some of the writing was indecipherable, words once permanent now eroded and crumbled, obscured by ivy.

A fresh grave, a few yards away, caught Lily's eye and she moved towards it, drawn as if by some powerful force. The grave was narrow, the grass growing over it bright and new. At the head of it was a white marble angel and at the angel's naked feet were propped bunches of ruined silk flowers, bedraggled dolls and feathers, white pebbles of chalk. Lily crouched down to read the inscription. *Lily Elizabeth Bell 1831 – 1851, Slipped from a Cliff, R.I.P.*

Lily stared at the words. The resinous smell of the yew tree, the soft brightness of the grass, the blue glass eyes of the dolls, all seemed extra-real, as if they had more substance than she. She felt as if she might be dreaming, or hallucinating, or perhaps it was true that she had fallen from a cliff, and this was what it meant to be dead.

'Where were you? Didn't you hear me calling?'

Stopping beside Lily, Faye looked at the inscription on the gravestone. She swayed as if she would fall, clutched at Lily's arm, a look of fear on her face. Walking back to the lodgings, her arm linked to the spinster's, Lily felt as if it was she that guided and supported Faye Salt.

Lunch was laid out on the table in the parlour. Faye said she felt a migraine coming on, and went to lie down in the bedroom. For what might be the last time, Lily chewed her way through cold beef, cold cabbage and cold blancmange, without tasting any of them. Her body was still in Mrs Webb's lodgings but her mind was one hundred miles away, in London, imagining the theatres she would approach, considering whether she ought to present herself at the stage door or the box office, rehearsing what she could say about her experience. Even the presence of the professor on the other side of the small table, the clash of his fork against his teeth, the sound of his swallowing, did not spoil Lily's mood. She didn't look at him or speak to him, had barely spoken to Erasmus Salt since what had happened that awful night. She wouldn't speak to him now, about the grave. Her mind returned to practicalities. No pawnbroker could assist her on a Sunday. The next day was Monday. She would slip out of the lodgings early, before Faye woke, and get what she could for the opal ring. Buy herself a one-way ticket on the Jupiter, the Eagle, or any of the steam packets bound for London, and be gone, lost in the crowds. Lily drank her cold coffee, got up from the table and hurried out to the privy in the yard. She came out feeling consumed with impatience. There was no blood. Not yet.

Upstairs in the bedroom, Miss Salt sat by the empty grate, her hands idle, her migraine cured or forgotten. She looked at Lily with an anxious, guilty expression.

'Miss Bell, I ...'

Lily raised her hand. 'I don't want to talk about it. What do you care for me? You only care for your brother. For obeying his orders and keeping me a prisoner.' She lay down on her back on the high bed and watched as the breeze lifted the long summer curtains at the French window, let them fall. Outside in the street a woman shouted and a child began to scream. Lily's buoyant mood began to fade.

That evening, playing Cribbage with Mrs Webb's visiting niece, who'd been granted admittance to the parlour in an attempt to cheer Lily up, the sensation came again, low down in her belly. It was slight but definite, had the quality of movement, as if deep inside her a butterfly struggled from a chrysalis.

'Your turn.'

The niece was looking at her over her cards, her brown eyes concerned. Lily looked blankly back at her. 'Pardon?'

'The game, Miss Bell. The game.'

Lily lost the next hand, and the one after. As the clock chimed nine, she excused herself and went back upstairs. Mechanically, she removed her blouse and skirt, laid them over the back of the chair, unhooked her stays. She bent to pull off her stockings and inside, the butterfly moved its wings, tentatively, and then with increased sureness.

Standing by the bed, in her chemise and petticoat, the only garments that were still comfortable, Lily stared at the stars on the wall, their unnatural geometric pattern. This was not her life. Her real life continued without her, somewhere far away from here, perhaps in the company of Mr Ames. She had lost or forfeited it, and in its place been handed this one, that was alien to her, that had led her into a deep, impenetrable fog, unable to see a way in front of her or on either side and obscuring any possibility of retreat.

Only one path remained to her. One course of action. She had seen it with her own eyes, in the graveyard, chiselled in stone like a message from God.

Twenty

'I should like to go for a walk. Up on the east cliff.'

'Of course, Miss Bell,' Faye said, feeling surprised. 'I'm sure the fresh air will do you good. When would you like to go?'

'Now. I want to go now.'

'As you wish.'

The girl was already dressed and Faye put on her own clothes, unplaited her hair and pinned it in a comb on the back of her head.

'Let us at least have a pot of tea first.'

'I want to go now, Miss Salt,' Lily said, her face set, her complexion very pale.

'As you wish.'

For weeks, Lily had refused to take a walk, other than to the theatre and back. The girl seemed unhappy and preoccupied and Faye was worried about her health. Faye had been horrified to see the gravestone in the church-yard. She hadn't dared to bring it up with Erasmus, or question him about the macabre death notice outside the New Tivoli. They put on their cloaks, their hats, and left, walking in silence along the crescent and over the road to the cliff top. Far down below, the sea was choppy and restless, surging and glittering in the sun, turquoise patches giving way to deeper, colder-looking drifts, opaque and gunmetal grey.

Behind her veil, Lily was quiet, her touch light on Faye's arm as Faye led her down the steep road into the town. They continued, past lodgings houses with their Vacancies signs turned outwards, unswept steps. On the other side of the harbour, by the obelisk, the Italian was at his post, turning the handle of the churn underneath a faded umbrella. The cart that had been such a cheerful sight all summer struck Faye now as mournful and she shivered under her mantle.

'Would you like an ice?'

'I might as well,' Lily said, as if talking to herself. 'Even ghosts enjoy ice cream.'

The Italian clawed out round balls of lemon sorbet with a silver scoop, dropped them into two scrubbed, ribbed scallop shells and stuck in little flat wooden shovels. Bowing to Lily, he handed her the ice as if it were a precious jewel.

'*Signorina,*' he said, in a grave tone before handing one to Faye in the same reverent manner. '*Signora.*'

Faye paid the tuppence and they sat down in a wind shelter, on a bench that faced out over the sea. Sheltered and facing south-east, catching the early sun, the little compartment smelled of warmed paint and iron. Faye hoped every day that Erasmus would announce his intention to close down the show. She was impatient for the end of the season, for the time when Lily Bell would go home to her mother. Faye couldn't yet think about what she would do. Search for another position, she supposed, if Ras no longer needed her. Get away from Nether Hall and continue the work of forgetting.

From down by the harbour, at the sailors' church, a half-muffled bell tolled.

'I wish I had eaten more ice cream,' Lily said, spooning it under her veil, seeming to savour it. 'I wish I'd eaten it every day of my life.'

'Are you ready to return, Miss Bell?' Faye said.

'I told you, I want to go up to the cliff top. To the east cliff.'

'Of course,' Faye said. 'If you like.'

The girl was in a strange mood. Returning the shells to Signor Pelosi, Faye held out her arm for Lily to take and they walked along the main sands. The beach was littered with heaps of seaweed and dry white blades of cuttlefish, patterned with the aimless tracks of gulls' feet. They continued on to where a section of the cliff had been clad in brown cement, smoothing out the jagged chalk face, giving it the appearance of an Alpine mountainside; between the boulders, pink sedums clung to life. Ascending the steps in silence, climbing up and up, they went past the Belle Vue Hotel with its Gothic arches and turrets, the deserted marble skating rink, and continued along to the wild, open cliff top, where a painted sign of a falling person warned of the sheer drop to the rocks below. It was bright and brilliant and windy under a great busy sky, the ground treeless and covered in tussocky grass. Pulling off her bonnet, flinging it to the ground, Lily removed her cloak and spread it on the grass. She kicked off her mules and lay down on the cloak.

'Do you think there is a heaven?' she said, staring at the sky, shielding her eyes with her hands.

'Of course,' Faye said.

'I don't. I wish I did.'

'Is something troubling you, Lily? Can I help you in any way?'

The sun disappeared behind a scudding cloud; the light dimmed momentarily and the air grew cooler. Lily's features hardened.

'No one can help me,' she said. 'It's too late.' Getting up, she walked in her stockinged feet in a meandering circle, plucked a blackberry from a bramble and squashed it in her fingers. Slowly, taking small steps, she went towards the cliff edge, pulling pins from her hair as she went, dropping them in the grass. At the edge, she stopped, gazing out towards the horizon. Her skirt and blouse, her white flag of hair, billowed from her frame as if she was held in the hand of the wind. She took a step closer to the edge of the cliff and her shadow – the top half of it, her head and shoulders and hips, disappeared over the side.

Faye felt suddenly nauseous. Scrambling to her feet, unable to breathe, she stumbled towards the edge of the cliff. The few steps seemed as long as a mile, and down below the sea appeared to have grown still; it lay, glittering and waiting. In a lightning movement, Faye lunged at Lily and caught hold of her, flinging her arms around her waist, dragging her back from the edge, tripping on her own hem. They both fell down on the springy, sweet-scented grass.

'Let go of me,' Lily said, attempting to cast Faye off, trying to get up. Faye kept hold of her arm, clinging to it with all her strength, her heart racing.

'If you go, you will take me with you.'

They struggled, panting with exertion, until Lily stopped suddenly, her body growing limp.

'I don't want to die,' she sobbed, tears streaming down her face, her breath coming in great, juddering gasps.

Faye helped her to her feet and led her away from the cliff edge, both of them shaking all over. Picking up the girl's cloak, she draped it around her shoulders. 'How could you even think of such a thing, when you have your whole life ahead of you?'

Lily gave a high, loud laugh and turned to face Faye, staring at her with wild eyes.

'Can't you see?' she said. 'My life is over.'

*

That evening, as Miss Bell lay asleep on her bed, calmed by a dose of the valerian pills Faye had administered, there was a tap on the door. Putting down her crochet, Faye stepped out onto the landing.

'What is it, Mrs Webb?' she said in a hushed voice, closing the door behind her.

'I cannot afford for my Betty to be set such an example,' the landlady said.

'Pardon?'

'Nor risk the reputation of my house.'

'Your house?' Faye said, coolly.

The landlady stared at her. 'Don't tell me you don't know.'

'Know what? What are you talking about?'

'I didn't like to speak to the professor.' Mrs Webb's chin quivered. 'I'm talking about the young lady. Her condition.'

'She isn't herself. She hasn't been for some weeks, but…'

The woman's eyes met hers and Faye's voice trailed away.

'I can give you one more week,' Mrs Webb said.

The landlady's feet thumped down the stairs. Faye remained on the landing. The desperate struggle of the morning presented itself afresh and she groped for the locket around her neck, gripped its smooth oval coolness in the palm of her hand, trying to gather herself. The painting inside of her mother as an infant had always been her talisman, always calmed and steadied her in times of trouble.

Re-entering the bedroom, she looked at Lily, curled up under the bedclothes.

'Is it true?' she said, softly.

Lily stared at the ceiling. Reaching for her salts, unstopping the bottle, Faye sniffed the sharp vapour deep into her lungs, first through one nostril and then the other. Erasmus had instructed her never to let Lily Bell out of her sight. She had not but ... As her head began to clear, Faye remembered the morning in early summer when she'd woken to find Lily gone from her bed. She had no way of knowing how long she'd been missing. Had assumed it had not been very long but it might have been an hour. Perhaps more. She'd gone looking for her immediately, found her down on the beach, wearing her own clothes, the little straw hat that set off her uncovered face. She'd been in the company of Tom Ames. Erasmus had been beside himself when he found out. He'd raged at Faye, accused her of wanting to ruin his life's work. Got rid of Ames shortly afterwards; the theft was a pretext, Faye understood. It concealed a worse crime.

She sat on the edge of Lily's bed, her mind racing, barely able to catch up with her new understanding of the situation. 'Mr Ames persuaded you into meeting him. He took advantage of your innocence. And the wicked, wicked man has walked away as if nothing happened.'

The actress regarded her with the same wild look that Faye had seen on the cliff top. She gave a harsh, hoarse groan and rolled over to face the wall.

'Please,' she said. 'Leave me alone.'

Twenty-One

Faye looked down at the pattern on the old Turkey rug, of lions baring their teeth. 'I never left her side, Erasmus. There was just that one time when I woke to find her bed empty. And you remember, I found her in the company of Mr Ames.'

'What are you talking about, Faye?'

'It was the only time,' she said, her heart in her mouth, her palms sweating. 'She claimed she was homesick.'

'What are you trying to say? Out with it, for God's sake.'

'Mrs Webb saw it. I didn't know. She hid it from me.'

'Hid what?'

Faye thought her legs would give way. 'Her condition,' she whispered, the lions jumping before her eyes. 'She is with child.'

The expected explosion of rage did not come. Erasmus for some time was completely still and then he kicked the table leg, sharply, flooding coffee into the saucer of his cup. 'Confounded little tart,' he said, getting up from his chair.

'The wretch has abandoned her without a backward glance. Mr Ames seemed such a gentleman. Who could have believed that he—'

'Quiet!' Erasmus barked. 'Let a man think.'

Faye sat down on the edge of the chaise, gripping the red velvet arm. Fearful of his reaction, she had for two long days put off telling her brother. The previous evening, Mrs Webb had knocked again, threatening to tell him herself. Faye had barely slept. She'd risen early and dressed, waited until she heard Erasmus on his way down the stairs and followed him, so she could speak with him in private before he left the lodgings. It was eight in the morning and Lily was still upstairs, in bed.

'I suppose you will send the poor girl home to her family,' Faye said, when she dared to speak again. 'But I fear they may not welcome—'

'Send her home?' Erasmus thumped the table. 'And lose another ghost?'

The atmosphere in the parlour thickened to mercury. Erasmus put a match to the bowl of his pipe, drawing on the stem with sharp, quick gasps.

'What's done is done,' he said, at length, pacing the room. 'You will attend Miss Bell until her bastard arrives. Then find a female that can give it a home. I will make a donation for its upkeep.'

'But why, Erasmus? Why should the burden fall on you? You must send her home to her family.'

Her brother looked at her through a plume of exhaled smoke, his eyes afflicted with that brightness that Faye had long ago come to dread. 'She has no home. Not now. Lily Bell is my ghost. Our work together has only just begun.'

Twenty-Two

Their new lodgings were down on the beach, in a sprawl-ing cottage built into the cliff. The back rooms were dark as caves, the front ones faced the sea; water and land squaring up to each other in an unequal contest.

Erasmus Salt had closed down the show at the New Tivoli, dismantled the blue room and transported Lily and Faye there, leaving his own bags and boxes on the back of the cart while he had an audience with his sister, behind the closed parlour door. Faye came out with an envelope in her hand, avoided meeting Lily's eye, and went straight up the stairs. Her brother remained in the parlour and through the open door, Lily saw him putting away his wallet.

She entered the room and closed the door behind her.

'You're leaving?'

'I have important work to do in London. I am to address a Next World Society conference.'

'What do you expect me to do, meanwhile?' she said

in a low, urgent voice, holding her belly with both hands through the cloth of her skirt. 'With this?'

He looked at her distractedly. 'I have instructed my sister to make arrangements.'

Lily stared out of the parlour window to where the grey sea and the grey sky merged, impenetrable, encircling, with no horizon. 'I thought my life was beginning when I left my mother's house. I was wrong. It was ending.'

'On the contrary, Miss Bell.' Salt smiled. 'We shall resume our work as soon as this inconvenience is over. In time, you will forget all about it.'

'I will never play the ghost again. You cannot expect it.'

'I can and I do. Mr Bell receives your salary every month. He is your guardian. And you are my ghost. Many of us believe,' he said, looking at her fixedly, 'that the conditions are right for the souls of the departed to begin to visit us freely and frequently. For us to commune with them at will.'

He put on his hat and adjusted it in the mirror over the mantel. 'I trust that in future you will avoid drinking wine. An unbecoming habit, in a woman.'

He left, ordering the carter to take him without delay to the railway station. The horse's hooves laboured up the slipway and as the sound died away, Lily stood in the hallway. She hated him, she understood with sudden clarity. She'd never known what it was to hate a person. She wished he would die. Their new landlady stood at the far end of the passage regarding her with shrewd brown eyes.

*

Lily had a small bedroom that led off Faye Salt's, a windowless room in which the back and side walls had been hewn out of the cliff. Forced out of bed every hour or two by the need to empty her bladder, she slept poorly at night and woke unrefreshed, the thing inside struggling with increasing purpose. She spent the mornings in the parlour, picking up magazines abandoned by previous guests, leafing through them, unable to concentrate. After lunch, Faye Salt forced her out for walks, the wind tugging at their cloaks and bonnets, the sands empty except for fishermen digging for bait, children collecting sea coals, solitary walkers with inexplicably joyful dogs. Behind her veil, under the voluminous cloak, Lily walked slowly, her gait ungainly, playing an ancient and rotund widow. Faye refused to let her go up the steps to the cliff top.

Despite the way he'd deserted her, Lily thought sometimes of Tom Ames. She heard his voice, clear and deep and humorous, and the light, agile tread of his feet. She pictured him in front of her, juggling, his shirt blowing in the wind and his hair, a figure on the edge of a raging sea, dancing a private dance with the elements. Walking on the beach with Faye Salt, Lily looked for him in the waves, in the caves that gaped like mouths in the face of the cliffs.

Except for Sunday mornings, when she went to take Communion at St Laurence's, Faye Salt never left Lily's side. During those hours, the door of the cottage was kept locked. Lily was enraged, the first time she realised it. 'Locked doors make no difference to me,' she shouted, when the spinster returned. 'Where can I go, in this condition? To the workhouse? To the streets? There is nowhere. All I can do is walk into the sea. Perhaps I should.' She pulled the brass curtain ring Faye had bought for her off her finger and hurled it into a corner. 'Your brother has ruined my life.'

'This situation is not his fault, Miss Bell,' the spinster said, her pale face aflame, her bony hands clenching each other. 'Mr Ames should have married you. The man was a blackguard. Blame him.'

The days contracted. They needed candles on the breakfast table, the tea table. Some days it barely grew light at all. Lily willed the tide to keep coming in, to flood under the door and along the hall, fill the rooms of the house and float the chairs and tables and beds and people up to the ceiling, carry them all away. The sea obeyed only its own invisible laws, waves teeming forwards, white-topped, surging with hungry intent and then hesitating, losing momentum and retreating back over the sand, erasing the footprints and circling paw marks, depositing heaps of tangled seaweed, frayed rope, old boot soles.

The sea's restless movement and constantly changing colours, the unfixed character of the water, reflected Lily's sense of herself as having dissolved, become amorphous, part of the great heartless movement of life. She could do nothing, could only be. Her mind had withered and become useless to her; she had nothing now to hope for. As her belly grew rounder and heavier, she felt her spirit grow thinner and lighter. She missed the streets of London and their relieving, impersonal layers of history. Missed the girl that had been so eager to leave her childhood home, filled with hope and faith, dressed in the gaudy finery she imagined an actress to affect. More than anything, with a keen sense of loss, she missed her mother. Sometimes, Lily sat with her eyes closed and imagined Ruth's quick hands dressing her hair; she heard her laugh or sing; pictured every detail of the old kitchen, from the worn brick floor to the lopsided range, the chipped glass vase in which Ruth put snowdrops in winter and roses in summer. She dared not write. She could not lie and she could not tell the truth.

Severed from her past, the dreams of her future ended, with only the present moment on which to sustain herself, Lily felt insubstantial, a shadow self that anyone might reach out and put a hand through. The ghostly green band left on her wedding finger by the brass ring seemed to mock her. She was nobody; the angel in the graveyard was more alive than she. Only her stomach – the skin stretched taut as a drum, the fluttering movements within turned to vigorous kicks and rolls – was real.

Twenty-Three

Lifting a knocker in the shape of a dolphin, letting it fall, Tom Ames stood back from the door. A lop-sided tread headed down the stairs and the door opened by a few inches.

'No single men,' said the woman who peered out at him.

'Thank you, ma'am, I don't need lodgings.'

'What do you want?'

'I am looking for Miss Bell.'

Her eyes slid past him. 'Never heard of her.'

'Miss Lily Bell. The actress. She was staying here, back in the summer.'

The door opened an inch further and the woman put out her head, glancing up and down the crescent. 'Disgraceful,' she hissed, her colour rising. 'How you have the brass neck—'

The door banged in his face. Tom felt puzzled. A pot lid clanged and a whiff of boiling cabbage drifted up from the kitchens. Descending the steps, crossing the road, he stood in the shadow cast by the houses opposite, looking up at the room on the first floor. The French windows were closed, the balcony empty except for a couple of dead geraniums, a discarded broom. Wherever she was, it was not here.

He'd been angry when Erasmus Salt sacked him. Angry at the injustice and disappointed that Miss Bell had passed his letter to the ghost professor. He'd thought they had the beginnings of an understanding, had felt a fool to realise that as far as she was concerned they did not. After following her home to this crescent, he'd drowned his sorrows at the Hovelling Boat Inn. Had woken after a night's hard drinking to find himself on the back of an open cart, moving along under a rosy sky, joined up – it turned out – with a band of strolling players who were his new best friends. He'd spent months with the troupe, juggling and performing tricks in provincial marketplaces, sleeping in barns and stables. On the road, he'd had time to consider. It had occurred to Tom that Lily might not have given his note to the professor of her own free will. That it might have been intercepted. The troupe had disbanded after three of them got into a fight at a fair at Canterbury and Tom had come back to Ramsgate, intending to try to see her. Make sure that she was all right. Try again, perhaps.

Still standing on the street, cursing himself for his own stupidity in imagining she would still be here, he got out from an inside pocket the picture he carried everywhere. Softened along the creases in her face but with her fair hair curling down past her shoulders, her eyes gazed out steadily, as if she looked not at every and any passer-by but at just one person. Himself. Looking at her eyes made him feel both more connected to her and more alone. She haunted him. Folding the picture back into his jacket, he set off down the crescent. Tom had heard about the grave back in the summer, seen the death notice Salt had displayed outside the Tiv, but felt no inclination to visit. The grave had been dug up, people said, the coffin found to be empty except for a few heavy flints. He wouldn't go to the churchyard. She wasn't there, thank God, of that he was certain. But where was she? Reaching the end of the crescent, he felt a tug on his sleeve. A brown-skinned girl of about eight years of age, wearing a blue dress, a red woollen shawl over her head, looked up at him.

'She's went away.'

'Who has?'

'All of 'em.'

She had a rag doll in her arms, floppy-limbed, with black hair like her own. Tom squatted down, his face at the same level as the child's.

'Where?' he said, softly. 'Where did they go?'

'Dunno. Missus said to her sister that Miss Bell's expecting.'

'Expecting what?'

A shout went up in the crescent and, the doll dangling from her hand, the child darted back towards the house.

At the end of the crescent, he was met by a blast

of clean, cold wind. Pulling his jacket around himself, turning up his collar, he zigzagged down the steps and made his way along the beach. It was sheltered inside his cave, the air still and cool and sacred, as if the cave was a church for drowned or lost souls, for mermaids and lovers. The lower parts of the walls were silked with emerald green weed, the upper parts soft white chalk striped with lines of half-buried flints. His initials were as sure and clear as if they'd been carved yesterday. Getting out his pocketknife, Tom began to carve another set of initials next to his, digging into the yielding chalk.

He worked for an hour or more, concentrating, feeling as if the act brought him closer to her, then finished, stood back and looked at the results. T.A. and L.B. He would bring her here. One day, he would enclose her initials and his within a single heart. First, he must find her. Wiping the blade of the knife on his handkerchief, Tom flicked it shut and made his way back under the cliff, jumping from rock to rock as the waves sallied in around his boots, hurrying to beat the rising tide.

Twenty-Four

'Miss Salt! Good morning!'

Faye tried to avoid her but Mrs Webb limped at surprising speed across the road, caught up with her outside the haberdasher's.

'I was only thinking about you.' She looked around. 'How is the unfortunate young lady?'

'Miss Bell? As well as can be expected. Her time is near.'

'What will she do with it?'

'I must find a suitable woman. There are advertisements in the newspaper but...' She hesitated. 'Do you know of anyone?'

'There's a widow. Takes in babies and raises them as her own.' Mrs Webb dug in her basket for an end of pencil, scribbled something on the back of her shopping list and handed it to Faye. 'Those that survive, that is.'

On one side of the scrap of paper was written: *potatoes, 3 yds scrim, white pepper.* On the other: *Mrs Parsons, Gull*

Cottage. Take cart track towards abbey. Faye walked along the west cliff, past the bandstand and the ornate wind shelters, past a sunken garden and the last tram stop, then turned inland. The track to the abbey was marked with an old wooden sign in the shape of a pointing finger and she followed it through flat, stony fields of sprouts and cabbages, peopled with scarecrows. After a mile or two, a long, low dwelling came into view, standing alone. A chained dog barked as she approached; a young girl, rosy-cheeked and prettily dressed, let her into a kitchen.

'I'm looking for Mrs Parsons,' Faye said, her spirits lifting at the sight of the child. 'Is she here?'

'I'll fetch Mother,' the girl said, calling for her.

Mrs Parsons wore layer upon layer of black clothing, fingerless mittens, a grey cap over greasy hair. She stared at Faye's stomach and Faye felt her face warming.

'I have a young friend. She finds herself in difficulty.'

'How old is it? I don't take them over two months.'

Faye bridled. 'It is not yet born, Mrs Parsons.'

The woman nodded. 'That's all right. Bring him up to me. She can board him here or I'll adopt him and your young friend won't have no more worries.'

Somewhere out of sight, an infant began to cry. A thick, sad smell wafted into the kitchen. 'May I see the accommodation?'

The woman shrugged and led her along the passage behind the kitchen into a low-ceilinged room. The air was rank, the only window closed. Two listless-looking babies lay top to toe in a crib, with a blanket thrown

133

over them. In a wooden pen on the dirt floor, a girl in a ragged smock – her skin stretched over her skull, her head too large for her body – stood holding onto the bars, looking up at Faye with a pair of ancient, hopeless eyes.

Mrs Parsons picked up a glass feeding bottle from a stool, shook it, and stuck the teat in the girl's mouth. 'I do my level best for them, miss,' she said.

Groping her way back along the passage to the kitchen, Faye hurried out of the cottage and into the front garden. She stood by the front gate, in the clear, salt air, retching into a clump of sea lavender. Mrs Parsons watched from the doorway, her own daughter standing next to her.

'Bring it up the day it's born,' she called. 'No questions asked. Ten guineas. Cash in advance. She can come and visit if she cares to.'

Faye walked back the long way round, through the old town. A low, grey-gold sun illuminated the dusty, salt-spattered windows of the houses; the smell of tar and rotting fish coursed up from the docks. The Tivoli was padlocked, a drunk passed out on the broad steps. She stopped by the window of a grocer's shop, looking at wooden boxes of dates and apricots and raisins, a patchwork of crimson and gold and orange. The smell of sickness and sorrow and dirt seemed to cling to her and, staring at the dried fruit, Faye saw only the despairing eyes of the little girl.

Twenty-Five

Erasmus walked through smog-shrouded streets, moving in and out of pools of yellow lamplight, his hands in his pockets. It was good to be in London, able to further his theories, receive inspiration from others in the field. New discoveries were being made all the time. He'd attended the Next World Society conference, a lecture series on Sir Walter Scott's understanding of immortality, and a number of scientific meetings. Had come that very evening from a spirit-rapping circle at Miss Penrose's establishment, where several present had received personal messages from lost loved ones. One woman had found on her lap a military medal – rusted and wet with saltwater. It had belonged to her late brother, she'd told the assembled company; he was never without it. He had drowned in a storm off the Canaries, a decade earlier.

No message had come for Erasmus. He didn't expect it. His mother was waiting, would appear to him in her own time, once he'd succeeded in summoning the first living spirit from the heavens. He was impatient for

Miss Bell to be delivered of her bastard and available again for the work. Before he took her from Alf Bell, Erasmus had hardened himself to the physical fate of the girl. Progress without sacrifice was impossible. Lily Bell was a member of the new generation; she belonged to the future, to the time when death would be defeated, the old human enemy vanquished and spirits called at will from the heavens – not announcing themselves through tappings and knockings, slate writings, delivery of trinkets such as those he'd just witnessed, but manifesting as beings of light, intangible yet visible, able to walk and talk, throw back their shining heads. In spirit, Lily Bell would live forever as a young woman, free of the burdens of age and decrepitude.

His last experiment had occurred too soon. He hadn't been ready and it had not been planned. The Hedges girl had taunted him. After a long evening's work, at the end of a long week, she had said she wouldn't come to Nether Hall any more. 'I'm sick to the back teeth of it,' had been her exact words. He had tried to explain to her about metempsychosis, that soon the souls of the departed would return in their full humanity, the glorious vision of which she was part. She had sat down in front of him in the library, parted her knees and flung up her skirts to her waist. Displayed her nakedness.

'This is what it's all about, ain't it, Professor?' she'd said, in her mocking country burr. 'But you don't want a real woman. Only a reflection of one.'

He'd commanded her silence but she'd carried on,

issuing a stream of obscenities about how he was no different from the grave robbers and corpse shaggers, only dressed it up in his ma's bloody clothes, gave it fancy names. Erasmus had moved towards her, compelled to stop the awful words that issued from her painted lips. Had reached for the first thing that came to hand, the veil thrown back over her head, and stuffed a corner of it into her mouth. He'd intended only to quiet her, stop the profanities, but he'd been possessed himself, with rage, had stuffed the silk on and on into the small mouth, tighter and tighter, barely aware of the bulging eyes, the bluing of the face. The hands that clawed at his neck then loosened. She had fallen at his feet, bringing him to his senses and Balthazar had sprung forward, moaning and yelping, dragging inch after inch of white lace from her throat like a conjuror.

Erasmus had worked with all his might to summon the spirit of Maria Hedges. He'd stood by the stage, issuing the invitation, the command, the entreaty that she return. With every flare of the lime, brought up to sit on top of the stage, he had expected to see metempsychosis occur. Believed that the soul of Maria Hedges would appear on the stage in the library, in her worldly form, whether clothed or naked, perhaps speaking in her old foul tongue. She had not come. As dawn approached, Balthazar had assisted him in removing the costume, rolling the lifeless body into a rug, carrying it out of the house and over the home pastures, into the woods. They had buried her not far from the old smithy at the crossroads, by the bank of a stream. Six feet deep, so the dogs and foxes would not sniff her out. Later, once the search parties had been called off and the commotion died down, hypothesising that those hours immediately following her passing to the other side had been premature, too soon to call her back, Erasmus had worked himself to the point of exhaustion to summon the spirit of Maria Hedges. Failed.

It had been a considerable setback but Erasmus believed now that he could explain it. The girl, brute that she was, lacked a soul. That was why – despite the long weeks of rehearsal, the training of her spirit for return – she had not been able to respond to the summons. It would be different next time. He felt hopeful, almost certain, of success with Lily Bell. After a run in London to publicise the ghost, and raise further funds, he intended to conduct the experiment properly. Balthazar, for the sum of one hundred guineas, had agreed to dispatch Miss Bell. The gasman would do the deed cleanly. Scientifically. The girl would know nothing about it. It would be done in Ramsgate, where her mortal resting place was already prepared. It was no mean feat, to dig a grave.

He'd missed the side street. Turning, lit by a halo of sulphurous light, he walked back and stalked down Love Lane, kicked open the door of the establishment. Madame Eve knew him. Understood his requirements. She had a little blonde tart on the premises, pliable and silent. White-skinned. White-haired.

Twenty-Six

The spinster laid out a game of Patience then sat in front of the card table as if she'd forgotten how to play, picking at her cuticles. It was a bitter night towards the end of February and Lily huddled close to the driftwood fire in the front parlour, trying to get comfortable. The creature inside her was still for once but the bulge in her belly seemed to have shifted, so low that it hurt to sit down. Lily knew the thing was male. If she pictured it at all, it was as a miniature version of the professor, tiny but aged, dressed in a dark suit of clothes.

Lily had no clear notion of how the baby would escape her body. As a child, she'd believed babies popped out of the middle of a girl's stomach, like peas from a pod. Later, she'd become aware that that wasn't so but her cousins, her friends, had offered no explanation of what happened. Her mother, when she'd asked her once, had slapped her. 'Babies are all born the same way,' Ruth Bell had said. 'Yours won't be no different.' She couldn't ask Miss Salt. The spinster would know as little as she did.

Their new landlady seemed to intuit Lily's unspoken questions. Mrs Ali was a foreigner, a sailor's widow, from the port of Alexandria. She brewed up tea with cinnamon and cardamom, thick with sugar, and brought it to Lily on a brass tray, patting her stomach, urging her in a guttural tongue to drink. She made alarming gestures, swishing her hand down over Lily's belly and between her legs, nodding, her eyes bright with secret knowledge.

About what would come after the birth, Lily could not think at all. One of her earliest memories was of seeing the body of a baby in the gutter at the end of Clara Street. It was naked, its chest torn open by the stray dogs that snarled at each other over the corpse. Ruth Bell had hurried her across the road but it was too late; she had seen it and could not unsee it. That wouldn't be this creature's fate. But what would?

Levering herself to her feet, she threw a twisted stick of wood on the fire, sending a shower of sparks up the chimney.

'Your brother said you would make arrangements.'

'I have found a woman,' Faye said, her voice strained. 'I will take the infant to her on the day of your confinement. It is the best way. The only way.'

Lily went up the stairs to bed, pulling her weight up by the bannister, each step an effort. She arranged herself in the bed, lying on her side with one pillow under her belly, another under her head. Some time in the night, she woke to a deep, smothering darkness and for a moment she was back in the blue room, convinced that the limelight was about to flare and she had missed her cue, forgotten her costume. She was in bed, she realised, in a nightdress that was sopping wet, the sheet underneath her damp. Pushing herself up into a sitting position, groping for the matches on the nightstand, she lit a candle and manoeuvred her legs over the side of the bed. She had no sensation of passing water and yet liquid was trickling from between her legs. As she stood up, a sharp pain rippled through her belly. The feeling passed and she crouched over the chamber pot. Indigestion, she told herself. Nothing more. It couldn't be her time, not yet. She wasn't ready. Pulling the sheets from the mattress, trying to think what to do with the damp bedding, the pain came again, uncompromising, like a warning. Feeling breathless, Lily leaned on the wall, pressing her hands against the rough surface of the cliff underneath the skim of plaster. The cramp faded, and then returned. For the next two or three hours, by the light of the single candle, she walked around the small bedroom, cupping the weight of her belly in her hands.

By dawn, the pains were regular. They were ruthless and inexorable, as if deep inside her an iron fist squeezed, informed her that her life was about to change for good. That her girlhood was over. Lily felt afraid, trapped in the house, the room, her own body, with no means of escape. When she could stand no more, she banged on the connecting door and in a moment Miss Salt appeared, her plait unravelling and nightcap slipping.

'Oh,' she said, her hand rising to her mouth. 'Why didn't you call me?'

Before Lily knew what was happening, Mrs Ali had been roused, candles lit, the range stoked into noisy life. The old woman laid a square of gutta-percha on the mattress, helped Lily into a dry nightdress. She felt Lily's belly with strong fingers, peered between her legs by the light of the lamp. Later, she said. Later. The day that followed was the longest Lily had known. Time ceased to pass; it stood still, stranding her in agony. Between the pains, she felt a pitiless clarity. Knowing it was not wanted, the baby refused to be born. Her own life, which had seemed an inexhaustible thing, was destined to end here in this windowless room. She would never see her mother's face again. Never hear her voice. She heard herself crying out for her.

Faye Salt stayed close, pressing a glass of brandy to her lips, dabbing her forehead with cologne, praying in a soft monotone for her safety and that of her unborn child. The spinster's face was grey, frightened.

'Please,' Lily said, between spasms. 'Don't tell my mother I was disgraced. I beg you – don't tell her how I died.'

The spinster gripped her hands. 'You will not die, Lily. Have courage.'

Lily let out a hoarse, rising shriek. The agony intensified, obliterating the bed where she lay, and the room;

it drowned the moaning sea and the gathering darkness outside. Nothing existed any longer, not herself, not a baby and not time. Only struggle. Exhortations now from Mrs Ali to push, and breathe, and push again. And then, the pain reached its climax and became, instantly, a memory. Time resumed.

Lily raised her head. The little room was lit like a ballroom, a dozen candles blazing, revealing distempered pink walls, watercolour pictures of a foreign land. Between her thighs, Mrs Ali was busy with a razor and a basin; a curved needle flashed in her fingers. Faye Salt stood by the door, with her back to the bed. Her head was bowed and her body racked with sobs.

'He is dead, isn't he?' said Lily.

The spinster turned around. In her arms was a small bundle of rags that she held up in the flood of light.

'It's a girl. A little girl.'

Twenty-Seven

She was coated in white grease, her shoulders smeared with blood, face wrinkled. Carefully, laying the baby down on the kitchen table, on the clean rags Mrs Ali had made ready, filling a bowl with warm water, Faye began to dab off the vernix, revealing mottled, mauve skin. She picked up the baby and rinsed her head over the bowl, rubbing it gently with her fingers, blotting it dry. In the dim glow of the lamp suspended over the table, the hair was red gold, like a nasturtium flower. The baby uncurled long fingers. Moved her dainty feet. She had an air of surprise, as if she'd swum up from the bottom of the sea and found herself beached on a strange shore.

Faye laid her in the pan of the scales, adding a five pound weight; two half pounds; an ounce. Another. The scales balanced at six pounds and two ounces. She wrapped her in a length of old sheet and held her in the crook of her arm, uncertain of what to do. A new life had entered the house. A new spirit. Lily's labour had lasted eighteen hours. A day had been and gone; it was past midnight and wild outside – the rain slapping against the windows, the gulls silenced. It was impossible to think of venturing out of doors.

In her own bedroom, emptying out one of the two small, paired drawers at the top of the chest, Faye lined it with a pillow, topped with a soft, well-worn chemise. The blanket lay on the chest, wrapped in brown paper, ready for donation to a worthy cause. She'd completed it only days earlier, had stitched together the squares, edged the rectangle with a crocheted border in the same wool. Tearing off the paper, Faye pulled out the blanket and swaddled the baby in it. It would keep her warm until the morning, she told herself. As soon as it was light, she would take her up to the Parsons woman.

She sat for some time and watched the tiny miracle of breath moving in and out, then got into her bed, hugging her knees to her chest, trying to warm herself. Her head filled with a fog that made it impossible to think, she fell asleep and woke almost immediately to a cry. The cry was rusty, as if long unused. It was insistent, summoned her with an authority impossible to resist. Leaning over the makeshift crib, she lifted out the baby, breathing in the hot-blood, newborn smell of her. The little creature's mouth was open, the lips stretched, the eyes screwed shut. A pulse beat fast in her temple. The high, struggling cry grew more urgent and the baby's face darkened.

A lamp still burned in Lily's room. She was alone,

lying on her side in the bed, facing the wall, a cup of tea untouched on the nightstand. Faye stopped in the doorway, rocking the light bundle, trying to soothe her.

'Your baby is hungry,' she said.

Lily rolled over and after a minute pulled herself up on the pillows to a half-sitting position. Her grey eyes looked empty, ringed with shadows. 'It's not my baby,' she said, in a hoarse voice.

'She is hungry,' Faye repeated.

'I don't want to see it. You said I shouldn't.'

'She cannot survive, Lily, unless you feed her.'

Lily held out her arms.

By morning, the storm was if anything more severe. Wind tore in across the sea from the north-east, ripping slates from the roof, battering the little house as if bent on destroying it. Sea spray and rain sluiced down the chimney, the fires first spitting and smoking then dying. Mrs Ali lit a charcoal brazier that she put in the centre of the parlour and Faye walked in circles around it, cradling the sleeping baby. At intervals, she presented her to her mother. Lily put the infant to her breast, grimacing, looking away while Mrs Ali positioned the baby on a pillow, supported her head. 'Take it away, Miss Salt,' she said, when the baby slept again, her voice soft and broken. 'I don't want to see it.'

The foul weather persisted. Faye winded the baby, wiped white dribbles from her chin. She changed a napkin soiled with a mustardy smear, rinsed the fleshy stump at the centre of the baby's tummy with warm salt water, swaddled her in the crocheted blanket and laid her in the improvised crib. In the evening, she sat watching her sleep as outside the waves hurled themselves at the shore, made a sound like thunder.

The next day, the landlady boiled up an aromatic porridge that she indicated would bring on the milk. She brushed Lily's tangled hair, swabbed between her legs with boiled flannels, issued admonishments to drink! Eat! Rest! She took a coal from the brazier with a pair of iron tongs and burned beads of frankincense, going from room to room, blowing smoke into corners and cupboards, behind the doors, incanting spells or prayers in her language. The damp little cottage took on the smell of a cathedral and Faye thanked God that the baby was alive, and her mother too. Lily wept continually – soundless, hopeless crying. When she didn't weep, she slept.

On the third day of the baby's life, down at the harbour, the bell clanged its iron summons. Faye watched from an attic window as the lifeboat and its crew set off, towed through the mountainous sea by a steam tug, the little cork-clad boat disappearing under the white-topped waves then miraculously reappearing. On the fourth day, the splintered remains of a schooner began to wash up on the shore; the beach filled with people hauling away barrels and crates, the women as strong as the men. Children picked over smashed china, collected spoiled rations.

The seventh day dawned calm and clear and still, the

sky an amnesiac blue. The receding tide had left the sands in front of the cottage carpeted in sea stars – thousands of them, pink and brown and ivory, all alike and all different, every last one dead.

'It's a punishment,' Lily said, turning away from the parlour window. 'From God.' She was out of her bed for the first time, wrapped in her old bright-patterned silk robe, a turban on her head and on her feet a pair of oiled wool socks that had belonged to Mrs Ali's husband.

'Nonsense,' Faye said, without conviction.

Lily lowered herself onto the sofa.

'You said you'd help me, Faye.'

'I am helping you.'

'You said you'd found a place for it,' Lily said.

The baby lay in her crib, in the wooden drawer that they moved from room to room. She was sleeping, her face serene and still.

Faye touched her cheek and the closed eyes flickered. 'I told you about the widow,' she heard herself say. 'I will take the baby to her soon.'

'Why not today?' Lily said.

'The baby has a little chill. I will send a note for Mrs Parsons to expect her shortly.'

'Will she be kind to it?'

'She'll do her best,' Faye said, her voice flat.

'Is the cottage clean?'

Faye could only shrug. Lily got up and ran from the room, slamming the door behind her. The baby began to cry.

Twenty-Eight

Tom began again, tossing a couple of balls in the air, catching one in front of him and one behind his back, throwing a third between his legs and over his head, adding a fourth. 'Just one lady or gentleman! If one man stops to watch I will juggle for his entertainment, free, gratis and for nothing.' Half a dozen gathered and he began, forgetting the crowd, their watching eyes, disregarding the ever-present possibility of failure, of the balls thumping to the ground, thinking only of the sky, its soft largesse and sailing clouds. Had there been a religion worshipping the sky, Tom would have joined it.

He fumbled, dropped a ball and caught the others, stooped for the one that had fallen. His cap lay on the ground in front of him, showing a scatter of pennies, the glint of a sixpence. Bystanders drifted away, their hands plunged into their pockets; small boys crowded around wanting to try their luck with the balls.

Lily's home was in London. He had heard her say so. Therefore it was in London that he would find her.

After a month in the capital, Tom had got into a routine. He went daily to Green Park, where fashionable men and women walked or rode, to the spot where on one occasion as he stopped juggling he had found a crown in the hat and which he'd designated as lucky. Bowing at the departing backs, he stooped for the coppers that were newcomers to the cap. Pocketed them. Began again and continued until the light began to fade.

In the evenings, he searched – loping around Victoria, along the Strand, back through Soho and north to King's Cross, scanning faces, returning by a different route, seeking out theatres and music halls, stopping at every place of entertainment, no matter how grand or how tawdry, checking the attractions, scanning billboards, studying posters pasted to the walls, collecting dropped tickets and programmes, searching for something – any-thing – that announced *The Return of Lily Bell*.

He got back to his lodgings late. He stayed in Chelsea, in a section of an old hayloft that had been fitted up with a bed and table and let out as suited to a bachelor. It reminded Tom of the garret in the backcloth at the New Tivoli, and he liked it for that reason. Each night, he spent an hour, sometimes two, practising new tricks, planning where he would search the following day, then got to his bed dog-tired but with his optimism replen-ished. Next day was a new day, he reminded himself, by way of prayer. A day in which all things were possible.

Twenty-Nine

Mrs Ali had warmed two gallons of seawater, filled the tin bath in front of the range in the kitchen. Lily sat in the water, squeezing a sponge over her shoulders, watching the water trickle down over a stranger's body. Her breasts were hard as apples, creamy drops leaking from the nipples. Her stomach was patterned with fine red marks and rounded, as if the creature had left behind a ghostly twin. She explored the prickle of catgut between her legs, felt the soft seam of flesh the stitches enclosed and grimaced. Lily's mind felt as traumatised as her body. She was in shock about what childbirth was, the horrific secret that women kept.

A piercing cry came from the other side of the door and she dropped the sponge and put her hands over her ears. She hadn't known that it would be like this. That once the thing was outside her, she would be more joined to it even than when it was inside, that inside it took care of itself but outside must be taken care of, every minute of every hour of every day. With the cry growing louder and more urgent, she got out of the bath, spilling water onto the floor, and dried herself, dragging on her chemise and drawers over damp flesh, retwisting her hair in a bun on top of her head. Mrs Ali had been right. She felt better for a bath. More human.

Faye came in with the baby and Lily took her, sitting on a chair and lifting the chemise. The baby searched blindly for the nipple, turning her head until she found it, trying to latch on. Succeeding, she began to suck and swallow, making soft, snuffling sounds, waving her free arm in the air, kicking her little feet. Lily gazed down at her. She'd meant not to look at the baby but it had been impossible to keep to her resolution. The silky cap of hair glowed in the light from the kitchen window. The paternity was unmistakable but Miss Salt refused to see it. Lily had never told her what had happened that night. She didn't want Faye to know. It made it easier to pretend to herself that the shameful event had never occurred. And that if it had, it was not with Erasmus Salt.

Lily was living day by day, hour by hour, waiting for this time to be behind her. As soon as Faye took the baby to the widow, she would escape the Salts and start her life again. She intended to return to London, find a cheap place to stay and look for a position with a theatre company. She would do any lowly thing – take a small, non-speaking part, mend the costumes, even sweep the stage – anything in order to further her experience, develop her craft. But until the thing was gone to its new home, she could do nothing.

The spinster sat down next to Lily at the kitchen table and they watched in silence as the baby's lids drooped, her arm ceased to move and her lips parted. Lily removed her nipple from its mouth, pulled down her chemise and began buttoning her blouse.

'You must take her to the widow tomorrow, Miss Salt. It is time.'

Thirty

The beach was deserted and the sea calm and still, the waves gentle. With the baby in her arms, Faye walked slowly and carefully, taking small steps, skirting outcrops of smooth white chalk, flints, a rusted anchor half buried in the sand. It was still early. Lily had fed the baby and gone back to bed, refusing to say goodbye to her child. Mrs Ali had made her a present of a rattle, woven from thin red twigs of willow, enclosing seven pebbles from the beach, making Faye understand that the sound of the rattle would keep away evil spirits. Faye had washed and dried the baby, tied a handkerchief around the head of silken hair, wrapped her in a clean, twice-folded length of sheet, and the white blanket, then bundled her up in one of her own old paisley shawls so that only her face showed. Dropping the rattle in her pocket, she had picked up the baby and let herself out of the cottage.

She wished that the widow's house was further away. The walk to the cottage on the west cliff was too short, the time before the surrender of the baby too brief. She

made herself keep on. Erasmus had written, demanding
to know that the 'inconvenience' had been resolved. He
was developing his vision, he said, had found a theatre
manager in London who wanted to display the ghost.
He would send for them soon. Approaching the harbour wall, Faye stopped. The winter sun was low, the
light on the sea bright and brilliant as if it spilled from
heaven. Cradling the warm, light weight against her own
body, Faye stared out at the swell pulsing under the
sparkling surface of the sea, the horizon beyond. She
stood motionless, watching the water, absorbed by its
rhythm, the waves seeming to break not outside her but
inside her, as if the sea had entered her and flooded her,
crashed and sighed inside her, breaching the dam that
had enabled her to live.

The bell over the Customs House broke her reverie,
ringing out over the men loading coal and cabbages onto
barges in the harbour, the rattling progress of the tram
up the hill. After a few seconds, Faye turned around.
She went back the way she had come, walking purposefully, passing a set of meandering footsteps in the sand
that belonged already to another woman, another time.
Continuing on past the lodgings, she walked under the
chalk cliffs. They towered over her, their ledges and
nooks and crannies resembling the grave, ancient face
of the earth, grey and silver plants clinging to life in the
crevices. Seawater ran in shallow eddies over gleaming
sands as if the world was washed clean. Absolved.

At a place where there was nothing but cliff on one

side and sea on the other, where no one could watch her or hear her, Faye sat on a ledge of chalk and looked down at the baby in her arms. She was awake; her eyes were open. When she was born, they'd been inky pools, not blue nor brown nor black. In ten days, they'd altered, lightened to grey, fringed with pale, silky lashes. Her complexion was fresh and pink, her expression content. She looked back at Faye, steadily, with curiosity, as if she was the first person in the world. The only person in the world.

Holding the baby close, Faye began to sob. Once she'd begun, she couldn't stop. She cried noisily, rocking backwards and forwards, her howls mingling with the desolate screams of the gulls until she didn't know what came from her throat and what from theirs. Cradling Lily's baby, her tears continuing to fall, Faye began to unforget.

It had started that evening in January, the ground outside the nursery window white with frost, the sky pinpricked with stars. Their parents were to attend a ball and before they left, Mother came up to say goodnight. Faye saw her in the doorway, in her ivory gown and feather boa, kid gloves pulled up above her elbows and her hair in ringlets around her face. She inhaled the creamy scent of her neck, felt the press of the gardenia on her cheek as Mother stooped to kiss her.

In the morning, she'd run down to the dining room, wanting to see her restored to her ordinary self, in her wrapper and lace cap. Mother wasn't at breakfast. Her place was laid but she didn't come and pick up the silver spoon, crack the top of the shell of a brown boiled egg, dab her lips with the damask napkin that lay on its side, rolled up in a silver ring that she'd had as a girl, that was engraved in flowing, flourishing letters with the initials CGP. Clara Grace Pepper. Pepper was her maiden name, for which foolish reason, she once told her children, she'd agreed to become the wife of Frederick Salt.

She wasn't in her bedroom, or the kitchen, or at the piano, or in the sewing room she sometimes used. She wasn't anywhere. Erasmus stayed in his room all that day and when lunch was served at one o' clock as usual, only Faye ate onion soup and shepherd's pie at the nursery table. That afternoon, she hung about the kitchens, asking Birdie where Mother was, but the servants were subdued and no answer came. In the evening, Father called Faye into his study and requested that she sit on his knee. Startled by the unfamiliarity of the request, she did as he asked. 'Your mother has gone away. She will not be coming back.' Faye heard the words but couldn't understand what he meant by them. From that day, Father refused any mention of Mother. Erasmus wouldn't speak of her either. A silence like stone settled itself around her absence.

The change in Erasmus had been sudden, from a carefree, kindly playmate to a morose and silent older brother. He woke Faye one morning saying that their mother had appeared to him at the end of his bed, in a nightdress, her face deathly white. He'd seen her, he insisted. Faye had covered her ears. 'If she is a ghost, she must be dead.'

'She isn't dead, Faye,' Ras had said. 'She's gone away.'

Father had died just two years later, in a hunting accident on the estate, his own gun discharged into his chest. After a funeral in the parish church, a brief season of attention from aunts and older cousins, they had been left at Nether Hall in the care of a series of governesses. Erasmus took to searching the great empty rooms, the dark staircases and corridors, for ghosts. He jumped out from behind curtains and cupboards, startling Faye, contrived flickering reflections with candlelight in mirrors and on paper screens, conducting what he called *experiments*.

Faye was transported back to those days, to herself at nine years of age, lying in her bed in the darkness. Over her head, a methodical scratching sound, human in its regularity and intent, grew louder. She cried out in terror and the scratching gave way to tapping, as if something or someone would come through the ceiling. As she began to scream, a voice spoke.

'What's the matter, Faye?'

Her brother stood over her, a nightlight in his hand. She couldn't speak, could only stare, her tongue clumsy, heart scrambling in her chest like a frightened mouse.

'Ghost,' she managed to utter. 'In the attic.'

'What did you see?' he said, his eyes bright.

'Heard it.'

Erasmus leaned in close. 'If you are afraid, keep your eyes tight shut. Reach out into the air. You'll know then there's nothing there.'

He'd left the room, taking the candle with him. Faye had lain under the weight of blankets, her eyes as tightly shut as she could make them. Later, as her arms and legs began to soften into sleep, a creaking board jolted her back to wakefulness. She heard a soft, brushing sound and made herself lift an arm and explore the space above her. Silken hair brushed the skin of her face. Strong fingers, clad in kid, seized her wrist. She heard someone screaming, uncontrollably, the sound terrorising her further until she realised that it came from her own mouth. Erasmus reappeared, holding up the lamp, staring at her. He held her hand but couldn't comfort her.

The torments inflicted by the spirits ceased abruptly when their guardian dispatched Erasmus to a school in the city of Rochester. Even when she knew that the sounds and sensations had been manufactured by her older brother, they retained their power. Faye had remained afraid of the dark, startled by sudden noises, fearful of life, of death, and of Erasmus. He went from school to university in Durham, returned as heir to Nether Hall and to their father's estate. At twenty-two, little of the boy he'd been remained. He turned the running of the estate over to a manager and went often to London to meetings at the houses of spirit mediums, lectures on reincarnation, making the old library his domain, filling it with books on the occult. Acrid smells wafted from open windows; beams of brilliant light escaped from under closed doors; quantities of glass and mirror, wrapped in layer upon layer of sacking, arrived from London.

Sometimes, Erasmus summoned Faye to the library. On a raised stage that he'd had constructed at one end of the room, against backdrops supplied by a Mr Bell, she watched a stuffed dog materialise from nowhere, and disappear; saw a china doll raise a china arm and vanish. Faye sat with a dry mouth, chills running up and down her spine, unable to bring herself to applaud. The apparitions frightened her and she felt they contained some inherent evil. When she said so, Erasmus grew angry, his eyes burning with some private obsession.

'This is just the beginning, Faye. You wait and see. One day, I will summon a real spirit from the afterlife. A human one.'

Thirty-One

Number ninety-seven, Wimpole Street, had white marble steps, men's names engraved on shining brass plates by the side of the door. A clerk took her umbrella, escorted her along a carpeted corridor to a room at the back of the building and tapped on an open door.

'Patient, Doctor Shilling.'

'Be seated, Mrs Bell,' said the doctor. 'What ails you?'

Ruth stared at him, struggling for words. It had started with the letter. From the day she received it, read the awful words, life had lost its urgent claim on her. Yet, uselessly, the body marched on. Food had lost its taste and that gave her the understanding of what she must do. She stopped eating. Alfred failed at first to notice but Jen remonstrated, made jellies from calves' feet, simmering them in the cauldron. When her maid went home, Ruth poured the viscous broth down the drain. In place of meals, she took nips of brandy, standing in the pantry, took them straight from the bottle, the ridges of the glass neck pressed on her lips. The campaign began to succeed. Her skirts loosened around her waist, her shoes slackened on her feet and her wedding ring when she soaped her hands slid off and lay shining and empty on the bottom of the sink.

Often, she dreamed of her daughter. Liza was walking beside her in a summer dress. Ruth greeted her, expressed her joy at her return, her sorrow that she had died alone, without her mother by her side, but Liza couldn't hear and didn't answer. Liza was behind glass, on the other side of a train window; the train pulled out of the railway station, leaving Ruth stranded on the platform. Liza lay in a coffin of soft black soil, laughing in the way she used to laugh. 'I'm acting, Mother,' she said. 'Can't you see?'

Alfred refused to talk about his stepdaughter. It was unfortunate, he said – briskly, as if they'd lost a kitten or a canary – but there was nothing to be done about it and it was no good dwelling on the loss. 'Won't bring her back.' He grew angry when he found Ruth sitting on the edge of Lily's bed, holding her daughter's old doll to her face, inhaling a faint, lingering scent of past happiness.

He'd noticed at last. Insisted that she see a doctor. He would pay for it. 'With the blood money you made from my daughter,' she'd thought but hadn't said. It was too late for that. Too late for everything.

'Is it your nerves?' said the doctor, impatiently, looking at her over his lunettes. He wore an old-fashioned stock onto which the skin of his neck pleated in soft folds.

Ruth smoothed her gloves on her lap, pressed the empty fingers against each other as rain pattered on the long glass window.

'Bowels?'

She'd made the diagnosis herself. *Broken heart.* He would see it in her eyes, if he only looked. She could see it in the mirror. Eyes from which the light had gone. Eyes deadened by the knowledge of what life could do to a person.

Indicating a high couch, he pulled a screen in front of it. She lay on the couch, breathing in the smell of formaldehyde, studying the plaster rose in the centre of the ceiling, the dust collected in its white intricacies, while the doctor's cold fingers pressed and pressed again. 'Does this hurt? Any tenderness here? Or here?'

Ruth rolled her head from side to side on the flat pad of horsehair. Dressed and buttoned, sitting again by the desk, she found her voice. Asked the only question to which she wanted an answer.

'How long will I live, Doctor?'

Dr Shilling rinsed his hands under a brass tap. He dried them on a linen towel and returned to his position behind the desk. 'I do not know,' he said, looking at her at last, with eyes magnified by the lenses of his spectacles. Ruth nodded. Men were helpless, more helpless even than women. It had taken her all her life to see it.

'Tell your husband you won't suffer. I'll make sure of it.'

Dr Shilling prescribed black drop, to be taken on

waking, before retiring, and otherwise as needed. Ruth took the small brown bottle and opened her purse. Passed over the guinea. She'd forgotten her umbrella, she realised, waiting on Oxford Street for the bus. Rain would fall on her best hat, would wet the felt, drench the silk roses. Climbing the twisting stairs to the top deck, as the first drops began to fall, she welcomed the prospect. Everything spoiled – milk, meat, human lives. It was the way of things.

Thirty-Two

The paddle steamer churned its way through the harbour, past the great stone obelisk dedicated to George IV that the townsfolk called the toothpick, and out into the open sea. Lily watched through a porthole as Ramsgate and the people that went about their business there – gutting fish or frying it, begging in front of the sailors' church, sweeping out seaside boarding houses, staring from attic rooms at the impervious sea – all disappeared. Despite everything, she had liked the little town. She'd been certain that when she returned to London, it would be as a free woman. But she was as much a prisoner as ever. Salt had sent two tickets, in a letter to his sister.

A little mew, like a kitten's, made itself heard. Lily looked down at the baby lying on her lap but made no move to straighten her lopsided cap, wipe the dribble from her chin. The creature had come from her own body but she felt disconnected from her, as if she belonged to someone else. Faye Salt had taken her up to the widow's house but had found the door locked and no smoke issuing from the chimney; the dog kennel empty. 'Mrs Parsons must have been called away,' the spinster had said, returning to the lodgings hours later with her eyes red and streaming from the wind, the baby crying for her milk.

Lily had suggested they go to St Laurence Church and leave her in the porch, or perhaps the font, if it was empty. She would be safe enough there, high off the ground, wrapped in the soft white blanket. A good woman would discover her and bring her up as her own daughter. Faye Salt had refused to even consider it. 'Anyone might find her, Lily,' she'd said, shaking her head, little spots of colour flaring in her cheeks. 'Anyone at all. We shall take her with us to London.'

'And what will we do with her there?' Lily had shouted. 'She would have been better off staying here, by the sea.'

'I am making enquiries,' Faye had said, and would not say more.

The other passengers were drinking beer, eating plates of roast chicken, tapping their feet to the tunes of a brass band. Some got up to dance, the women's brightly coloured skirts swinging out, their laughter floating on the air. Through the crape, Lily watched. She was fully dressed for the first time since the confinement, her skirt sponged by kind Mrs Ali, her hair washed and curled, her boots buttoned onto her feet. She'd worn the veil of her own free will, afraid that someone she knew might see her, that word of her shame would reach Ruth Bell.

Even to think of it made Lily feel sick. If Ruth Bell was ever to learn what had happened, it must be from her own mouth.

'She is hungry, Lily,' Faye said.

Lily looked down and saw that the baby was crying, the sound drowned by the music. Reluctantly, moving to the curtained-off bunk that was their private cabin, she lifted her blouse and held the nipple towards the creature's face. Clamping her gums, staring up at Lily, the baby began to suck as if her life depended upon it. Which it did. Looking down at her, seeing her intense focus, the little scatter of milk spots on her cheeks, her tiny, waving fingers, Lily felt something inside her soften. She'd thought she would hate the baby. Would see in it only what had happened to her at the hands of its father. It wasn't like that. She did not love her but nor did she hate her. It was impossible to do so. She was innocent and beautiful, uncorrupted by her origins. Lily wouldn't have believed that something so perfect could come from herself.

The sucking slowed and stopped. The baby turned scarlet, eyes squeezed shut, milk running down her chin. Lily moved her to her other arm but she refused the other breast, her arms flailing, her features contorted. Lily got to her feet, pulling down her blouse, yanking the veil back over her face.

'Here,' she said, returning to the saloon, thrusting her at Faye. 'You take her. I don't know what's wrong with her.'

'She has wind,' Faye said. 'That's all.' Laying her over her shoulder she rubbed her back until she stopped hiccoughing, then sat with her in her arms, cooing and murmuring in the voice she used only for the infant – sweet, high-pitched, infinitely patient. Just before they left Mrs Ali's house, to Lily's surprise, Miss Salt had produced a layette. Half a dozen little dresses with yokes worked in smocking; six each of shirts and shifts hand-sewn in soft lawn, their edges scalloped. All the garments appeared unworn.

'Where did you get these?' Lily had asked, as the spinster eased the baby's head through the neck of a shift, made a bow with the ties at the back.

'I sent for them,' Faye had answered, after a pause.

'Who from?'

'A friend,' the woman had replied, pulling a cotton bonnet onto the baby's head, speaking briskly. 'You must give her a name, Miss Bell, before she leaves us. You can at least give your baby a name.'

Lily had refused. She was afraid that if it had a name, the creature might start to become real – her daughter and her mother's grandchild. Afraid that some well of maternal love might open up in her that she could not withstand. It was better that the baby remained, 'she'. Sometimes 'it'.

The musicians put down their instruments and gathered round a table with plates of food in front of them. Through the veil, Lily scanned their faces. She'd continued to look for Mr Ames, searching the beach for a familiar figure with his face turned to the sky, staring out of the cottage window dreaming that she would see him approaching the door, that he would come for her and they would leave together. It comforted her to remember Mr Ames. She felt when she thought of him as if somewhere in the world she had a friend.

'Did you ever hear anything of the actor, Miss Salt?'

The spinster's face stiffened. 'Mr Ames? He ran off to London, I believe.'

Lily felt an irrational moment of hope. 'He had an engagement? At a theatre?'

Miss Salt's face flushed, from her high collar to her hairline. 'Forget about him, Lily,' she said, with sudden fierceness. 'He was unworthy of you. And of his poor little infant. He wasn't what you thought. It will do no good to think about him.'

Clasping her hands together and digging her nails into her palms, Lily looked out of the porthole. They'd reached the estuary. The boat chugged past a herd of cows up to their knees in mud; a slow-turning windmill; a gang of men in striped jackets erecting hop poles. If Faye Salt wouldn't find a place for the baby, she must do it herself. Near where she had grown up, there was a workhouse, a sombre-looking stone building that took in orphans and old women. 'And sent them out in boxes,' her mother used to say. Lily used to pass it on her way to school, sometimes seeing little girls peeping out from behind the high gates, dressed in drab pinafores, their hair shorn like boys. She couldn't understand then how any mother could ever abandon her child. It had seemed to her worse than murder, the wickedest crime a woman could commit. She understood now.

At the top of Tower Steps, a stooped figure in a black hat was pacing up and down, his hands linked behind his back. Lily spotted him from the gangplank, her heart turning over at the sight. Remembering how she'd given him her unearned respect when she first left London, had trusted him and believed he would launch her on the stage, she felt almost as angry with herself as with him. 'Idiot,' she muttered as they walked towards him. 'How could you have been so stupid?'

'Late,' he called, catching sight of them. 'Been waiting for an hour.' He saw the bundle in his sister's arms and his expression darkened. 'What the hell is that doing here, Faye?' he said, as they joined him. 'Told you to make arrangements.'

'There was nowhere suitable, Erasmus,' Faye said, her words rushed and anxious. 'She is delicate. I know of a place in London where the infants are well cared for.' Breathing in the tainted city air, Lily looked down at the toes of her boots, the flagstones splashed with birdlime and river water, a basket of wriggling eels at the feet of a nearby fisherman. Salt hadn't examined the infant swaddled in the blanket, or touched her. He wanted to pretend that she was nothing to do with him.

Their boxes were loaded onto a cab and they set off, Lily and Faye inside with the baby, Salt riding on the box next to the driver. On the other side of the glass, the streets were crowded with liveried carriages, well-dressed people hailing cabs, tradesmen in long aprons. Lily had thought she was coming home but looking out at the crowds going about their important business, she felt small and insignificant, as if London had forgotten her, wouldn't have noticed if she'd never returned.

The driver turned into a side street and pulled up the horses. They got down, Faye loosening the ribbon under the baby's chin as Salt hauled on the bell pull of a dingy-looking house with a tree on the pavement outside.

'My sister,' he said to the woman who came to receive them, indicating Faye with his hand. 'And her infant.' Faye looked startled. Her mouth opened then closed.

'Good afternoon, Mrs...' the woman said.

'Brown,' he said. 'Mrs Brown.' He nodded at Lily. 'This young lady is helping with the baby.'

Lily kept silent. Soon, the baby would belong to someone else. It was what she wanted more than anything so she must get used to it, play the part of nursemaid. They followed the landlady to a room on the first floor, cluttered with small items of furniture that left just enough space for two beds on either side of it and a table in the middle. The baby began to struggle in Faye's arms, arching her back, letting out a confused cry. Faye unwrapped her from the blanket and a shaft of light streamed in through the dusty window, lighting up the small form.

'Got your hair, bless her,' said the woman, peering at her, touching her cheek. 'What's her name?'

Faye looked at Lily. Lily stared back, impassively.

'Grace,' Faye said, suddenly. 'Her name is Grace.'

In the doorway, Professor Salt began to cough. He requested a glass of water, claiming a dry throat from the ride on the box of the cab, and he and the landlady left the room. Throwing off the bonnet and the cloak, Lily almost toppled a large china umbrella stand.

'It wasn't your business to name her,' she said, hanging the cloak on a peg on the back of the door.

Sitting on the bed, settling the baby on her lap, Faye kissed her forehead. 'Every child has a right to a name, Lily. There is a foundlings hospital,' she said, her voice indistinct. 'I have written to them.'

'We could go there now,' Lily said. 'Can they take her today?'

'I'm to visit in the morning. There are procedures.' Faye got out the rattle, shaking it gently, and the baby waved her arms, kicked her legs under the white dress. She stretched her lips in what looked like a smile.

'Stop it, Faye.' Grabbing the rattle, throwing it on the floor, Lily snatched up the baby. There was a rap at the door and with the baby in one arm, Lily whirled around and flung it open.

'Yes?'

Erasmus Salt stood on the landing. He'd taken off his hat and coat, was in his shirtsleeves. Lily felt a sense of dread at the realisation that for a short time they would once again be residing in the same house.

'Due at the theatre shortly, Miss Bell,' he said, his voice displaying some of its old silkiness. 'Can have a look at the blue room before we start rehearsals. Everything is prepared.'

She stared at him. 'I told you before. I won't do it. You can get yourself another ghost.'

'Leave us, Faye,' Salt said.

Faye took the baby from Lily's arms, muttering about arrangements for a cot, and went down the stairs. Stepping into the room, closing the door behind him, Salt stood in front of Lily. He was closer than she had been to him since that distant, cursed night, so close that she could see the crooked downwards lines on his forehead, the intense expression in his eyes as he reached for a lock of her hair, his fingers brushing the skin of her neck. 'You are my ghost,' he said, as if explaining something to a simpleton. 'You and no one else. You appear when I command it. You will disappear when I will it.'

He looked insane, Lily thought, with a heart-stopping sense of fear.

'There was a ghost before me,' she said, trying to move her head, free her hair from his grip. 'And there will be another after me, Professor Salt. As soon as the child is placed, I will return to my life.'

Erasmus moved his face closer to hers.

'You have no life,' he said, softly. 'You are dead. Buried

at Ramsgate. The certificate was signed by your father. You have no life, except with me. And I will give you eternal life.'

Lily stared at him, unable to breathe or speak. A chill ran through her, to her marrow; every cell in her body told her she was in peril. Footsteps approached up the stairs and Salt let go of her hair. As Faye re-entered the room, he stepped back and straightened his collar. Bowed.

'Rehearsals begin tomorrow. We shall visit the theatre this evening.'

Thirty-Three

Rain overtopped the mossy gutters and spilled from the rain butts, backed up the storm drains, created muddy lakes where there had been paths, obscuring corners and running down steps, hurrying into basement kitchens and coal cellars. In Ruth's bedroom, the damp spot on the bedroom ceiling broadened. Ruth thought of Noah's ark. Wondered how big it must have been to accommodate all those beasts, and how he kept them fed.

Easing her feet into her slippers, she sat down in front of the dolls house. The stairs needed a carpet. She could find a scrap of something, a green heathery tweed or red woollen worsted, cut it to size and pin it down with tacks. But she wouldn't. There was no use any more in mending and making and hoping. Only this was real. The rain outside and herself inside; a woman in her bedroom, alone.

Reaching for the dropper, she filled it and with a deft squeeze emptied the contents into her mouth. Soon, the opiate coated the back of her throat, numbed her tongue.

A welcome sense of removal, of release from cares, began to spread inside Ruth's head. Inserting her hand into the kitchen, she turned a rigid figure round from the range.

'Cook,' she said, leaning her against a mangle. 'I have bad news.'

'Yes, ma'am.'

'Yes,' said Ruth. 'The thing is ... Well, the thing is, Cook, that I am not long for this world.'

Cook wrung her apron, an expression of concern flitting across her impassive features. 'Is there nothing to be done, ma'am?'

'No,' said Ruth. 'But I would like a cup of tea.'

'Yes, ma'am,' said Cook, toppling to the floor, exposing her wooden legs.

Ruth stood her up, turning her round to face the range again. She unhooked the copper kettle from the rafters and placed it over the painted flames. Arranged the tea set on the tray.

'We shall take tea together, Cook. Milk? Sugar?'

Cook made no answer. Ruth got into the feather bed and lay under the gaze of the people on the walls. These were her companions. Her mother and her father on their wedding day, small and hopeful; her beloved younger brother; two sisters, taken one after the other in childbirth, a third by a shovel blow to the back of her head from her husband. One by one, they slipped out of their frames and filled the room, a welcoming committee crowding in on her, beckoning and chattering, tugging at her hands and heart, closer now than they'd ever been in life.

Only Liza did not appear. In her bed, Ruth groaned. She should never have allowed her daughter to leave the house. Should have laid her body over the threshold to prevent it, or run after her, made a spectacle, shouted for someone to fetch the police. It had been the worst mistake of her life, letting Liza walk out of the door.

It would be put right soon enough.

'She waits for me,' she said aloud. 'When it is my time, I will go to her.'

'Still raining out,' Cook said, in her sharp little voice. 'Cats and dogs.'

Thirty-Four

Faye had written to the foundling hospital from Ramsgate, indicating that she was considering making a bequest and wished to see for herself the charitable works. A letter had arrived by return inviting her to join one of the occasional tours provided for supporters. She'd arrived a few minutes late, joined the group in the hallway as the lady president led them around a large old house, past well-appointed kitchens where children stood at low sinks scrubbing potatoes, a steam-filled laundry that made the ladies' eyes water, on through the trustees' oak-panelled meeting room and into the chapel. In a private sitting room, a table had been laid with a lace cloth, a vase of primroses. Tea was poured from a silver pot, Madeira cake passed around by a maid introduced as a beneficiary; the woman seemed cowed, her hair scraped back, a wooden cross dangling at her neck.

Three little girls, attired in thick brown dresses, came in and sang hymns. Two boys in pantaloons followed, racing through the creed and the sacraments, looking at the cake. The boys departed, backing out of the room, their eyes still hungry, and the other ladies began chatting, talking quickly and loudly, laughing. They wore silk day dresses in green and purple checks; plumes of bright feathers swayed on their hats as they lifted their teacups. Faye felt hollow. She ought to have stayed away. Putting down her cup, excusing herself, she left the room and set off down an echoing corridor. She'd intended to make her way directly to the exit but seeing the boys ahead of her, she followed them, her feet squeaking on polished parquet that as they went up the stairs to the first floor gave way to cork tiles. Halfway along another corridor, the boys disappeared through a door. Faye stood outside, her head bent, listening to the murmur of children's voices.

After a minute, she opened the door. The room was large and functional, the lower section of the walls clad with white tiles, the long windows barred. Oilcloth covered the floor and nestling on it like a flock of starlings settled on a field were innumerable small children, all dressed in brown. At the sight of her, one of the nurses shrilled on a whistle and the children got to their feet, arranged themselves in lines and stood to attention, their arms stiff by their sides. Only one, a little girl, neglected to join a line or even to try to stand up. Engrossed in her game, she sat on the floor building up a pile of wooden bricks. Her hair, in the dull window light, was a halo of fire. For a moment, Faye forgot how to breathe.

She moved towards her, making her way between lines of children, compelled by an instinct to pick her up. A white-aproned attendant swooped and hoisted the child by one arm.

'Stand up for the visitor,' she said, knocking down the tower, sweeping aside the bricks.

The girl began to wail.

'Please,' Faye said. 'Please, I—'

She left the foundling hospital and walked back to Islington. The route by which she returned was the one by which she had come, yet everything was altered, the streets unrecognisable. The trees waved their branches in urgent semaphore; the horses raced to their destinies; a shower of rain fell directly from heaven. Every small and great thing was charged with life.

Lily was sitting on the edge of her bed, one of her play books in her hand.

'Well?' she said, putting aside the book, jumping to her feet. 'Will they take her?'

In the iron cot the landlady had produced for her, Grace lay on her back, awake but content, her grey eyes watchful. She was listening, Faye felt. Laying her mantle on the back of a chair, Faye removed her hat and smoothed her hair from the parting, looking at her reflection in the mirror on the wall. Right and wrong was not the simple affair she had once believed it to be. Sometimes, to lie was the right thing. The godly thing.

'There is an epidemic at the foundlings home,' she

said, her face in the glass impassive. 'Scarlet fever. The committee is unable to admit any new children, at the direction of the medical officer. We are to enquire again in a month.'

Lily slumped down on the bed, her head in her hands.

The unforgetting, once it had begun, would not cease. Memories rose in Faye's mind at times of their own choosing; unbidden, unwished-for, they assailed her, the claims of the past more urgent, often, than those of the present. Her head and heart ached, her guts churned. She bought notebooks, ink and a pen, and in the lodgings in Islington – late at night, while Lily and the baby slept – tentatively, almost fearfully, resumed her old habit of journaling. To write what she remembered, to set it down on the page, in the small, precise handwriting that was decipherable only by herself, gave Faye relief.

Maria Hedges had been barely out of girlhood, skinny, with bony hands and knees, freckled cheeks, teeth too big for her face. A foul mouth on her, picked up in old Ma Hedges's cottage and at the village pump. She'd had the same peculiarly colourless hair as Lily Bell, white-blonde, falling to her waist. She came to the house three or four nights a week, arriving in her own unsuitable clothes, being brought up by Birdie to what had been their mother's dressing room. She was tall, five feet and seven inches, her legs too long for the old gown of Mother's that Erasmus insisted Faye dress her in. But her narrow waist fitted the bodice, her feet slid into the satin slippers. Faye made up her face from the box of stage paint Erasmus had brought from London, following the directions in the manual, smoothing her white lashes and brows with pigments, reddening her lips and brushing contours onto her cheeks. Dressed and made up as Erasmus instructed, at times the girl resembled their mother, in the painting in the dining room.

Faye stayed away from the library while he conducted his experiments with lights and mirrors. More than ever, she loathed his obsession with ghosts. It was sinister and could lead to no good. Maria Hedges didn't object though. The girl came to the house a dozen times or more, in her best dress and shawl, her hair curled. The routine was always the same. Faye applied the stage paint, dressed her, and delivered her to the library. Erasmus worked, assisted by Balthazar. Later, when he rang the bell, Faye collected the girl from the library and in the old boudoir cleaned off the paint and powders and helped Maria back into her attire: usually, she wore a blue muslin dress patterned with yellow daisies; a silky, long-fringed shawl, embroidered with more flowers; a pair of soft blue shoes, worn down at the heels. When Maria was ready, Faye saw her off from the side door to walk back down the lane to the village, about four miles away.

She hadn't done so on the night of her disappearance. She'd waited up as usual but the bell had not rung. Erasmus had gone on late with his work and didn't wish to disturb her, she'd decided, as she went to bed. Early the next morning, old Ma Hedges had come to Nether Hall, banging on the side door, asking for Maria. Birdie had woken Faye and called her down. 'What do you want?' Faye had said to the woman, a cold, sick sensation flooding her body. 'She's not in her bed,' Mrs Hedges said.

Erasmus had arrived behind Faye in the stone passageway, still in his dressing gown, his pipe between his teeth.

'What has happened?' he'd said, irritably, puffing blue smoke into the cold air.

'She's not in her bed, sir,' the woman said again. 'She isn't anywhere.'

'You saw her off, Faye,' he said. 'As usual. Didn't you?'

'Yes,' she'd said, after just a moment's hesitation. 'Yes, I did.'

'She must have got lost,' Erasmus said. 'On her way home. We must search for her.'

Terrible days and nights had followed, with the men crossing the fields with flaming brands in their hands, fanning out through the woods and the lanes. Erasmus led the search parties, coming home with wild hair and wild eyes, his clothes singed by burning pitch, the skin of his neck torn by thorns. The police arrived to interview him, and later asked Faye what had happened that night. She lied again, her heart in her mouth, told them that Maria had left as usual, dressed in her own clothes, shortly before ten in the evening. Was it so? Could she have seen off the girl and forgotten that she had done so? Was her mind failing her?

That evening, late, the veil and gown and satin slippers had appeared back in the dressing room, piled in a heap. Faye stared at them for a long while, feeling sick. Erasmus had made no reference to them but she understood what she must do. By candlelight, she brushed tendrils of dry bracken from the deep, flounced hem of the dress, sprinkled it with patchouli oil for preservation and rolled it in brown paper. Bundling up the lace veil, she packed everything – the kid gloves and pearl choker, the white feather boa, the button hook – away in the chest that had been their mother's, softly closing the lid, turning the silver key in the lock. She extinguished the candles and went to her own room, her mind racing. She did not know what had occurred exactly but she knew that Erasmus must be innocent. It could not be otherwise.

Here, another memory struggled but failed to rise to her mind.

The police came again, this time to interview the mute. Ras had recruited the fellow from London to operate the limelight; he lodged with the groom in the cottage behind the stables. Faye listened outside the closed doors of the library, heard Balthazar grunting and groaning, heard the officers raise their voices.

'He didn't tell them anything,' she said to Erasmus that night when he returned from London from one of his scientific meetings.

'How could he, Faye?' he'd said, his voice cold and collected. 'There is nothing to tell.'

She'd kept quiet for the rest of suppertime. Forced down the cold game pie Birdie had served up, a glass of sour wine.

'Ras,' she had said as he got up to leave the room. 'This morbid obsession... Why don't you... Could you not... take up some other form of employment?'

'Such as?'

She rose from her chair and stood in front of him, her arms rigid by her sides. Faye felt a loyalty to her brother so deep she could barely articulate it even to herself. Therefore, she must speak. She owed him that.

'You might run the estate, like Father did.'

Erasmus delivered a slap to her face that sent her sprawling on the stone flags. 'This is my work,' he bellowed. 'My life's work. Bringing back the dead. If you don't like it, then go.' As Faye struggled to her feet, under the watchful image of their mother, he sat down and relit his pipe. Pungent smoke curled towards the ceiling. 'Remember, Faye,' he said, his voice soft, 'that you were the last one to see the Hedges girl alive. If anyone knows what happened to her, it is you.'

Shortly afterwards, intending never to return, she had fled Nether Hall to take up a post as governess in the household of their distant relatives, the Mordaunts.

Thirty-Five

In his new rooms, the oil lamp burning bright under a clean glass mantle, Balthazar attended to his work. He had a rag tied around his mouth and nose but still his eyes smarted as he whittled the lump of quicklime into a cylindrical shape, holding the stone in a pair of tongs with his left hand, using a chisel with his right, catching the chips of lime on a sheet of old newspaper spread on the table for the purpose. The lime had arrived that day – Nottingham lime, the best there was – and he was preparing new cones for the device that had, when he started in his trade, been known as the *phoshelioulam-proteron*. Now, in these reduced and coarsened times, it was known as the limelight.

His attention was half on the lump of inert matter in his hands, and partly on what it would later that day illuminate. Miss Lily Bell was to play the ghost again. Just for a short while, Salt had said. A month at most. Balthazar felt a shift in his guts, a queasy wave of something unpleasant, and was forced to remind himself of the code by which he lived. There was no sentiment in business. When the professor gave the word, Mr Pook would be ready.

The cones shaped, he set about them with his gimlet, carefully, drilling a hole through the centre of the first one. The young lady would not suffer, he would make sure of that. He'd use the cheese wire. Or perhaps the gimlet. He pulled the spike out of the lime and turned it in his fingers, tested the point on the palm of his hand. Either way, she would barely know what happened. It wasn't pretty, but for the hundred guineas Salt had promised, it would be worth it. With a *monkey* in his pocket, he intended to leave the ghost professor's employ and embark on the life of a gentleman, with a good suit of clothes on his back and a short memory.

The job done, Balthazar put down his tools and wrapped the cones tightly in two layers of waxed paper, secured them with string. The air in London was damp and dirty as the people, had the capacity to spoil the lime.

Thirty-Six

The blue room underneath the stage of the Empire Theatre on Old Street was similar in size to the one at the Tivoli, lined with the same black velvet, the single limelight replaced by two. From the corner, Balthazar grunted a subdued greeting.

Positioning her feet on the chalk marks on the floor, her reflection faint in the great mirror, Lily felt numb. The dressing room – with its bright gaslights and running water, a carpet on the floor – had given her no pleasure. She'd squeezed her body into the costume, Faye Salt tugging the bodice over her breasts, inserting cotton pads over her nipples. Her face was whitened with greasepaint, her hair fresh out of the curling papers, eyes darkened. Next to her, in a hastily procured rush cradle, little Grace lay asleep. Salt had announced that until such time as she could be admitted to the orphanage, the baby might as well feature in the performance. Otherwise he would be forced to convey regrettable news to his old acquaintance Alf Bell, he'd said, looking at the baby for what seemed the first time, staring at her. Lily hadn't dared to object. He'd rewritten the cameo, made Lily Bell the ghost of a young wife who had died in a fire along with her infant.

'Ladies and gentlemen! You will shortly behold the late Lily Bell and, for the first time anywhere in the world, that rare, unique, and most affecting ghost – the unfortunate lady's baby, which perished with her in the fire.' The boards flexed as the impresario walked off stage, the curtains rose and the footlights went up. As the trapdoor opened silently downwards into the blue room, at a knock on the wall, Balthazar lit the first gas jet, the flame burning blue.

'Wife,' the actor on stage called out. 'I would give my life to see you one last time.'

Balthazar ignited the second stream of gas and Salt's voice echoed through the auditorium, intense and charged. 'Late Lillian Bell. Come back to us, we beseech you. We mortals await your visitation in spirit form.' Standing under the stage in the blue room, Lily's skin prickled; she felt a chill, as if her blood ran cold in her veins. He meant what he said. Erasmus Salt spoke not like a showman, an entertainer, but as if he were a priest, a priest of darkness summoning someone from the dead.

The limes glowed white-hot and as the gasman focused a beam of brilliant light on her, Lily forced herself to open her arms, as if to embrace her widower.

'You are back,' groaned the actor, trying to seize her,

finding that his hands passed through her. 'Yet you are not here. And what of our beloved child?'

Balthazar focused the second limelight on the cradle and Salt's voice came again, soft and sinister. 'Return to us, spirit child.' The crowd grew restive and from outside the pool of light, Faye whispered urgent prompts. Leaning over the crib, Lily lifted out Grace. A deep, awed silence fell in the auditorium. The baby was dressed in a lace Christening gown, the long fall of the skirts reaching almost to the floor. With her face framed by a matching lace cap, her cheeks daubed with greasepaint and her lips reddened with carmine, Grace looked like a beautiful china doll.

'We have left your ill-fated world,' Lily said, holding the baby close, her voice hoarse. 'You see before you our everlasting spirits.'

On stage, the widower reached to take the infant but found the child to be as immaterial as his wife, a weightless spectre that his hands could not seize. A single male voice jeered that it was a doll, not a ghost baby, and as rehearsed, Lily pinched the baby's arm through the sleeve of the dress. In her drugged sleep, Grace twitched; she jerked her head and raised her arm, and from the auditorium a rumble went up, a sound that was neither joy nor sorrow nor longing but some heartfelt blend of all three. Women moaned; there was a thud as one in the front row fainted and fell forward against the flimsy partition. A scuffle broke out as the ushers tried to keep people from rushing the stage.

At the tap on the wall of the blue room, Balthazar extinguished the oxygen jet. The cones of lime cooled and in a short time Lily stood in near darkness, the baby limp in her arms, her ears ringing with the noise of what sounded like a riot in the auditorium. Grace's eyes were half open, the lids heavy, her expression dazed and vacant.

Faye arrived with a bottle of Mother's Friend and a teaspoon. 'She's to have another drop,' she said, taking out the stopper. 'Erasmus insists.'

'No,' Lily said. 'No more.' And Faye's arms fell to her sides.

In the final scene, as the limes began to glow, Salt's summons reverberated again through the auditorium. 'Come to our earthly abode,' he intoned. 'Oh fair spirits, make yourselves known to us.' Lily and Grace appeared to the audience and overhead the actor jumped up, playing a man torn between joy and terror.

'Stay,' he cried. 'I command it as your husband. Give me my child.'

'She is no longer your child,' Lily answered. 'I am no longer your wife. Do not try to detain us in your world. You will never succeed. We are feminine spirits, free to come and go as we please.'

The theatre filled with a gale of women's sighs. As the widower moved towards her as if to try again to snatch the baby, Lily stepped back.

'We do not live as you mortals live. We shall not obey your laws. Farewell!'

They were not the lines Salt had given her, but they were the words she'd felt impelled to speak. Balthazar closed the jets and the light in the blue room dimmed. Under cover of the continuing roars, the sheet of glass was lowered and the trapdoor closed. As the curtain fell, women sobbed, their cries rending the air. Men bellowed, demanding that the ghost professor return their lost daughters, their beloved sons.

Amid the tumult, Lily looked up to see Faye. She was standing in the corner of the chamber with a candle in her hand, her eyes fixed on Grace. She looked like a wraith, her eyes haunted and filled with longing. Faye had altered, since the baby had been born. Her old certainty of manner was gone and sometimes, as she rocked the baby, she shed silent tears that she attempted to conceal, wiping her face with the side of her hand.

Taking off the veil, Lily noticed again the long, right-angled tear in the lace, mended with Faye's neat handiwork. She touched the mend, feeling the raised bump of the stitches, as if she might read in them a message, from another young woman. Since they came back to London, she had been thinking more and more about Maria Hedges. Lily pictured Salt's eyes, his fixed expression as if he looked not outwards but inwards, at some twisted vision of his own creation. She had a bad feeling about what had happened to Maria, and at whose hands.

'What happen to the other ghost?' she said, her voice low and urgent. 'Tell me, Faye.'

Faye's gaze fell to the floor. 'She went away. I told you before.'

'Where? Where did she go? I need to know.'

Faye made a convoluted movement of her face and shoulders and a low, awful groan came from the corner. Balthazar was beating his chest, shifting from foot to foot. Lily went and stood in front of him. Held up the rush light so it illuminated his face. 'What happened to her, Balthazar?'

The gasman looked at her with bright cunning. He made no sound but threw back his head on his shoulders as if he swung from a gallows, his mouth gaping open, his eyes rolling back in his head. Lily felt chilled, fear creeping along her spine. Seeing the shock on her face, the gasman began to laugh, noiselessly, holding his sides, bent double.

'Stop this nonsense, Balthazar,' Faye whispered. She turned to Lily, her cheeks flushed, her eyes wide, glancing around as if she feared she might be overheard. 'No one knows what happened to Maria Hedges. She went away somewhere. That is all.'

Thirty-Seven

The crowd thinned. People dispersed, buttoning great-coats, blowing noses, marvelling or quarrelling, hailing cabs, queuing for omnibuses. Outside the tavern at the side of the Empire Theatre, leaning against a wall, Tom Ames drew on a hand-rolled cigarette, his eyes fixed on the stage door.

Some time after midnight, the door swung open. Tom watched as a figure emerged, veiled and cloaked but unmistakable. She stood for a moment, silhouetted in the lit doorway, a bundle in her arms. The spinster came behind with a bag on her arm and the thickset, menacing form of Erasmus Salt lumbered ahead of the women to the front of the theatre, raised his stick. A cabbie drew up and the spinster got in first. Miss Bell handed up the baby then climbed in herself, Salt shutting the door behind her. Salt installed himself beside the driver and at a crack of the whip, the horses took off down the street and vanished round a corner. Taking a last, deep draw on his cigarette, Tom flicked the end of it upwards, showering crimson sparks into the darkness.

He set off along the new embankment towards his lodgings, walking by the side of the river that flowed deep and silent in the darkness. The previous evening, going home soaking wet after a cloudburst, he'd stooped to pick a discarded playbill from a puddle. It was limp, the ink on the engraving smudged, but the eyes looking out with an expression not ghostly but mortal seemed to stare up at him, calling him to her. She had a baby in her arms. *Salt's Ghost. Back from the spirit world and now with a spirit child* said the print underneath.

Tom had been first in the line that formed for tickets, first through the theatre doors, had sat in the front row of the pit. When the show began, he'd been dazzled, happy beyond measure just to see Lily again. In the second act, he gathered his wits, saw that she looked drawn, her acting strained. She appeared reluctant to pick up the baby from the cradle and more than once, she forgot her lines or sounded as if she improvised. She was more beautiful than ever, with a new aura of graveness and sorrow about her, and Tom felt a wrenching sensation in his chest. She was not happy. He knew it. And if he hadn't been so obtuse, all those months earlier in Ramsgate, he could have persisted, helped her get away.

Reaching World's End, climbing the ladder to his room, he considered the baby ghost. It had been waxen-looking, so deathly still he'd believed at first that the heckler in the audience was right, it was a china doll. Suddenly, in an unmistakeably human movement, it had raised its arm, moved its little head. The crowd had erupted with some suppressed emotion, moaning and sighing; women fainted, their heads dropping to their knees, and had to be revived by their friends. A punch-up had broken out in the row behind him. There was no one there, it seemed, who hadn't lost a precious infant. The effect of the appearance of the infant ghost was even greater than that of Miss Bell's manifestation. But where had Salt found a baby?

Removing his jacket, hanging it on the nail on the back of the door, Tom sat on the edge of the bunk and his thoughts rose into the still air of the loft and tumbled there. Later, he lay awake, looking through the skylight at silvery, moonlit clouds, wishing Miss Bell would appear in his garret. They scarcely knew each other and yet he felt bound to her. She lived in his heart and his imagination. Even if she didn't want his attentions, Lily Bell might want his help. He pictured her on the beach that early morning, in distress. God only knew what Erasmus Salt might be capable of. With his aristocratic voice and manners, his important-sounding title, Tom hadn't realised at first that the man was a scoundrel. A charlatan duping the public and, he suspected, abusing the actress.

It was Saturday. The Empire Theatre would be dark the following day. He would return on Monday, would wait near the stage door in a cab and follow the party home. As soon as he knew where she lived, he would call on Miss Bell. Refuse to leave until he had seen her, and offered his assistance, his hand, and the only fortune he possessed – his life, to join with hers. If she said that she was content with her circumstances, told him to his face she had no interest in him, only then would he accept defeat.

Thirty-Eight

Grace cried out in her sleep and was quiet again. In the dip in the middle of the mattress, in her underclothes, Lily lay motionless. Scurryings came from behind the wainscot. The nightlight flickered. As the clock in the hall downstairs chimed two, she pushed back the covers and silently swung her feet to the floor.

Faye lay facing the wall, her hair spread over the pillow, her breath regular. Lily pulled on the skirt and blouse she'd left on the chair, reached under the bed for her boots and fastened them, matching the loops with the buttons. She groped for the sling on the bedpost, slipped it over her body and stood up. Grace was too big for the sling but it would have to do. The rattle lay on the table, attached to its own long shadow. Carefully, so the stones wouldn't tumble, Lily picked it up and slipped it into her pocket. She'd leave it with her as a token, so one day Grace might understand she had come from somewhere. Someone.

As she moved towards the door, a board squeaked.

Lily froze but the spinster slept on and she began to breathe again. Unhooking the cloak, she slid it over her shoulders and reached for the bonnet, jammed it on her head. She was ready. If the baby stirred and cried, woke Faye, she would grab her and make a dash for it. Barely breathing, she turned to approach the cot and as she did so the hem of the cloak swung against the umbrella stand. The china column toppled, a crash resounding through the silent room. The Professor's sister sprang from her bed and in one lightning movement snatched Grace up from the cot.

As the nightlight flared, Lily had a peculiar sense that she saw Faye Salt for the first time. The woman's face was alight, her eyes bright with purpose, her body entwined around the baby. Lily held out her arms.

'Give her to me, Faye,' she whispered, urgently. 'I am leaving.'

Faye backed up against the wall, her shadow close behind her. 'It's the middle of the night. Where will you take her?'

'There's a place near my mother's house. I'll explain to the matron that I cannot care for her. Beg her to take her in.'

Faye stared. 'I was going to tell you tomorrow, Lily,' she said, her voice low and hoarse. 'I know a lady, unable to have a child of her own. She is a good Christian with a private income. She wishes to adopt Grace.'

On another floor, a door closed. Water ran in the pipes and for a sickening moment Lily thought she heard footsteps coming down the stairs. She looked at Faye in confusion. 'What's her name?'

'Valentin. A Mrs Valentin.'

'Where does she live?'

'At White Horse Street,' Faye said, after a moment. 'Number nine.'

A picture of the shaven-headed girls in the exercise yard flashed through Lily's mind, followed by an image of Grace aged two or three, in a pink dress and kid shoes, picking flowers in a garden. She saw her sitting at a piano, walking in a great park. Saw her as a woman, with her gaze clear, her head held high. If the woman was wealthy, if she grew to love her – Grace might have a life. A good life.

A timber creaked somewhere in the old house. Again, Lily thought she heard the tread of a man's foot. She glanced at the door, almost fainting with fear. Tried to swallow. 'It might be for the best. When would you take her to Mrs Valentin?'

'Soon,' Faye said. 'Very soon.'

Lily tried to think. She could leave her here, safe with Faye. Walk away, knowing she had a home waiting for her. She would escape. And it would be best for Grace.

'Go, Lily,' the spinster whispered, glancing at the door. 'Go now, before the whole house wakes. This is your chance.'

Her heart racing, head hammering, Lily crept towards the bedroom door and opened it. Noiselessly, moving like a thief, she crept down the stairs and along the hallway, unbolted the front door and let herself out into the night.

In his bed, Erasmus woke with a start. He had a sudden vision of Miss Bell, slipping away through the filthy city streets like a living ghost, hidden under her mourning attire. Rolling over, pulling the sheet over his head, he discounted it as impossible. Faye was with the girl. He must have been dreaming.

Thirty-Nine

The front garden was filled with sunlight, the leaves of the poplar tree fluttering like tambourines. In her crib, Grace was beginning to stir. From when she was born, Faye had had the sense that the child, wordless though she was, knew everything, understood everything. Would one day remember everything.

'Just a few minutes, Grace,' she said. 'There are things I must do.'

Sitting at the table with a pen and sheet of notepaper, Faye wrote a note in a large, clear hand that could not have been more dissimilar to her own. She blotted it, folded the note into a square and still in her nightgown went down the stairs.

'Busy, Faye,' Erasmus barked as she entered the room. 'Leave me.'

Taking no notice, Faye closed the heavy door behind her. The dining room was as overcrowded as the bedroom, with an unlit gas lamp hanging low over the table, patterned wallpaper, elephant's foot stools on either side of the hearth. Faye had always found those stools singularly pathetic. At the table, Erasmus was half hidden behind heaps of books and papers.

'She's gone, Erasmus.'

'Who has?'

'Lily.'

Erasmus looked up. 'What do you mean gone?' he said, irritably.

'Miss Bell has run away.'

He sat for a minute then got to his feet, toppling his chair behind him.

'And where the bloody hell were you?'

Faye steadied her breathing. Held up the empty bottle of Mother's Friend. 'She must have dosed my tea. I slept like the dead. Woke just now and found her missing.'

Erasmus stared at her. He kicked the fender, ran his hands over his head, scraping his fingers through his hair. 'Took her bastard with her?'

Faye looked past her brother to a plant stand where a fern spread its fronds, tentatively, as if it reached for something. Ferns could survive, thrive even, in conditions of little light. Faye had always admired them for that. 'No,' she said, her voice clear and strong. 'She has abandoned it.'

Erasmus seemed to flinch. 'Poor little brat,' he said, at length. 'A mother that deserts her. A father not worthy of the name.' He rubbed his eyes. 'I shall go to Alf Bell this morning. Fetch her back. If she left the kid, it means she has gone to her mother.'

'No. You are wrong.' Faye held up the letter. 'I found this by the door. She dropped it as she fled, I suppose.'

Unfolding the note, Erasmus read it aloud. *My beloved Lily, everything is ready. I will wait for you tonight at the agreed spot and we will leave London immediately. We shall tour the fairs together, I will perform magic tricks and you will be my assistant. Salt will never find you. Yours always and forever, Tom.*

Erasmus screwed up the paper and tossed it at the grate.

'I'll go after her,' he said. 'Won't stop until I find her. We'll close down the show today. Dismantle the blue room. You can leave the baby at the foundlings home, Faye, measles or no measles.'

'Scarlet fever.' Faye went to the window and lifted the curtain, looking up at the poplar leaves, their movement full of some ineffable hope that seemed to transfer itself into her own heart. 'Have you lost your head, Erasmus?' she said, coolly. 'The marvel must continue. You will display the infant ghost at the fairs. Until the day we find her mother, I will look after Grace.'

Mr Valentin had been at the dining table. Faye saw dark curly hair, a narrow face composed in a scowl, eyes that looked darkly up at her. The matron, upholstered in yellow satin, got up from her seat and came to the doorway, taking Faye's hand, drawing her into the room.

'What a charming rig-out,' she'd said, looking Faye up and down. 'How was your journey?' She turned to the dining table, addressed the people assembled around it. 'Children,' she said. 'This is Miss Salt. Miss Salt, meet my husband, Mr Mordaunt.' The middle-aged man at the head of the table nodded. 'Evening, miss. Pleased to make your acquaintance. How's your brother?'

'And this is Mr Valentin,' the woman said. 'The drawing master.'

The scowler said nothing but rose from his chair and only resumed his seat when Mrs Mordaunt had indicated a place at the far end of the table and Faye had sat down. A maid brought in a tureen of mushroom soup and ladled out dishes, withdrawing when she had finished. Faye touched the soup spoon to her lips.

'I don't suppose you will always wish to eat with us, Miss Salt,' Mrs Mordaunt said in a ringing voice, as if she could read Faye's mind. 'The children dine with us on Sunday evening so they can practise their manners. During the week, they take their supper in the breakfast room. I hope you will be agreeable to joining them.'

'Of course, Mrs Mordaunt,' Faye murmured, as a piece of white fish arrived in front of her. Between mouthfuls, and during them, Mr Mordaunt talked to the table at large about the foxhunt he had undertaken earlier in the day, how it was a poor sort of man that didn't enjoy the chase, didn't Mr Valentin agree? Mr Valentin did not agree at all; he thought it brutish to kill defenceless animals for sport. Mrs Mordaunt issued a running commentary on the temperature of the food, the children's table manners, the tardiness of the maid.

By the time the sponge pudding came, Faye felt as if her nerves were out on stalks. There were eight children. She longed to be back in the little faded boudoir where 'all the governesses stay', Mrs Mordaunt had informed her, and be on her own to consider her impressions of the family. The oldest child – a serious-looking girl of twelve or thirteen – said grace and with a feeling of relief, Faye folded her napkin and got to her feet.

'I will say goodnight,' she said.

She had taught the younger Mordaunt children in the mornings and the older ones in the afternoons. The smaller ones – there were four with less than twelve months between each of them, fought and bit and kicked. Her attempts to separate them, begging them not to fight, were in vain and before long Faye grew accustomed to having bruised shins, teeth marks on her wrists, scratches on her face.

'They are bored, miss,' said Mrs Mordaunt, coming up to the schoolroom after an episode in which a cricket ball had been thrown and a window glass cracked, a disturbance that had been heard as far away as the drawing room. 'I'll take the cost of repair from your wages,' she said as she left the room. 'You wouldn't expect any different.'

Faye devised a programme of nature study and before sitting them at their desks took the younger children for rambles around the Mordaunt estate. They were to gather egg-shaped pebbles or search for four-leaved clovers, find forked sticks for the making of catapults. Often, as they walked, she would encounter Mr Valentin with the older children, sketching buds and caterpillars or, as the year wore on, flowers and butterflies. At first, they exchanged no more than polite greetings but, imperceptibly, and Faye wasn't sure afterwards quite how, they started to stand and talk, watching the children occupied in their different pursuits, listening to their high cries.

'Do you like children, Mr Valentin?' Faye said.

'I can't say that I do,' he replied and she heard herself laughing, softly, and could not stop.

Mr Valentin was not handsome but Faye found that his was a face of which her eyes didn't tire. It was expressive, large-lipped, his forehead high and his dark hair beginning to recede. He wore no perfume that she could discern but smelled faintly of cloves, mingled with something male. Animal. Faye began to anticipate her meetings with him; their exchanges, made standing up as they leaned on the trunk of a smooth-barked beech or a rough-skinned oak, became the centre of the day, the moment around which all other moments were constellated.

The afternoons, when she stayed in the school room with the girls, the air stuffy with breath and effort, the sound of breaking lead punctuating the youngest's sniffing, were claustrophobic. She watched as outside the window the sun sank red behind the trees, waited eagerly for the bell to ring for nursery tea and went to bed at nine, looking forward to the next morning, to seeing Mr Valentin, every day the same, every day different.

Mr Valentin was a painter, of landscapes. Short of cash, he said, one of his patrons having died and the other having gambled away his fortune. He owed money for art materials to a shop in town, at 9 White Horse Street, and had agreed to teach the Mordaunt children what he could of the principles of drawing for a year. Then he would be off, back to Paris where the light was sent from heaven, free of charge, for the benefit of painters.

On hearing that, Faye had looked away.

'And how long have you been here?' she said, lightly, affecting the low tone they used with each other, as if all of their exchange was secret.

'A few months. I arrived just before you did.'

'Are your pupils progressing?'

'There is hope for one or two of them. Lottie has talent. The others not a jot. Except when I take the pencils from their chubby hands and execute the study for them. Then Mrs Mordaunt thinks their efforts quite passable.'

'Will you see out the contract, Mr Valentin?'

'Don't call me that. It sounds so stiff. Call me by my first name.'

Faye blushed. 'I might, if I knew what it was.'

'It is Pyramus,' he said. 'My mother was afflicted with the Greeks.'

'My Christian name is Faye,' she said.

'What was your mother thinking?' he said.

'I can't tell you. She was gone from my life by the time I was of an age to form the question. She ran away and we have never known what befell her.'

'Ask Pater then.'

'He died soon afterwards in a hunting accident. I was eight and my brother twelve.'

Pyramus reached out a dry, warm hand and took hers and they stood in silence, leaning on the tree, the yells and shouts of the children tumbling in the air.

The first time she heard the knock on her door, Faye thought she imagined it. She sat up in bed and looked around the room by the glimmer of the nightlight. With the two great volumes of her dictionaries on the bookshelf, the addition to the mantelpiece of dried grasses and round silver seedpods collected on the walks, drawings the children had given to her, the room had become homely. The sound came again – not a knock but a light, intimate tap. One of the girls, she thought, suffering from a nightmare or a tummy ache; none of the boys could have made such a restrained sound.

'Come in,' she said, softly.

The door opened and Pyramus entered, closed it behind him.

'I'll leave now if you want,' he said.

'No,' Faye said. 'You can stay. Turn around while I get out of bed.'

He complied and she got up, put on her dressing gown and lit two candles. As an afterthought, she brushed her hair. 'You may turn around.'

He drew the low chair away from the window and sat down on it, stretching his legs out before him, leaning his head back on his hands, as if he was in a drawing room.

'I wanted to hear your voice in a bedchamber. See you with your hair down.'

Faye's mouth was dry; she could hardly speak. 'Well, now you have heard it. Seen it.'

'Yes. And I wish I'd brought my sketchbook.'

She sat on the edge of the bed.

'What do you hope for, Faye? What do you dream of?'

'I have never dreamed of anything,' she said. 'Except to see my mother again.'

'Don't you long for children, like the members of your sex are supposed to?'

'No.'

'Marriage?'

'For its own sake, no. I do not.'

'You are good, Faye,' he said. 'You are good. And I am a reprobate.'

And before she could ask Pyramus Valentin what he dreamed of, he had brushed the fingers of her right hand with his lips, and gone. The room looked different because he had been in it. Where it had not been empty before he came, now it was. It wasn't true that there was nothing she dreamed of. Her dream couldn't easily be articulated; it was simultaneously both the most humble and the most exalted aspiration. Faye hoped, if it were possible, to become her real self. To live, for better or worse, her own true life.

Forty

Clara Street was narrower than Lily remembered, the houses huddled together. Somewhere out of sight, cockerels crowed a ragged greeting to the day. A woman walking towards her gave her a lingering, curious glance and through the darkening screen of the veil Lily recognised Mrs Dyer, a neighbour who'd known her all her life, been present when she was born. Lowering her head, Lily hurried past her.

The privet hedge was untrimmed, the front gate lurching off its hinges. In the hallway, under the slanting, moulded heads of two angels, Lily removed the bonnet and cloak and hung them on the coat stand. She stood for a moment listening for the sound of her mother's voice, the chink of the teapot and – hearing nothing – moved towards the kitchen.

'Mother? It's me. I'm home. I need to talk to you...'

The kitchen was empty, the range unlit. Lily went through to the scullery and stood at the sink, running a glass of water. The garden looked different and it took her a moment to realise that the apple tree was gone. That leafy being that had been a guardian outside her bedroom window, whose branches she'd sat in and whose fruits she'd picked and eaten, had been cut down. Only a low stump remained, the top raw and pale. In the workshop, his eyes fixed on his canvas, Alfred Bell raised his brush.

Her room was as she'd left it. Lily picked up the doll lying on the pillow and held her, breathing in the scent of sawdust and woollen hair. Her breasts were full and aching. Grace would be awake by now, her eyes sleepy, cheeks flushed. She'd be crying, her napkin sagging down to her knees, her shift rucked up and damp.

'Grace,' she said, softly. 'My Grace.'

'Liza? Is that you?'

Lily put down the doll. She'd decided, on her long walk through the dark streets, to tell her mother everything. Ask for her forgiveness. She couldn't stay long. Erasmus Salt would come after her, Lily felt certain. Walking along the landing, she pushed open the door of her mother's bedroom. The room was dim, the curtains closed, and at first she didn't see the woman hunched on the stool in front of the dolls house, looking at Lily as if from some faraway place, across a continent or a century.

'At last,' she said. 'I've been waiting for you.'

The querulous voice sounded like her grandmother's. But she'd been dead for years. 'Mama?' Lily went to her.

She kneeled by her and put her arms around her, gently. 'You're ill. I didn't know.'

Ruth Bell reached out a sparrow's claw and touched Lily's cheek.

'Not ill, Liza, I am dying. Leaving this world. I long to come to you.'

'Come to me? What do you mean? Mother...' Lily stood up. She must speak now, before her courage ebbed away. 'I have to tell you something. Something that will hurt you. I have a daughter.'

'Daughter?' Ruth said, her dull eyes brightening. 'God bless her.'

Lily stared at her. Ruth Bell hadn't understood. She must make herself more plain. 'I was wrong, Mother, about Professor Salt. And you were right. He was not to be trusted.'

'Didn't I say so, Cook?' Ruth Bell said, looking into the dolls house. 'That my Liza would come for me, when it was my time.'

She reached into the pocket of her robe. Unscrewing the lid of a little brown bottle, she put back her head and squeezed drops from a pipette down her throat, her movement sure and quick. Before long her shoulders slumped, her chin rested on her chest.

From the doorway, came a jarring voice.

'Turned up like a bad penny, have you?' said Alfred Bell. 'Just as well. Your mother needs you. Your little adventures on the stage are over now.'

*

Milk squirted in thin streams into the bottom of the bowl and puddled, bluish and watery. Lily had been away from Grace for a week and the amount was less every day, the intervals between having to empty her breasts longer each time. Soon, the milk would have dried up. Buttoning her blouse, Lily opened the bedroom door and carried the basin downstairs, emptying the contents into the sink in the scullery, watching as the cloudy liquid ran down the drain.

Lily stoked the coals, filled the kettle and put it on the range. She felt jumpy, expected at any moment a violent banging on the front door, the sharp sting of Turkish blend tobacco from the hallway. Reaching down for the pot sprinkled with rosebuds, she set out on a tray a milk jug and two cups and saucers, a bowl of sugar, the old silver tongs. She hadn't understood that her mother could change too. She'd relied on her to be unchanging, like a rock or a hill. Had assumed that while her life continued, her mother's stood still until she needed her once more.

She had told Ruth Bell again and again about the baby, explaining what had happened, hoping that her mother would take it in. She longed for her to come back to her old self for a short time and give her advice, tell her what she should do and send her on her way with her blessing. But Ruth Bell was lost in a drugged dream, convinced that Lily was a spirit come to fetch her to the afterlife. She had no wisdom to impart.

She would try once more and then she must get away,

before her luck ran out. Carrying the tray upstairs and along the landing, Lily pushed open the bedroom door with her foot and entered the room, softly. 'I've brought you tea, Mama. Will you take a cup?' The figure under the covers did not move. Setting down the tray on the dressing table, Lily parted the curtains and looked up and down the street. It was empty except for one of Mrs Dyer's girls scrubbing the steps at the house opposite, her skirts tucked up to her knees, suds spilling into the gutter.

'Mother,' Lily said, turning from the window. 'I need to explain to you again, about my situation.'

A shaft of light fell on her mother's face. Her eyes were open and staring, her lips blue. Lily crossed the room, slowly. She touched Ruth's shoulder and found it stiff. The eyes did not move. With a sense of unreality, she took the mirror from the dressing table and held it to her mother's lips. No breath misted the glass. Dropping the mirror, Lily lay down next to her on the feather bed, pressing her face against the soft cheek, hugging the frail body as if she could warm the chill flesh. Minutes passed. Lily couldn't cry or wail. She was invaded by intolerable feelings, as if the world had ceased to turn and she tumbled through nothingness, lost and alone. The brown bottle stood on the bedside table. In a desperate effort to reach her mother, be near her again, Lily reached for it. She filled the pipette as she'd seen Ruth do so often and emptied it into her mouth. A tarry substance coated the back of her tongue, crept down her throat. As she lay there, clinging to her body, feeling its awful rigidity, she started to feel relaxed and calm, as if nothing could hurt or threaten her. Her mother's face began to alter. The shadows under her eyes lightened; the lines on her forehead softened. Her face flushed with pink. Her mother was alive, Lily realised without surprise, and younger than she was. After a while, Ruth Bell sat up. Her hair was thick and shining, coiled over her ears, her eyes lively.

Come, Liza, she said, getting out of bed. Time to get up. She was wearing a white summer dress that she wore often when Lily was a girl, and she was tall, so tall that Lily reached only to her waist. Come, Ruth said again, taking Lily's hands. Dance with me. And she began to turn in a circle, Lily following her movements, her mother singing in her tuneless voice. Lily was swinging through the air, her feet lifted from the floor and her legs flying out behind her into the street. I will fall, she called, and her mother threw back her head and laughed. Disappeared.

I have fallen, Mother, Lily said, opening her eyes, her head still spinning. An old woman lay beside her on a bed, asleep. A stranger. Lily felt detached. The woman was no concern of hers; nothing was. Her father appeared, the real father that she never knew, stooped down, so that his head and shoulders should not go through the bowed ceiling, his elbows poke through the walls. Where's Ruth, he said. I'm looking for her. She was here, Lily said, silently now, aware that there was no need to speak, because her thoughts would be heard clearly by anyone who was nearby; everyone's thoughts always were the loudest thing about them. She discovered she could see neither her father nor her mother, only smell violets in the air, strong and sweet; she breathed in the heady perfume, filled with a sense of ease. Nothing in the world was amiss and nothing in herself was lacking or ever could be.

Her own daughter, a child of nine or ten, her hair tucked behind her ears, her grey eyes solemn, sat under a tree, reading a book. Lily called out to her and Grace looked up and smiled. Can't you see I'm reading, Mama, Lily understood her to have said although no words had passed her lips. She felt the sun on her hands and realised she too was outside, lying on the ground beneath the apple tree of her childhood solace. She lay under the gaze of the branches as buds formed and opened, blossom drifted down and apples swelled, ripened and fell, and in this state of peace, understanding that every living and unliving thing was its own timepiece, she remained.

Later, lying by her mother, holding her marble fingers, Lily talked to her. She told her in a soft voice everything that had happened since she went away, crying, laughing, begging for forgiveness, for advice. The cheek she kissed and kissed again was smooth, the forehead untroubled, as it once was on Sunday mornings when the cares of the week were put aside and Ruth Bell sought God's blessing.

Getting up from the bed, Lily struggled to absorb the treachery of the empty body. Her mother was gone and all that would pass between them had happened already. Lily closed Ruth's eyes and drew the sheet over her face. She stopped the hands of the clock on the mantel so that the spirit could move into eternity, threw her mother's shawl over the mirror. Moving to the window, she realised that the day had passed. Outside in the street, the lamplighter ran from post to post, lighting up little faltering moons.

She'd got everything wrong again, Lily understood as she drew down the blind. It was not ordinary life that was important, or freedom, or privacy. It was love. Ruth Bell had given her life, had done her best to protect her while she grew. Lily thought of Grace, alone in the world. Mrs Valentin might be cruel or given to rages. Might have a husband that couldn't be trusted. She must get her back. Kissing her mother's cold hand one last time, Lily asked for her blessing. She was no longer a daughter but with a conviction that surprised herself, she knew that she could become a mother, protect her own daughter as best she could until she grew. Life demanded it.

Alfred Bell rested his elbows on his knees. He smelled of turpentine and linseed, the oily aroma mingling with the scent of violets, the unmaskable smell below.

'I've got no one,' he said, 'and I can't live alone, like some fellows do. Can't even coddle an egg. Not that I ever had much fondness for coddled eggs.' He looked across the still body of his wife. 'I've a right to some comfort in my old age, surely?'

Lily remained silent.

'I like a pie,' Mr Bell continued. 'And a pie takes cooking. Plain cooks aren't what they were. Then there's wages. Money doesn't grow on trees. You'll stay and look after me. Take on the housekeeping. It'll be useful, having a female in the house.'

A plank of wood was balanced between two chairs in the front parlour, made up with a white sheet and a pillow to look like a bed. Lying on the bier was the body that once housed Ruth Bell, her silver hair drawn back from her face with black satin ribbons, her skin powdered, her gaunt cheeks pinked with rouge. She wore her black bombazine, the one she'd worn to other people's funerals for as long as Lily could remember, with bunches of her favourite white violets pinned to the bodice, arranged around her head, placed between her fingers.

Lily had washed her and with help from Mrs Dyer laid her out. The body was all bones, the skin hanging from it translucent, too thin now to contain her, a chrysalis from which she had emerged. Sitting by her, Lily knew her mother was still in the room, escaped from life in its old form, flowing around the parlour where she had laughed and cried and played piano, filling it with her presence.

'Forgive me,' Lily murmured.

'What for?'

She looked up at her stepfather.

'I am leaving, Mr Bell. I won't be coming back.'

As she spoke, Lily had the sense that her mother vanished, that she by some mysterious means departed the room, in advance of the funeral she'd saved for all her life. Her spirit no longer filled the atmosphere, only a corpse remained. The room was empty. Lily was free.

None of her brothers had arrived yet and Lily felt a pang of regret that she wouldn't see them. In her childhood bedroom, she donned the old cloak, collected the bonnet, and went to her mother's bedroom. The brown glass bottle stood on the bedside table, half full. Lily left it where it was. Opening up the front of the doll's house, she took the baby from the cradle and slipped it into her pocket.

At the top of the stairs she stood, listening to the sound of neighbours, relations and acquaintances making their way along the hall and into the parlour, checking for a silky, cold voice, a whiff of pipe tobacco. The hallway cleared and she ran down the stairs, almost falling down the last two, and let herself out of the front door. Walking as fast as she could up Clara Street, she saw a neighbour going the other way, a bag of potatoes clutched against her chest. It wasn't potatoes, Lily saw, drawing closer. It was a baby. She slowed her step until the woman had passed, then turning onto the main road, passing under the railway bridge as a train thundered overhead, she began to run.

*

The doors of the Empire Theatre were padlocked, the steps unswept. Posters in the glass-fronted display cabinets for *The Return of Late Lily Bell with her Spirit Child* were stamped with the word 'Cancelled'. Lily's heart skipped beat after beat. Faye Salt wasn't at the lodgings. Lily had been there first, going down the area steps and knocking at the kitchen door, asking in a whisper for Miss Salt. She had been informed by the landlady that the professor and his sister had left, leaving no forwarding address.

'And they took the baby with them?'

The woman looked surprised. 'Of course,' she said. 'Mrs Brown took her little daughter.'

Lily had stared at her in disbelief. She'd been certain that she would find Faye there, alone with the baby. That the spinster would come down the stairs with Grace on her hip and that Lily would tell her that she had changed her mind about Mrs Valentin, take the baby from her and leave. Once she had Grace in her arms, had put some distance between them and the Salts, she would be able to think about what to do next.

'Where are they, ma'am?' she'd said to the landlady. 'You must know where they were going. Tell me, I beg you.'

'Dismissed weren't you, Miss Bell?' said the woman, dabbing her lips with a napkin. 'I wouldn't be looking for them if I was you. Anyhow, I don't know where they were going. They left suddenly, soon after you.'

She'd set off from the lodgings to the theatre, rushing through the steets, and in her distraught and agitated state had lost her way. The air was heavy; clouds hung low and sullen over the spires and chimneys; thunder boomed again and again. Empty hansoms bounced past, their drivers sitting up at the rear in their shirtsleeves, horses twitching docked tails. Suited men walked in pairs, wiping their brows. Women emerged from shops, fanning glistening faces, servant girls following behind laden with parcels.

By the time she reached the Empire, she'd felt on the edge of panic. She didn't know which frightened her more: finding them, and seeing Erasmus Salt. Or not finding them. They were not there. Sweat ran down her back under the heavy cloak, dampened her hair beneath the bonnet. The ground seemed to tilt beneath her feet and feeling herself swaying, gripping the handrail to prevent herself falling, Lily sat down on the steps. The theatre is dark, she repeated to herself. *Dark. Dark.* She couldn't take it in.

There was a tug at her sleeve. 'Miss. Have pity.' It was a girl in a short red dress, the bodice tight over childish breasts, holding out a grimy palm. Lily felt in her pocket, found a sixpence. 'Where's your mama?' she said, softly. Snatching the coin, the girl flitted away. It was dusk and the street had emptied of respectable women, the shoppers and nursemaids gone to their homes. A man standing outside the tavern over the road tipped his hat at her and Lily looked away. Other men were beginning to circle. She must act purposefully; go to White Horse Street and ask to see Mrs Valentin. Grace must be with her already. The woman must be persuaded to give her back. She had no birth certificate for the child, Lily realised, nothing to prove that Grace was hers. Only her own marked and altered body attested to the truth. Her growing will.

Standing up, pulling the veil over her face, she began to walk.

Forty-One

Arkwright's Travelling Theatre stood close to the Thames in a water meadow outside the city of Oxford. The river had risen in the rains, spilling over the fields and creeping under the wooden walls of the theatre, causing the cancellation of a production of *A Midsummer Night's Dream*, afflicting half the cast with influenza. Erasmus's old acquaintance Harry Arkwright needed a new production, in a new location, and the two men were deep in conversation.

Faye stood to one side of the auditorium, rocking the perambulator she had bought, its suspension squeaking gently. Erasmus and Mr Arkwright were joined by Miss Henrietta Arkwright and Faye pushed the pram over to the group.

'My sister,' Erasmus gestured towards Faye, 'is recently widowed. Her infant appears as the ghost baby.'

Mr Arkwright removed his hat. 'Must be a consolation,' he said, looking at Grace. 'Spitting image. Deepest sympathy.'

'Thank you, Mr Arkwright.'

'My ghost is temporarily unwell,' Erasmus said. 'She will return shortly. Meanwhile, someone will have to stand in for her.'

The canvas roof snapped overhead. Mr Arkwright stroked his whiskers. Miss Arkwright sneezed into her handkerchief. She was a pretty young woman, strong-featured, with thick brows and a quick laugh. Dark brown hair. 'I would like to play the ghost,' she said, when she'd recovered herself. 'Until Miss Bell returns, that is.'

'Are you an actress, Miss Arkwright?' Faye said. 'I am certain you would make a delightful ghost.'

'I'm not averse,' her father said. 'What d'you say, Salt?'

Erasmus looked up at the tilt. When he spoke, he sounded irritable.

'Temporarily, she might substitute for the ghost.'

Leaving them negotiating terms, Faye pushed the pram back along by the side of the river, her feet squelching in the mud. The floodwaters had receded, leaving a layer of silt and weed over the path, blurring the boundaries between water and land. The baby waved her arms at a line of waddling geese, burbling at them. Putting down the hood so Grace could see them more easily, propping her on the pillows, Faye felt relieved to see her happy. Grace hadn't taken well to the feeding bottle; she disliked the rubber teat and when she could be persuaded to take it, more often than not, the milk came too fast and half choked her. Since Lily went, she'd been listless and fretful in the mornings, worse in the evenings.

Teething, Faye told herself, setting off again, bumping the pram towards the graceful spires on the horizon. She was too young to miss her mother. Even if she retained some faint memory of Lily, it would soon fade. Faye would devote herself to her wellbeing. Providence had given her a child to look after; she would adopt her as her own daughter and one day, when Grace was old enough to understand, she would explain everything to her. Almost everything.

From that night on, she and Pyramus had met twice in each twenty-four hours. They met in the morning, most often by the handkerchief tree in the arboretum. 'Good morning, Miss Salt,' Pyramus would say, stiffly, the older girls still nearby. 'I trust you slept well.' 'Good morning, Mr Valentin,' Faye would reply. 'Passably well. And did you spend a comfortable night?' 'I cannot complain, Miss Salt. Although sleep evaded me.' If Mrs Mordaunt came into view, cutting blooms for the table or taking the air, they nodded at each other and went on their ways.

They talked only when the children were out of earshot; Pyramus told her about the places he'd visited – Venice and Paris and the Rhine, how superior they were to English cities, English rivers. He talked about painters, the closed doors of the Academy to young artists, the safe and stale tastes of the market. Art was his love, he said, and painting his perfumed mistress.

Within his head, Mr Valentin carried world upon world. Faye felt her own world growing larger not from his descriptions of the Palace of Doges or the treasures of the Louvre, but from what was happening inside herself, her mind and heart and body thrilling to this man. She had believed it was not her fate to experience love.

At night, she sat on a spindly chair at the escritoire in her room, writing in her journal. She'd kept a journal since she was a young girl, recording the events of the day, whether great or small, finding it a way of affirming that although her mother and father had perished, she lived, that each day while similar to the one before, the one after, had its own character. Now, her diary was filled only with Mr Valentin, what he had said and not said, how he had looked at her with an expression she couldn't read, which made her nervous.

Before midnight, she rose from the writing desk, brushed her hair, applied rosewater to her neck and began to move around the room, noiselessly. Pyramus no longer knocked. He simply entered and they no longer spoke but moved straight into each other's arms. It didn't feel sinful to Faye, to have Pyramus's lips on her lips, his body pressed against hers. It felt as natural as the groans of the foxes outside in the night, the dawn chorus of the birds as they disentangled their bodies and he went from her narrow bed back to his own room, whistling softly.

*

Spring came. The handkerchief tree bloomed, producing a profusion of limp white flags hanging under the light green leaves. Pyramus was silent and Faye content to stand next to him, watching the children playing hide and seek, running from tree to tree, peering around the great trunks.

'I'm going away, Mouse,' Pyramus said, looking into the distance.

'When?' she said.

'Tonight.'

Faye felt as if she had had every last bit of breath knocked out of her.

'For how long?'

Pyramus extracted a letter from his pocket. 'My patron has won back his fortune. Paid off my bills in White Horse Street. I am summoned to spend the summer in the Alps, painting.'

He was there already; she knew it from his voice. He was hiking up a grassy mountainside listening to the sound of cowbells, his palette in one hand and his easel strapped to his back. If it hadn't been for the solid trunk of the tree at her back, Faye felt she must have fallen, fallen to the soft ground, tumbled through its unreliable surface and down, down into the comfort of the earth and stayed there, perhaps forever.

Mrs Mordaunt walked past at a little distance; she stopped and turned in their direction, regarded them with suspicion. 'Looks like rain,' she called out, her voice rending the air, making the handkerchiefs tremble over their heads. Faye gathered up some shattered fragments of what had been her self.

'Lottie,' she whispered, to the oldest girl. 'Gather the children. We shall go inside.'

Mr Valentin's departure did not at first seem real to Faye. She couldn't, when she came down to the breakfast table in the morning, restrain her eyes from flickering to his place, to the empty chair where a setting was no longer laid for the drawing master. Couldn't keep her ears from listening for his tread in the hallway, the clash of silver as he lifted the lid on the chafing dish and declared the kedgeree fit only for pigs, kids and starving artists.

'Don't look so gloomy, miss,' Mrs Mordaunt would call out from the other end of the room. 'It might be contagious.'

Worse than thinking she saw Pyramus in the grounds, more painful than believing any sudden movement or disturbance in the shrubs presaged his return, was waiting for letters from him. Faye received one letter, from the port of Calais. She took it up to what she by then thought of not as her room but as the governess's room and opened it, wild with hope. She had cruelly misjudged him. He was summoning her to be by his side. *Come, as quick as you can, for things ain't the same without you.* The note was dated a month earlier, written in pencil. 'We had a passable crossing and will be on our way shortly. Oils are reasonably priced here and

I've been torturing the natives with my French. They drink wine as if it were ale and coffee like tea. Draw like angels. I am happy. Don't ever miss me, dearest Mouse, for as I told you, I don't merit it.' Underneath was a sketch of a mouse, its soft eyes sad, its expression wistful. The signature was the one he made on the bottom right corner of his paintings:

P. Valentin

Forty-Two

The railings were painted glossy black, the steps whitened; polished brass doorknockers gleamed in the lamplight. Lily walked soundlessly along the pavement. She passed number 1, number 3, number 5, and slowed her step. With all her attention focused on finding White Horse Street, asking directions, she hadn't considered what she would say to Mrs Valentin or how she would say it. She could not rehearse, she realised. She wasn't playing a part. This was her life, her one and only life. She must speak the words that came. The prospect of seeing Grace again, taking her in her arms, doing battle with anyone that tried to dispute her claim to her, made her feel like a lioness.

Number 9 was not a house but a shop, selling art materials. Despite the hour, lights were on inside. Lily looked through the window at wooden easels, portable cases open to display coloured chalks or tubes of oil paint, an earthenware jar stuffed with brushes of every size. She felt confused; the fierce courage that had been building in her seeming to ebb. It was possible she had misremembered the address. She was certain she had not. White Horse Street. Number 9. She could hear Faye's voice saying the words. Pushing open the door, she went into an emporium filled with furled canvases, jars and tubes and cakes of paint, watercolour sets, bottles of linseed oil, palettes and brushes and folding stools.

'Can I help you?'

Lily pulled back the veil and saw a man sitting behind a desk at the back of the shop. Noticing his embroidered waistcoat and pale silk bow tie, she remembered her shabby cloak, her dreadful hat.

'I am looking for Mrs Valentin.'

'Who?'

'Mrs Valentin. She is … a lady that lives here.'

The man shook his head. 'These are the premises of Mr Sycamore. No one of that name here.'

'But there must be. Mrs Valentin has recently taken in a baby, I believe. A little girl.'

The doubt in his eyes turned to pity, then distaste. 'Not here,' he said, returning to his ledger. 'Mr Sycamore is a confirmed bachelor.'

Everything in Lily refused to believe him. She wanted to sit down on the ornate carved chair next to the desk, remain there until he produced Mrs Valentin, a kind honest woman who would listen to Lily's story and return her child to her, offer to help her in any way she could. She left, feeling numb, walking slowly. She had no idea where to go. What to do. She felt as if she might have arrived in the world that very moment, a stranger to everything and everyone.

On Piccadilly, a great church was set back from the thoroughfare behind a courtyard that contained trees, a fountain. Stained-glass windows glowed red and blue and gold. Lily crossed the flagstones and opened the unlocked door. The air inside the church was still, fragrant with incense and prayer and stone; from somewhere in the valuted, galleried space came the sound of snoring. She edged into the first pew she came to and for a long while sat without moving; later, overcome with tiredness, she lay down on the scarred oak, pulled her cloak around her and slept.

Forty-Three

The theatre doors opened and the crowds dropped all pretence of manners and surged forward, shoving and pushing their way inside. Women were the worst, elbowing past each other, tripping on each other's hems. Leaning on one of the great fluted pillars that looked like stone but he knew to be Plaster of Paris, Balthazar watched as they pressed towards the double doors, eager to secure their seats in the stalls, get a close view of the ghost girl.

He'd conveyed Salt's technique to a Mrs Epiphany Diamand in the form of drawings, notes, diagrams; written answers to her questions. Had kept up the pretence of being dumb, just as now he kept up the pretence of being poor, although the widow Diamand had paid well for the secret. Scanning the crowds, Balthazar was looking for one woman. He was waiting for the night when Miss Bell came to witness a performance of the show called *Ghost Girl*, waiting for that moment when he might step forward, greet her as his old acquaintance, enquire how she was keeping and where she stayed these days.

Then he would telegram Salt for further instructions.

The doors to the stalls and the circle closed; inside, the performance began. Balthazar watched from an empty box. On an otherwise bare stage, against a muddy backdrop, a man and a woman in mourning clothes sat beside a closed coffin. An unseen clock struck a loud midnight, waking them from their dozing.

'Husband, is it day?' said the woman.

'Wife, I know not,' said the man, 'now that day and night to me are all alike and both unwanted.'

'Mother!' called a muffled female voice. 'Father!'

A glimmer at the back of the stage brightened and a young woman in a lurid green dress, her arms full of roses, appeared. The old couple – underlit, it was hard to make them out at all in their weeds – rose to their feet and clutched each other as their daughter discarded the blooms, sat down at a piano and began to thump out a tune.

Balthazar sat in the darkness, smirking. This ghost was a cheap and tawdry creature that left no mark on the heart. The gasman's technique was crude and the audience were left in no doubt that they witnessed not a returning spirit but an illusion. To thuds and squeaks that clearly emanated from below the stage, ghost girl disappeared. Balthazar left before the crowds. Not a patch, he whispered to Mary, at home in their new lodgings – two rooms and a kitchen, fully furnished, in a tree-lined street near a garden square.

Balthazar Pook was coming up in the world. He had one last job to do. The ghost professor had promised him a hundred guineas, a *monkey*, for the dispatch of Miss Bell. First, he had to find her.

Forty-Four

A gusting wind chased Lily along the pavement, raising flurries of dust. Towards the end of the great wide road a pair of wrought iron gates with crowns at their centres stood open. Beyond them, in a green park, ducklings waddled in lines behind their mothers; uniformed nursemaids pushed perambulators along sandy paths. Gardeners tended bright, well-ordered beds of flowers. At a bench a little way inside the park, Lily sat down.

For a week, she had sheltered at night in the church, under the gaze of kindly disciples, listening to the sleeping breath of the other men and women hidden in the pews, their coughs and cries. Early in the morning, she joined the queue as black-garbed nuns distributed cocoa and bread rolls and prayer tracts from a barrow in the courtyard. She must make a plan, Lily instructed herself every morning, sitting under the tree, sipping the cocoa and eating the roll slowly, bite by small bite, combatting the urge to cram it whole into her mouth. Her hands were dirty. Her hair matted. Her ankle throbbed. Two days earlier, she'd tripped on a paving stone and gone sprawling on the ground. Been helped up by strangers with concerned faces, set on her feet next to a fountain splashing water from the mouth of a horse.

Boots crunched on gravel. A police officer was walking along the path towards her. She had seen him before, making his rounds, a pair of silver handcuffs dangling from his belt, a red and gold truncheon under his arm.

'Afternoon,' he said, walking by.

Lily sat perfectly still, watching a sparrow fluffing its feathers in the dust, the daisies with their faces turned to the sun. She felt detached, unable to do more than exist moment to moment. The breeze ruffled her veil; the weight of her body rested on the wooden seat; her ankle ached. Hunger came and went; she was growing accustomed to it. She was still alive, she reminded herself. Alive in her own strong body through which another life had come. She would find Grace and become her mother. A way would present itself.

A sound rose nearby that sounded like trickling water. Near a spreading tree, a crowd had gathered. They were clapping. Beyond them, red balls rose in the air and fell and rose again. The crowd swelled; the applause grew louder. Getting up from the bench, Lily moved towards the people, edged her way through to the front of the circle. The juggler wore soft leather shoes, a striped shirt without a collar. Woolly locks of hair fell to his shoulders and his hands were quick and deft, his eyes turned to the sky.

Lily turned and fled. Pushing her way back through the crowd, moving as fast as she could, she limped towards the gates of the park. The police officer stopped in front of her on the path, spreading his arms to block her way.

'Not so fast, miss,' he said. 'Been observing you. Where is your home?'

'I have no home,' she said, surprised by the sound of her own voice.

'Where did you sleep last night?'

'Nowhere.'

'What is your name?'

'My mother used to call me Liza.'

The officer made notes in a pad and Lily looked over her shoulder. As the last of the crowd dispersed, a tall, straight figure loped off, a rucksack slung over one shoulder. It hurt to see him go but she was relieved that Tom Ames hadn't seen her. She didn't want him to pity her.

The police officer's pencil ceased to write. Putting away his notebook, he linked his hands behind his back.

'Got daughters myself,' he said, looking up at the sky. 'Going to be a cold night, by the look of it. There's a place not far from here for servant girls put out by their mistresses.'

'I'm not a servant. I'm an actress.'

He rattled the silver handcuffs. 'Yes, you are,' he said, taking hold of her arm. 'A maidservant put out this morning without a word of warning. Come with me, missy.'

Forty-Five

On Sundays, after Matins and Lauds but before Vespers, inmates of the House of Mercy were allowed two hours free time. Lily hurried through the streets of Soho, passing a closed barber's shop with tins of pomade balanced in a pyramid in the window, a padlocked pawnbroker's with an iron grille over its doors. Outside the Alhambra Theatre, she stopped to rest her ankle. Pasted on a hoarding was a poster of a dark-skinned, almond-eyed man. He wore a wide-sleeved red satin coat; striped black and white pantaloons ballooned under his coat and were gathered in cuffs at his ankles, over pointed slippers. *The Egyptian Enchanter! Straight from the Casbah of Cairo! Never before seen in London!* White birds perched along his arms and one balanced on the top of his scarlet fez, poised for flight. At the bottom of the poster was a handwritten notice. *Conjuror's assistant required to tour England. Enquire within.*

Moving on to Piccadilly, Lily walked past the church that had sheltered her before she'd been arrested by the police officer and delivered to the night matron at the House of Mercy. She was in training to become a parlour maid, was wearing a uniform – a printed cotton dress, brown shawl, a small hat with a single band of ribbon. Passing quickly by the entrance to White Horse Street, she crossed the road, dodging between carriages, slipping through the gilded gates and into the park. The light was greenish through the trees and the grass soft underfoot after a night of rain. Her old bench was vacant. She sat and watched as near a large, spreading tree a circle of people gathered. From inside the circle, red balls flew into the air like tumbling robins.

In the distance, a clock struck four, the tones commanding the still air. The juggling balls seemed to hang as if suspended, then fell, one by one. As the last peal of the bell died away, the crowd parted to reveal a figure, packing a rucksack, filling it with his props. Raising his head, the man looked at Lily and began walking towards her. His step was light and buoyant; he slanted towards her, the tip of his shadow falling at her feet and travelling on up her body until he stood in front of her.

They greeted each other with no more than their eyes and began to walk in looping circles around the park, his step matched to hers, her breath paired with his.

'How did you know me?' Lily said, as the grass soaked her boots, her stockinged feet.

'I'd know you anywhere.'

In De Castro and Peach, Tom Ames ordered two cups of coffee. His hands were strong and long-fingered, browned by the sun. His face was serious, particular in a way that memory hadn't prepared her for.

'Are you well, Miss Bell?'

'Quite well.'

She remembered the declarations of love they'd made for each other so many times. Now, they must speak like strangers. Sitting opposite her across the table, he took something from inside his shirt and unfolded it. The paper was softened and creased, the face in the engraving once familiar.

'I'm not her,' she said, looking at the ghost, remembering the day she'd put on the make-up and the costume for the first time and stood in the photographer's studio. 'I never was.'

'It's not her I've been searching for,' he said. 'It is you.'

The waiter arrived with a tray, set down china cups and a bowl of sugar crystals. Tom poured the coffee and placed one of the cups in front of her.

'Salt said that my letter to you caused offence. I didn't know whether you—'

'What letter?'

Their eyes met and Lily felt a charge of feeling run through her.

'I saw the new show,' he said.

'You know then,' she said, her voice low and quiet.

'Know what?'

'I'm ruined. I have a child.'

'Was it him?' he said. 'Salt?'

Coffee splashed hot on her hand and he pulled a

clean handkerchief from his pocket and passed it to her. 'I ought to have killed him when I had the chance,' he said. 'I wish I had.'

In the distance, the bell chimed the half-hour. Her time was almost up. The doors of the House of Mercy were locked at five.

'Do you hear anything of them?' she said.

'I met the gasman not long ago. Salt's gone on the road from what I understood. Touring England in a travelling theatre. Balthazar was looking for you and seemed to think he would find you with me. I had to disappoint the little fellow.'

'Did they take the baby with them?'

'Balthazar said so. In his own fashion.' Tom made a rocking movement with his arms and the gesture was so unexpected that Lily thought for an instant she would break down. Pushing back her chair, scraping the legs on the floor, making a discordant, ugly sound, she got up.

'They tricked me. Took my daughter. I must go now.'

He got up from his chair, followed her to the exit, held open the door, stepped outside after her. They stood facing each other, the space between them charged and full, the passing carriages and buses, clattering hooves and jingling harnesses, fallen silent.

'Will you look for them?' he said. 'Get her back?'

'Yes. When I find a way, I will. I'm in training to be a housemaid.'

'I'll help you, if I can.'

Lily couldn't speak. How could he help her when she

could not help herself? Had no idea what to do or how. Tom Ames looked at her with his complicated eyes.

'I must go,' she repeated.

'Will you be in the park next week, at the same time? I cannot lose you again.'

'I will try. Keep my picture by you, Mr Ames, will you?'

'Always.'

'And I would. If I had one of you.'

Meeting his eyes had an effect on her that Lily couldn't name, as if somewhere deep inside, her life stirred and woke. Their fingertips touched and splashes of rain wetted her face, his bare head.

Forty-Six

Drawing on the cigar he held between thumb and forefinger, the Egyptian Conjuror blew out a ring of smoke that rose and floated over his head. His skin was the colour of walnuts and his long black hair was oiled, brushed back and tied behind his head.

'Would've said so, if I wanted a female.'

'I'm hardworking,' Lily said. 'I have stage experience. I will assist you to the best of my ability, I give you my word.'

'That's as may be, miss.' The ring stretched and thinned. 'But I'm looking for a lad. We'll be on the road all summer, touring the fairs, ending up in the north country. It's too hard for a lass. One that ain't accustomed to it. And a female on stage is a distraction. Takes folk away from the magic.'

Behind him, a cupboard door hung open, spilling bright silk scarves, tassels, a stack of fez caps. On the floor next to him, in a wicker cage, a pair of white doves

murmured and cooed, raising and resettling their feathers.

Lily held up her head and put back her shoulders. 'I
belong on the stage. I'll do the job as well as any male.
Better.'

'We're going far from London, and—'

'That's why I'm here. I want to tour England.'

'And leave thy family behind?'

She looked at the floor. 'I have no family.'

The conjuror blew out a last round ring. Stubbing out
the cigar in a brass pot, he sighed as he got to his feet.
'Position isn't open to females. I am sorry, miss.'

As she left the room, the conjuror came to the door,
leaned his head out. 'Become a young man!' he called, in
his north country accent. 'Then I'll tek yer on.'

In the corridor, hissing gas lamps threw pools of light
over framed, sepia-tinted photographs of actors and
actresses. Lily walked along the thick wool carpet, past
the handsome men, the beautiful women. This had been
her girlhood dream. This muffled, lit world of drama
and artifice, this improvement upon life, was where she
had wanted to be. Fate had not granted her admittance.

At the corner of Dean Street and Old Compton Street,
three golden spheres were suspended beneath an awning.
Lily pushed open the pawnbroker's door and stepped
inside. Emerging soon afterwards, without the opal ring
her mother had given her when she first left home, she
proceeded to Berwick Street. Costers stood by carts

and stalls and barrows piled high with old clothes. Rummaging in the heaps, ignoring the scratch of coarse fabrics on her hands, the stale smell rising from the garments, she found a white shirt that looked clean, if on the large side. A corduroy cap, smaller than average. With the items tucked under one arm, she continued to search. Before long, a small pair of dark trousers, hardly worn, emerged from the bottom of the heap, with a brown jacket, narrow in the shoulders.

'For my brother,' she said, to the stallholder. 'He's the same build as myself.' The man examined the clothes. He was dressed in a long black coat and had ringlets on each side of his face.

'Two,' he said, holding up his fingers. 'Two shillings.'

Lily left with a parcel wrapped in brown paper, tied up with twine. Four pounds, seventeen shillings and sixpence remained in her pocket, the coins heavy against her hip. The barber's shop was empty of customers, the air hazy with scented steam coming from a vaporiser in a corner. A young man dozed in one of the raised chairs, his feet propped on a basin. Lily jangled the bell on the door.

'Barber's at a funeral,' he said, scrambling to his feet. 'I'm the 'prentice.'

'You can cut hair, can't you?'

After a brief conversation with him, Lily went into a back room and closed the door. Emerging in the clothes she'd bought, with her own tied up in the parcel, she felt something of the old stage fright. Bound against her chest with one of the barber's flannel bandages, her breasts did not betray her but without the familiar weight of petticoats and skirts, she felt unanchored, as if she could float up into the atmosphere. The close-fitting breeches displayed the outline of her legs and despite the sturdy cloth she felt exposed.

The apprentice averted his eyes from her ankles and gestured towards the chair.

'Here, miss.' Lily freed her hair from its bun and ran her fingers through it. A woman looked back at her from the mirror, a woman dressed in boy's clothing, with her oval face framed by shining white hair down to her elbows, and a defiant expression in her eyes.

'You can begin,' she said.

The young man hesitated.

'Go on. Start.'

The apprentice lifted a hank of hair and closing her eyes Lily heard the blades shear through it. It wouldn't be enough to change on the outside. She must begin from the inside. Become a male. She kept her eyes shut as, length by length, the apprentice sheared off her hair. Kept them shut as he ran a comb across her head, made adjustments around her ears, the side of the blades cold against her skin, the cuts slow and careful. He moved round to the back of her neck, instructed her to tip her head forwards and took the razor to the nape of it. Lily continued her silent dialogue with herself. From now on, she would be on stage all the time. The streets would be her theatre; she would never step out of role. Until the day she found her daughter, she would think like a man; walk like a man; act like one.

A soft-bristled brush flicked over her ears and neck. Lily opened her eyes. In the mirror was a male in that fleeting moment between boyhood and manhood. His grey eyes looked determined; his expression conveyed all the challenge and hope, the unspoken rebuke of his elders, of any young man of his age. Lily Bell had disappeared.

The barber slid his scissors into the pocket of his apron.

'Suits you, miss. That is to say, master ...'

Jumping down from the chair in one agile, unrestricted movement, Lily stooped to the silky white heap lying on the floor. She felt an ache of loss; her hair had been part of her, had accompanied her all her life, been part of her feminine power. Without it, her face and ears exposed, she felt naked. Picking up a single lock of hair she coiled it into a ring, put it in the inside pocket of the jacket, with the baby from the dolls house. These would be her tokens, her lucky charms.

The apprentice paid her two pounds for the rest of her hair, counting it into her palm in half crowns. The boss would sell it on to a wigmaker for three times that, he assured her. Such a colour, that was – lack of colour – was rarely seen. They shook hands and Lily pulled on the cap, settled it over her ears and left.

A few yards from the shop, at a place where seven narrow streets ran off a central space, she stopped.

Leaned her shoulders against a wall. Her hips thrust out, feet apart, toes turned out, she swivelled her head from side to side, staring at anyone she found of interest, one cheek swelled as if with chewing tobacco. A woman walked past her without a second glance. Two men were approaching, in conversation. Lily wiped her nose on the back of her hand, coughed from the back of her throat and spat, aiming unsuccessfully at the gutter. 'Whippersnapper,' one of them said, stepping round her.

Her neck felt cold. She reached inside the shirt, into the woman's chemise she still wore underneath, and drew out Tom Ames's blue and white spotted handkerchief. Lily folded it into a triangle and wound it round her neck, knotted it at the front. With her head high, her fingers pushed into the pockets of the breeches, she crossed the road and retraced her steps, heading for the Alhambra Theatre.

Forty-Seven

'I am returned from the spirit world. With my child.'

Half of the baby disappeared. Etta Arkwright was standing in the wrong place, outside what could be reflected from the mirror onto the tilted glass. Erasmus sat forward on his seat, grunting with annoyance. He couldn't be in two places at once, had instructed his sister to stay in the blue room, outside the lit area, to prompt the actress to stand in the right spot. Faye must have said something, because the girl took a step backwards and the infant was restored to wholeness. Behind him, someone began the Lord's Prayer.

They were at a fair in the town of Worcester. The travelling theatre had arrived loaded onto three wide flatbed carts, each pulled by a team of four horses. Behind those came another cart, bearing the huge sheet of glass and enormous mirror, wrapped in sacking and packed in heavy wooden frames. Faye and the infant had travelled by stagecoach with Miss Arkwright; Erasmus had gone with Arkwright on the cavalcade, resting the horses frequently, eating mutton with onion sauce at a succession of tawdry inns, keeping his eyes peeled for a head of white-blonde hair. He'd seen one that turned out to be a boy. Another was a woman that when she turned around was forty if she was a day. Erasmus was angry with Balthazar. He had expected results by now.

'We do not live as you mortals live,' the ghost said loudly. 'Nor love as you love.' Etta Arkwright was pretty enough, with her shapely body, her brown eyes and dark hair, but her appearance left Erasmus unmoved. Etta Arkwright would never progress to being a real spirit. Arkwright had refused point blank to allow the drawing up of a death certificate for his daughter. The training of her spirit was in vain.

The limes faded late, leaving the ghost still visible on the stage while the actor lamented her disappearance. The gasman responded at last to Erasmus's urgent tapping; the ghost and her comatose child disappeared back to the spirit world. Three violinists, recruited that afternoon from a gypsy camp outside the town, struck up a cheery polka in place of the mournful melody he'd instructed.

In the blanketing darkness, Erasmus took another mouthful of brandy. He had collected from Poste Restante a letter from a colleague from the Next World Society, a medical doctor who was working in a similar way to himself, although with pet dogs. The fellow wrote that he intended shortly to take his experiments to the next stage, invited Erasmus to come and witness the occasion when for the first time he would call back a spaniel from the afterlife. Reading the letter, Erasmus had felt enraged. He would be the first one to call a spirit from the afterlife after the process of training. It would be Lily Bell's, not some woeful hound.

The swagged velvet curtains came down; a stagehand threw open the side door of the travelling theatre. Night air and a damp, rural drizzle gusted into the theatre. A woman accosted him, wringing her hands.

'Saw them,' she moaned. 'Saw them with my own eyes.'

'Saw who?' Erasmus said curtly, wrinkling his nose at the whiff of unwashed linen.

'My daughter and her little one. Taken on the same day, by the whooping cough.' The biddy fell to her knees on the muddy sackcloth. 'Bring them back to me, sir. I beg you. I cannot live without them.'

Erasmus signalled to the stewards to remove her. If people wanted to be duped, wanted not to know that this was a mere rehearsal for glories soon to come, it was their own affair. He couldn't be held responsible. Taking another anaesthetising draft from the flask, he left the theatre, intending to telegram Balthazar Pook, enquire urgently what news he had.

Forty-Eight

The conjuror walked by the side of the horses. Despite the clear morning sunshine, he wore an old brown coat down to his knees, a fur hat with flaps over the ears. 'Where's the magic man?' boys shouted, seeing the picture painted on the side of the van of him in a red velvet cloak and fez cap, white doves on both shoulders, a wand in his hand.

'Asleep,' Conjuror shouted back. 'And I'll thank 'ee not ter wake 'im.'

The conjuror's wife followed behind the second van, collecting wild herbs as she went, dropping them in a pocket at the front of her apron. Lily walked next to her, her cap pulled down over her eyes. It was easy in breeches to walk, her stride long, her hands pushed into her pockets, not worrying about the wind getting under her skirts, her hem trailing in the muck or getting caught in the cart wheels. She'd got the job, for the season at least. 'You make a canny lad,' the magician had said, when she returned to the theatre. 'Better than most. You'll come with us, as far as the north country.'

They joined a great road out of the city, following it under a towering railway viaduct and on through vivid green patchworks of market gardens, fields of purple lavender, dusty yellow brickworks. When they came to hills, Lily lent a hand pushing the props van, leaning into the wooden frame, putting all her strength into it as the covered wagon juddered into potholes and over ruts. She'd discarded her stays, rolled them up and stored them inside the bundle of her old clothes. Freed from their grip, she could bend and turn at will, breathe deeply. Since her milk dried, her breasts had grown small and soft. Bound against her chest, they didn't betray her.

They walked all day and at dusk, Conjuror pulled up the horses by a wide grassy verge running along the edge of a field. He unharnessed the beasts from the vans, hobbled them and turned them loose to graze.

'Rest tha' self,' he said to Lily. 'You walked long, for one that's not accustomed to it.'

The conjuror's wife moved around, making a fire with the sticks, setting an iron griddle over the flames. Mrs Mo was wiry, with hoops in her long ear lobes, a loose dress, an embroidered shawl in purple and red and gold wound over her head. After a supper of flatbreads and cheese and pickled roots, the conjuror and his wife sat by the fire, him plucking the strings of a mournful-sounding instrument while she smoked her clay pipe, drank sweet coffee. They talked in their language, the unfamiliar sounds hanging on the air like birdsong, and sometimes they laughed.

Conjuror bunked in the props van; Lily was to sleep with Mrs Mo in the living van – a dark cave, the roof festooned with branches of leaves, stems of dried berries, round cheeses in cloths. A row of narrow wooden shelves, with lips on their fronts, was packed with jars and caddies; below, teacups swung from hooks. In the back of the van, two pairs of white doves cooed and preened in their cages, sometimes hopping out of the open doors and fluttering up to a wooden rail across the corner, or drinking from the bowl of shallow water left out for them.

On the top bunk, Lily lay under a rough blanket with her body aching, her feet blistered. She wouldn't be defeated by physical discomfort. Somewhere in this land, her daughter waited for her. Despite her terror of whatever evil the professor had planned for her, she would keep searching until she found him and his sister, would find a way to get Faye on her own, and claim Grace back from her. Breathing in the smell of birdlime and damp wool, looking up through an open hatch at a patch of starry sky, the dependable line of the Plough, Lily renewed her vow that when she found her daughter, nothing and no one would part them again. Salt would have to kill her first.

Forty-Nine

Hansom cabs were lined up in the middle of the road outside the railway station. Faye took one, climbing up inside with Grace in her arms, the driver loading her box at the back. The roads were rough and she held the sleeping infant tightly as the cab jolted and bounced along the streets of Nottingham, past clanking, rattling factories and the austere, silent walls of the castle, heading for the address Erasmus had given her.

The cab pulled up outside a wood-framed inn, its front bowing out over the narrow pavement. Their room was on the second floor, quaint, with a low ceiling and chintz curtains at leaded windows. With the box brought up and the key to the room handed over to her, Faye laid the sleeping child on the bed and began to unpack; she unwrapped a new bar of transparent soap and put it on the washstand, draped Grace's nightclothes to air on the towel rail. She lit the portable spirit lamp and half filled a pan with water, put an egg to boil.

Arrivals in new cities were unsettling, no matter

how many of them she went through. She feared bed bugs and rotten floorboards, disreputable fellow guests and tainted meat but more than anything Faye feared a letter from Balthazar Pook, addressed to Erasmus. She'd thought her brother would forget about Lily Bell, once he had a new actress. He had not. Erasmus was determined to find her. He'd sent Mr Pook out as his scout, scouring the country. The thought of it made Faye uneasy.

Grace woke and rolled onto her tummy, raising herself on her arms. She looked around her, as if perplexed by where she found herself, in a way that reminded Faye of the night she was born. She seemed not happy or unhappy, but puzzled to find herself here. The baby had a sore on her top lip, shadows under her eyes. Her appetite had been poor ever since her mother left and her growth had slowed. Faye gave her the crocheted blanket and propped her in a sitting position between two pillows. As the egg bumped on the sides of the pan and steam began to mist the windows, she sat watching Grace chew a corner of the blanket.

They'd been with the travelling theatre for what felt like months although it was only weeks. After Oxford, they'd gone on to Banbury, then Worcester, and Shrewsbury, each run lasting a fortnight, Grace appearing as the infant ghost every night except Sundays. At each new site, audiences crammed into the bench seats of the travelling theatre, bought tickets to stand along the side aisles and at the back.

Twice, Faye had sat in the raked seats for a performance, watched the actor on stage reach for his wife, his
hands appearing to pass straight through her. The effect
was astonishing and even knowing how it was achieved,
Faye felt shivers run down her spine. She watched Etta
Arkwright lift Grace from the cradle and turn her sleeping face towards the limelight so the audience could
get a good look at her. Saw the actress pinch the child
through the lace, make her jerk and twitch. It was at
that moment, when Grace proved not to be a doll, that
audiences went wild. Women fainted or wailed, fell to
their knees and prayed, begged the ghost professor to
spare them a glimpse of their own lost angels. Men
choked up, demanding Erasmus bring back their lost
sons and sisters, or on occasion a beloved mare or dog.

In Shrewsbury, on the last night, after the performance finished, a gale had got up, howling into the theatre
through the open doors, the canvas tilt billowing over
their heads as if the wind might lift up the whole structure, whirl it away and them with it. It felt to Faye
as if it were a warning, a symbol of the flimsiness of
their existence, both physical and moral. Arkwright had
been in the small hut they used as a box office, counting
the takings, and her brother sat alone in the front row,
writing in his notebook.

'Is it right, Erasmus?' Faye had said, sitting down next
to him, with Grace in her arms, still in a drugged sleep.

'Is what right?' Erasmus said, coldly. Her heart thud-
ding with the old fear, Faye had freed one arm and

gestured towards the stage. 'All of it. All of this ... pretence.'

'Not a pretence,' Erasmus had said, getting to his feet, staring down at the baby. 'A vision of the future. We shall see the dead return to us, Faye. That day will soon come.'

The pan had boiled almost dry. Removing it from the flame, Faye lifted out the egg and put it to cool. She understood Ras's longing. She had hoped all her life that one day her mother would return to her, that she would see her again. In Faye's imagination, her mother was as she'd been at the time of her disappearance – a young woman, younger than Faye was now, radiant in her ivory gown, her face framed with curls. Clara Grace Salt had never come back to Nether Hall, never sent her children a letter. There had been no word of her from any quarter. Faye supposed she must be dead. The knowledge had grown in her slowly, almost imperceptibly, over the years. It was something she knew without knowing.

Slicing the top from the egg, Faye peeled off fragments of shell. She sat Grace on her lap, offering a little of the yolk on a teaspoon, blowing on it to cool it. Grace closed her eyes, flailed her arms and after two mouthfuls refused to take any more. Faye ate the remains of the egg herself, without tasting it. She put a bottle of milk to warm by the fire while she undressed the baby for bed, taking off the little gown that was growing tight around her arms and neck, changing her sodden napkin and pinning on a fresh one, sitting on a low chair to give her the milk.

'In the morning, Grace, after your bath, we'll go out for a walk. We will look for pussycats! And puppy dogs!' She spoke to Grace as if she understood every word. 'Drink up your milk, there's a good girl.'

Before long, Grace slept, clutching her blanket to her face, her limbs making sudden, involuntary starts. Faye put her in the bed, extinguished the spirit lamp and got in next to her, leaving a nightlight burning. Dark shapes scuttled across the ceiling over her head and she pulled the sheet up over their faces. She'd thought joining Arkwright's Theatre would be a good thing, that even if she tried, Lily Bell could never find them, performing at fairs in sooty provincial towns and cities. She hadn't anticipated how gruelling it would be for the child, constantly moving to new places, staying in dirty lodgings and existing on bakery bread, watered-down milk. She was worried about her.

Faye slept and dreamed of a child that was hers but not hers, crying for her mother. *Mama*, the piteous cry rose again and again. *Mama*. In the dream, she was compelled to go to the child yet found herself unable to move, incapable of taking a single step towards her, even though she knew clearly where she was. She woke in the small hours, on the very edge of the bed, with Grace lying sideways across the mattress. Eventually she rose, lit the lamp and, sitting at the table with her notebooks, the gathering pile of them, continued to write.

*

Her condition had announced itself through the onset of a violent and persistent nausea. Mrs Mordaunt brought in the family physician and the old gentleman announced to them both that Faye was *enceinte*.

'Ancient?' said Mrs Mordaunt. 'I hardly think so. Past the first flush, I grant you.'

'*Enceinte*, Mrs M. With child. Expecting.'

Words, for once, failed Hester Mordaunt.

'You must keep her here,' the doctor said. 'This violation has happened under your roof and you must shelter the lady until her confinement.'

Forbidden all contact with the children, although Lottie visited at night, creeping down from the nursery with saved buns, wilted posies, Faye had stayed in the room. She'd thought at first that she must surely die, of shame and heartbreak. As day succeeded dreary day, she understood with regret that she would not. To keep herself from going mad, she had occupied her hands with sewing, stitching little smocks and chemises, forming scalloped necks and hems. It was all she could think of to do for the child that would be born of her love for Pyramus. As her time approached, she completed the layette. One afternoon, her employer came in without knocking, found Faye wrapping the little clothes in tissue paper. Mrs Mordaunt snatched up the garments and threw them in a heap on the floor.

'Your infant is a bastard, Miss Salt. A bastard does not wear clothes such as these.'

When she'd gone, Faye retrieved the baby clothes and rewrapped them. She hid them at the back of a drawer at the bottom of the armoire, nestled in the darkness, with a note to whichever future governess might find them that she would one day send for them. Outside the window, under a round silver moon, the black-limbed trees reached up to the sky as if they prayed for her. Faye searched the dictionary for a word that described her – broken of heart, swollen of body, an animal woman keening at the moon. She found nothing.

Fifty

Dressed in a red robe, a tasselled fez, his hair oiled and his fingertips stained orange, the conjuror emerged from the back of the booth and took his place in the middle of the stage. Feeling unsure, Lily stepped up behind him. By the light of a seven-branched candelabra on the table, the conjuror began.

'Good evening, ladies and gentlemen. I will perform marvels from the East. Marvels that come from the land of the pyramids and desert sands, from the learning of ancient kings...'

A hundred or more people were packed onto rows of plank seats, craning their necks to see the narrow platform on which Lily and the conjuror stood. Bellows wheezed behind Lily and as Mrs Mo scattered beads of incense on a glowing coal, fragrant smoke began to plume onto the stage. Inhaling the resinous scent, Lily began to feel light-headed. In the blue room, she'd heard the audience but had never seen them. Now she stood before real people, looking at her with hungry eyes that seemed as if they would devour her, rapt faces distorted by the glimmering light of the candles that lit the booth. They were country people, the young women pretty and fresh as wild flowers, the old ones ruddy and weathered as the men.

Lily had spent all day getting ready, Mrs Mo opening trunks in the props van and pulling out tunics, Morocco slippers and lace ruffs. Wordlessly, they'd agreed on her costume: a white shirt with a frilly jabot at the front, waistcoat striped in red and green and mustard, with red satin breeches and a pair of high, snug-fitting leather boots with turned-up toes. Mrs Mo had fitted the satin breeches to Lily's hips and waist. If she noticed, as she pinned and tucked, her mouth full of pins, the crimson marks that still scarred Lily's belly, her features didn't betray it. She darkened Lily's face and hands with a bitter-smelling unguent, slicked her short hair with oil, her fingers quick and gentle. Back in the living van, peering at her reflection in the glass, Lily had felt as if she'd always been brown-skinned and black-haired, always been a boy that might have been a girl, his grey eyes startlingly light.

Conjuror tapped his wand on a brass bowl, sending a low, resonant note humming through the air. 'Abracadabra!' he cried, raising his arms, his voice altered from its usual gentleness to something stern and grave. 'I hereby summon the birds of the ancestors.' Lily held up a small brass bell and rang it three times, muffling it with her hand after each peal. With fresh clouds of smoke enveloping him, Conjuror reached upwards and held out his palm to the audience. A white dove stood on it and cries and shouts emerged from the watchers' open mouths.

'Where by Allah did that come from?'

As he scratched his ear, in apparent puzzlement, another dove appeared on his other hand. 'These doves have flown from Egypt,' he announced, releasing them onto the table, the pair pecking at the grains of corn Mrs Mo had scattered earlier, concealed in the furrows of the crimson chenille cloth.

'At a sign from my assistant, you will see these sacred birds, these birds of peace, disappear in a single enchanted moment.'

Lily stared at a woman in the front row. Her mind was empty, as if a fog had descended in it and rendered everything invisible. She couldn't remember what she was supposed to do or even why she was here.

'Sound the magic trumpet!'

The trumpet. Putting out her hand for it, she knocked the instrument off the table and as she stooped to pick it up, the stage seemed to rock beneath her feet and she stumbled, almost fell. Regaining her feet, Lily blew into the instrument and produced a feeble squeak. Someone in the audience jeered; a piercing whistle came from the back.

Conjuror tapped his wand on the brass bowl. 'The sacred messengers need no human hand,' he intoned, his voice lowered now, altered again, as if he were in a trance. As the eyes of the audience swivelled back towards him, he waved his wand and made a rapid, swooping movement with his long, sleeved arms. The doves vanished from the table.

'See that?' exclaimed the large woman in the front row. 'Didst thou see it?'

All eyes were on the conjuror and Lily began to be able to breathe again, felt her concentration return. From then on, time passed quickly. The audience applauded as Conjuror caused balls to remove themselves from underneath upturned cups; he produced ribbons matching those on her hat from the sleeve of the large lady, and restored to wholeness a glass that had shattered at the high, whistling sound he produced from its rim. For the finale, Lily passed him – as rehearsed – a curved dagger with a jewelled handle. The knife was razor-sharp and Conjuror had warned her to handle it with extreme care. 'This here in't a prop,' he'd explained. 'This here's a lethal weapon. This here could kill a man.'

From the front of the low stage, the magician bowed, reaching as he rose towards the tall hat of a gent in the front row, slicing the crown from the hat with one lightning movement. 'Hocus pocus,' he intoned as he rose, laying the severed crown on the table. 'Tontus talontus.'

The white doves emerged from the amputated hat on the man's head and fluttered through the air to the table, landing, spreading their wings and dipping, as if they curtsied. As Conjuror replaced the hat, whole again and intact on the man's head, the birds rose in the air and fluttered there as if poised for their flight. Conjuror bowed, the bellows wheezed, and in a final cloud of mystical, scented smoke, as Lily extinguished the flames on the candelabra, the magician left the stage, his cloak a swirling flash of scarlet. He exited the booth through the back, scattering a crowd of boys who'd been peeking through gaps in the wooden shutters, and disappeared into the props van.

Lily took a bow, then stood motionless as the people departed. She'd appeared on stage for the first time in her life – not in the way in which she'd dreamed of since she was a girl, not in any way she could ever have imagined or if she had imagined it would have wanted, but she had done it. If only her mother could have been there to see her.

Half an hour later, dressed in a plain shirt and breeches, hands stuffed into her pockets against the chill night air, Lily walked the fairground, what Conjuror called the *tober*. She half expected someone to challenge her, ask her what she thought she was doing and where she was going. Lily still hadn't grown accustomed to the freedom she had as a boy, to the novelty of walking alone without shame, her head up, free to go where she pleased.

Sauntering around the pitch, she tried to look as if her interest was casual. The fair was a large one and the range of entertainers dizzying. There was a pair of Siamese twins; a Camel Girl who walked on all fours; a bearded lady, her pretty face displayed in an advertisement, her eyes large and feminine, nose neat, cheeks and chin invisible behind a luxuriant growth of soft-looking black hair. Wrestling booths stood next to shooting galleries, stalls selling hot peas and baked potatoes; a bent old woman wandered the ground with a tray strung round her neck, her back bowed by the weight of humbugs and honeycomb.

From the corner of her eye, Lily saw a short fellow clad in a bright green suit picking his way between the booths, his mop of black hair swivelling. He reminded her of someone, but after the exertions of the performance, she couldn't think who. The milling crowds were beginning to thin. Some were drunk, men and women staggering and singing and quarrelling. As Lily made her way back to where the line of vans were drawn up, to the area roped off for the fairground people, she spotted the bearded lady from the picture, sitting on the steps of her caravan. The woman beckoned and Lily walked over to the van and stood in front of her.

'Evening,' she said, from underneath her cap, her voice as gruff and low as she could make it.

'I don't mean nothing by it,' the woman said, stroking a little dog. 'But I'm a strange-looking woman. And you're a funny-sounding lad. We should stick together.' She held out her hand. 'Violet Spratt.'

Lily took her soft fingers and – aware that her own were still almost equally soft – quickly dropped them. 'Pleased to meet you,' she said, unable to come up with a name for herself. Conjuror called her *Walad*. It meant boy in his language. Mrs Mo called her *Bint* and that meant girl. She wasn't Lily Bell any longer. She had no name.

Violet patted the space next to her on the step and Lily sat down. They stayed there, watching the performers make their way back to their vans, and Violet shared her bag of humbugs with Lily. There were the born freaks, Violet explained, of whom she was one. Then there were the made freaks: the fat lady, whose flesh fell in rings around her wrists and ankles, whose rolling hips could knock children flying; the human giraffe, her neck elongated by a stack of brass rings so that her head appeared disconnected from her body, as if she was in two parts.

'So he's a made freak,' Lily murmured as a man walked by, naked from the waist upwards, pictures inked along the length of his arms, over his neck and chest and back, patterns of green and blue ink obscuring his face and one black teardrop under his eye.

'You're learning,' Violet said, crunching sugar between her teeth.

Sitting in the darkness, Lily knew who it was that she'd seen earlier. It was the gasman. Balthazar. She leaned forward, feeling suddenly sick, looking at the crushed blades of grass in front of her, the daisies with their white eyes closed tight against the night.

'Ever seen a ghost professor, Miss Spratt?' she said,

straightening up again. 'Goes by the name of Salt. Putting on a spirit in a travelling theatre?'

'Can't say as I have,' said Violet, without curiosity.

Fifty-One

Balthazar did up the buttons of his jacket and adjusted his wig, tugging it more firmly over his ears. He was travelling in disguise. He'd been looking for the girl without success, moving from fairground to fairground, criss-crossing the country by stagecoach and trains and on occasion Shanks pony. He'd scoured this fair, found nothing, and the previous evening, to pass the time, had bought a ticket to a magic show. Packed onto an uncomfortable bench, between a couple of bony old scarecrows, he'd scarcely seen the Arab's voodoo. A boy in breeches and a striped waistcoat, hair hidden under a red fez, top lip darkened with a moustache, stood to the side of the stage. It wasn't the face Balthazar recognised as the assistant stepped forward with a glinting, jewelled dagger in his hands, nor the hair – cropped and dark, it bore no resemblance to the ghost's. It was the set of his head on his shoulders, the gesture as he held up the weapon for the conjuror.

Next morning, walking through the field where the

fair was being held, Balthazar spotted her again. She was dressed in a white shirt and black trousers, a corduroy cap pulled over her head, and was walking with a foreigner woman. They went together towards the stall selling coffee and jam tarts and Balthazar followed, watching from under a tree as the two joined the people crowded around the stall. He lounged there, luxuriating in his find, considering the curves under the boy's jacket, the narrowing of waist and ankle. The secret place half hidden by a pair of men's breeches and half revealed. It was a pity to pluck a flower before it hadn't hardly bloomed, but then again there was no sentiment in business.

A waft of frying doughnuts, hot oil and sugar reached him and he closed his eyes and leaned back on the tree. He'd watched the previous night's performance to its end, had extracted from the lad sweeping up outside the booth the information he required; this stage of his mission was complete. He had to find her and Salt would get her to the place where she would meet her journey's end. He would take a cup of coffee, he decided, and a doughnut, before he set off back to London.

'Balthazar?' He opened his eyes to see Mister Lily Bell walking towards him. 'I thought it was you. What on earth are you doing here?'

Balthazar performed a short jig. He widened his eyes, thumped his chest in the region of his heart, opened his mouth in feigned surprise, trying to conceal his fury. In the *syrup*, the new *whistle and flute*, he'd thought himself unrecognisable. Lily Bell glanced around.

'Professor Salt...' she said. 'Is he here? Are you with him?'

Balthazar let his mouth go slack. Gave a half shake of his chin.

The young master swallowed. Stood a little straighter. 'Have you seen them?' she said, gruffly. 'Him and his sister? The baby...'

Squeaking a denial, shrugging his shoulders, Balthazar brushed his palms together in a gesture of finality and for good measure made a scissoring gesture.

'You have parted company with them. Salt cut you off.' She stared at him and some of the tension seemed to leave her. 'Balthazar, for old times' sake – do you know where they are now? I must find them.'

He resumed the slackness of expression, staring at her dully, and her face fell. She was more beautiful as a boy than she had been as a girl. More nervous than he remembered; the hands clasped before her white-knuckled and raw, the nails bitten. He needed to put her at her ease. Balthazar remembered another old acquaintance he'd seen, working the crowds in Green Park, drowning his sorrows in a tavern in Soho. He made a show of juggling imaginary balls.

Lily Bell gave a wan smile. 'Mr Ames. Have you seen him? Is he well?'

He made an enthusiastic grunt of assent. Carried on the charade of throwing and catching.

'I would like to send him a letter,' she said, after a minute.

Balthazar hesitated and then saluted. There was no harm in an extra few bob on the side. No harm at all. He intended to make Erasmus Salt wait for his prey anyway. He thought of Lily Bell dead, lying on the ground with the life gone out of her, eyes wide with surprise. Pictured himself lifting the limp, warm weight on one shoulder, staggering through the dark to the graveyard, to where her place awaited her. Salt wanted the deed done in Ramsgate.

The ghost professor had laid the Hedges girl in the ground himself, shovelling the earth in on top of her with furious energy and tramping it down with his patent shoes. 'Her own fault,' he'd said again and again, on the long trudge back over the fields and hollows, streaks of bloody pink and orange striping the horizon. 'Brought it on herself.'

The girl was looking at him, he realised, with a puzzled expression on her face. He resumed the juggling action, hoping his features had not betrayed him.

'So you can take a letter to Mr Ames?' Miss Bell said.

Balthazar agreed and by means of further clowning with gestures and facial contortions, confirmed the information he had and extracted more. Salt's ghost was assisting in a magic show, heading for the great fair at the town moor in Newcastle-upon-Tyne. At the season's end, she would look for new employment. She urgently wished to find Faye Salt and the little baby but did not wish on any account for the professor to know her whereabouts. He, Balthazar, would understand. After all, and here she had hesitated, hadn't he tried to warn her, that night in the blue room, what the ghost professor was capable of... Her words trailed away.

Balthazar gave her to understand by grave noises of assent that he would be honoured to take a letter to Mr Ames, undertook to deliver it by hand when he returned to London. Bring an answer perhaps, to the town moor fair, if it should be his fate. She could rely on him to attempt to find out where the old rogue Salt was. He gave her a ghoulish smile and again her face took on a look of puzzlement. Even, he thought as he made his way back to the caravan he'd rented, suspicion.

That evening, Balthazar considered his next move. He intended to string Salt along, tell him just enough to keep him hopeful but not so much that he, Balthazar, became dispensable. He wouldn't put it past the professor to undertake the dispatch himself, save some money. There was a knock at the door of the caravan and Balthazar opened it to see a woman who would have been decent-looking if it weren't for the *strange and weird* creeping from her ears to her chin. She extended a white wrist.

'Letter for you, mate,' she said. 'From the conjuror's assistant.'

Glancing at the envelope Balthazar saw, written in a neat copperplate, the name of Mr Tom Ames. The caravan rocked as the bearded lady descended the steps. Balthazar closed the door behind her and bolted it.

Wiping his hands on his breeches, he broke the seal on Miss Bell's letter and retrieved a single sheet of paper, carefully folded. The writing was fluid and even, as if the letters had written themselves, following their own natural course, every character joined to its neighbour. As he unfolded it, a small, pristine square of blue and white spotted cotton fell to the table.

Dear Mr Ames,

I left London in haste, in search of Salt and his sister, and was unable to meet you as we planned, or to say goodbye. My search for my daughter has so far been unsuccessful. I am still looking.

I enclose a section of your own handkerchief, which I have kept close by me, so that you know this letter comes from me and with it the hope that the handkerchief, cut up, may one day be restored.

It is my dear hope that one day soon we may meet again.

Yours,

Lily Bell

(PS You recall old Balthazar? Am entrusting this note to him.)

Balthazar put the scrap of cotton into his wallet then tore the note into pieces that he fed into the pot-bellied stove. He left the door open, watched as they flared and fluttered in the flames, then banged it shut, burning his thumb. He would make a quid or two out of Ames but there was no need to arouse false hope in the young fellow. At the notion of himself sparing the feelings of another, the gasman began to shake with mirth. He opened a bottle of pale ale, foam spurting from the neck, took a sheet of paper and got out his pen.

Fifty-Two

Tom waited under the spread arms of an oak tree. Dressed in his best, he had left his knapsack of conjuring kit back at the lodgings, brought only a brown envelope containing the picture he'd had made for Lily. He kept his eyes fixed on the ornate, gilded gates, scanning the people that walked into the park, each and every one of them disappointing to him because they were not her.

He waited until it got dark and left the park. He waited every Sunday. He would continue to wait. Continue to hope. Back in the lodgings in Chelsea, in the room that reminded him of the stage garret where he first heard Lily's voice, he got out the photograph and propped it on the mantelpiece. He'd stood stock still for two minutes, in a studio in Glasshouse Street, one juggling ball balanced in the fingers of each outstretched hand, his eyes cast up at two more balls that hung in the still air, suspended on cotton threads.

A foolish-looking fellow, he decided, his striped shirt marking him out as someone not serious, not wealthy.

The balls in the air – that should have been moving – were unnaturally still and solid. The two in his hands, that should have been still, were soft-edged, as if in motion. Staring at the image, Tom saw something else.

A crack ran through him, from his left ear and down across his chest, extending through his right wrist, severing his hand from his arm. The photographer must have dropped the plate, cracked it in two. The fault had been repaired with brush and ink on the print, but was clearly visible. It was a broken portrait of a broken man.

Fifty-Three

Grace's crying grew louder and in the room above, someone banged on the floor.

Faye finished putting on her dress and stockings, twisted her hair up at the back of her head with a comb. She pulled Grace's blue woollen coat on over her night-clothes, adding a knitted cap to the only part of her that flourished – the silky red curls that with each passing week grew longer, thicker, brighter in hue. Jamming on her own hat, locking the door of the room behind her, she carried Grace down the stairs of the inn.

In a stone-flagged hallway that reeked of drains and bacon, she strapped Grace in her perambulator and let herself out, bumping the carriage over the threshold and up the street. They'd returned from the theatre late the previous night, arriving at the lodgings in the dark-ness, and Faye couldn't immediately place where she was. Pushing the pram underneath the timber frames of overhanging houses, seeing two great Gothic towers rearing up in front of her, she remembered. It was the city of York. They had been there for several days, staying in what they called the Shambles, the theatre pitched at a fairground occupying a large meadow near the river.

A team of drays stood in the marketplace, between the shafts of a laden cart. The great beasts hung their heads, pawed the ground, steam rising gently from their haunches. Behind them, men were unloading barrels, thumping them down onto the cobbles, rolling them towards a cellar entrance in practised movements, as if they'd done the same thing a hundred times or more. Sometimes Faye felt surprise that places she'd never heard of or dreamed of were solidly peopled and full of life, citizens eating and dancing and marrying. Working. She put the brake on the pram and stood leaning on the handle while Grace gazed at the horses.

A woman stopped and peered into the pram.

'Spit of you, isn't she?' she said.

Faye attempted a smile. Grace needed ever-larger doses of Mother's Friend to keep her quiet through the performances. Fifteen or twenty drops, half an hour before the curtain rose, spooned down her throat in warm milk sweetened with sugar. Sometimes by the start of the show the child seemed almost unconscious, her eyes rolling back in her head, her little mouth open. In the mornings, she was tetchy and tearful, couldn't be consoled.

The woman rubbed her gloved hands together. 'There's a travelling theatre. A ghost comes, with her wee ghost baby. Have you seen 'em? Looks a bit like your little one.'

'Never,' Faye said, taking off the brake.

'You ought to. It's a miracle. I'm going again tonight. I lost three myself.'

The doll catapulted from the pram and landed in a puddle. A wail rose from under the hood. 'I'm sorry to hear it, ma'am,' Faye said, picking up the doll. 'Good morning.'

She set off again, bouncing the wheels over the cobbles while Grace held onto the sides, the breeze ruffling her curls. Heading back to the lodgings against the wind, Faye pictured Grace restored to health, the colour back in her cheeks. An image came of the baby tottering towards Lily, uttering a word that hadn't yet passed her lips, despite Erasmus's efforts to teach it to her. *Mama.* Ras wanted Grace to say it on stage, to Etta Arkwright, but Grace so far had spoken no words, only her own formless language.

Back in the room, Faye removed the child's hat and coat, put her on the floor with her damp doll and for some time sat watching her play. She'd trimmed her hair for the first time, cut a straight line across her forehead; the fringe accentuated her wide brow, her clear grey eyes fringed by curled lashes. Often, caring for her, Faye thought of her own mother, Clara Grace Salt. She had so few memories of her. Feeling for the catch on the chain round her neck, she took off the locket and opened it. Untethered from her body, held at a little distance, Faye saw the miniature afresh, looking as if for the first time at the tiny girl's broad, creamy forehead, the large eyes under a head of copper curls. Grace sat on the floor, propped on her cushions, talking to her doll. Faye looked at the child and looked at the enamelled portrait. They were almost identical, so alike that the painting might have been of Grace. Yet, how could that be? For a long time, she studied the picture and then the child, the child and then the picture.

Closing the catch on the locket, Faye returned it to her neck. Drawing Grace up onto her lap, holding the little girl close, she kissed her head and her hands, but could find no words to speak to her. Faye forced herself to remember the night she had left Lily alone with Erasmus, drinking wine. She'd seen no harm in it – Erasmus cared nothing for the girl and never had, was interested only in his ghost. Thinking about Lily's face, covered in greasepaint, looking like a mannequin, an image came to Faye's mind of the line of bruises she'd seen on Lily's cheek, marks spaced as if they were made by the fingers of a man's hand. Marks for which she had blamed Mr Ames.

Groaning aloud, sickened with a kind of helplessness, as if the floor was falling away beneath her feet, she stood up and went to the window, staring out without seeing the street outside, the broken down stables opposite with the nags' heads hanging out of the open top doors.

Mrs Mordaunt had accompanied her. They'd travelled by train to London and taken a hackney from Paddington Station. Mrs Mordaunt knew the lady chairman of the trustees and had written to plead Faye's case, stressing her former good character, her family background, her Christian contrition.

The baby was small and slight, unmoving as a doll. In Faye's arms, she weighed almost nothing. She'd dressed her in one of the shifts she had made, a name embroidered into the hem of the dress in blue thread, with the date and place of birth, in tiny, tight stitches that could not be unpicked, and wrapped her in the shawl she'd crocheted that was light as a spider's web. Faye had wished the carriage ride would last forever.

The driver helped her down and they stood for a moment under the branches of a line of plane trees, looking at the long, low white building that stood in grounds behind iron railings. Mrs Mordaunt knocked on the door of the porters' lodge and gained admittance, looking over her shoulder to check that Faye followed her. The sun was high in the sky and the shadows of the trees fell in circles on the ground. The baby stirred and settled, her eyes tight shut, her face complicated with dreams.

The next minutes occurred in a blur, obscured by the smell of carbolic, a rubber-aproned nurse, cheery voices echoing off tiled walls. The sound of screaming – her own, Faye understood later by the hoarseness of her throat. In what seemed no time at all, they were leaving the building, walking back through the grassy grounds by the shadow-pooled trees, the porter saluting. The small weight and warmth that had rested against Faye's body, in the crook of her arm, part of her, was fiercely, intolerably absent.

'Good day, Miss Salt,' Mrs Mordaunt had said, on the pavement outside. 'These are yours.' She passed Faye the valise containing her dictionaries and walked away, quickly, as if from the scene of a crime.

Fifty-Four

Erasmus received a telegram. The gasman had met 'the little runaway'. She could be found at the forthcoming fair at Newcastle town moor. Balthazar waited in London, ready at the professor's instruction to 'accompany her to her journey's end'. Sitting in front of a plate of stewed kidneys, re-reading the telegram, Erasmus cursed the fellow for the lack of detail. He experienced a familiar sense that the gasman toyed with him. Still, the knowledge that he was closing in on his prey, that Lily Bell was within his sights, threw him into a state of anticipation. They were still in York. Arkwright wanted to proceed to Sheffield, where he had a pitch for the winter, but Erasmus would insist that they go north, to Newcastle-upon-Tyne.

Picturing the ghost's painted face, the gash of red in the white oval, Erasmus had a sense of a tide having turned in his run of bad luck. Arkwright's daughter's acting had improved and the gasman's timing was more accurate. Audiences went wild for the infant ghost; the takings were piling up. Even the London critics had taken notice at last; several had trooped out to muddy fairgrounds, squeezing themselves onto the front benches, their cambric handkerchiefs clutched to their noses. Mr Gilbert of *The Times* had been effusive. *The infant ghost is utterly natural, in the movements of her head and limbs. It is impossible to imagine her an automaton and the manner in which she appears and disappears from the ether – as I personally witnessed last night, in a damp, travelling theatre, on the edge of a damp field, in that notably damp county known as Northumberland – defies all rational explanation. A remarkable phenomenon that must be seen to be believed.*

The time was right to move to the next stage. He must proceed with his vision and summon a real spirit, before one of his rivals beat him to it. Correspondence between members of the Next World Society had become cryptic and secretive, several claiming they would shortly be proclaiming significant developments in the field. Erasmus snorted at the thought of the blasted spaniel. He would track down Miss Bell at Newcastle. Balthazar would dispatch her to the next world in Ramsgate. And on a London stage, Erasmus would call her spirit back, the paraphernalia of mirrors and glass made redundant. He spent some time picturing the scene – the stage dressed only with simple but elegant bouquets of white flowers, a chair suitable for a lady's boudoir. The air scented, perhaps, with rose oil. An exquisite silk rug, in pale colours, laid on the baize ready and waiting to be graced by a pair of spirit feet. No hidden room. No clumsy mechanics. Only a limelight in the corner of the stage, to illuminate further the perfect beauty of Lily Bell's ghost.

The door opened and his sister came in, the infant squirming in her arms.

'I must speak with you, Ras.'

Erasmus folded the telegram back into its envelope. 'What is it, Faye?'

Faye held the baby tightly, looking at Erasmus over its head of red curls.

'I'm going. I have decided to leave.'

He looked at her without expression. She was becoming opinionated. Getting above herself. She'd raised her voice to him, the previous week, on the subject of the infant. Said she couldn't survive touring round the country like a raggle-taggle gypsy and must have a proper home. The brat looked all right to him and if she was not over-rounded, so much the better. A spirit baby ought not to appear bonny. He took a mouthful of tea.

'Leave for where?'

'Nether Hall. I am going home.'

Faye looked tired. Her dress hung on her frame; her undressed hair displayed threads of silver. His sister grew old. A younger woman would be better able to look after the baby. Its mother was within his sights, Erasmus reminded himself, and given what was to come it might be better if Faye was out of the way. It had been a close call with the Hedges girl.

290

'As you wish. Go home if you must.'

Faye's face brightened. 'Thank you. We'll wait until the next fair ends, to give you time to find a replacement. We'll travel south by train and when we—'

'We?' he said, coldly.

'Myself and Grace. I don't expect you to accompany us.'

'No one will accompany you, Faye. You will leave alone.'

Faye stared at him. 'What do you mean?'

'Grace is my ghost. There are plans for her of which you have no knowledge. Important plans.'

'Erasmus.' His sister's tone of voice changed. It was not fearful as he anticipated but stern. Reproving, even. 'The sins of Grace's mother and of her father are not her fault. She ought not to suffer for them. She has the right to grow up like a normal child. Almost as if she were part of our own family.' She looked at him levelly. 'Do you not agree?'

Erasmus experienced an uncomfortable sensation as if in his heart something curdled. Rising from his chair, moving around the table, he grabbed Grace out of Faye's arms. 'Ain't a normal child,' he said, over the sound of startled screams. 'Never will be.' The creature was damp, puking and puling in his arms; an unpleasant smell rose from it. He shoved it back in his sister's direction. 'Go home, Faye, as soon as you want. I'll find a nursemaid.'

Fifty-Five

A boy ran out of a cottage and stood at the side of the lane, pointing, jumping, shouting. From below the sagging thatch, a woman came after him, clouting the boy's head, grabbing him by his collar and dragging him back inside the cottage. 'D'you want to be stolen away by them gypsies?' she shouted, delivering another blow. Lily kept her gaze on the horizon. Once, she would have been the same – half fascinated by the fairground people and half terrified of them, fearing that one might give her the evil eye, slit her pocket or her throat. Now, she felt safe with them. They worked hard, said what they felt, didn't try to hide behind manners or affectations. Many were brilliantly talented, but in skills the world thought little of – swallowing fire, walking on the high wire, divining the future.

They were on their way to the town moor fair at Newcastle-upon-Tyne, had come from Durham, a city with a castle and a cathedral staring at each other atop a severe, craggy hilltop, black-gowned scholars and clerics hurrying through lanes in the town below, a noisy, rushing river turning a series of water wheels in the ravine. Before that was Darlington, with its railway station and iron foundries, and before that a fair on the coast at Hartlepool, where once the townspeople hanged a monkey brought ashore from a shipwreck, accusing him of being a French spy.

Often, they never saw the centre of the town, the grand, newly built libraries and chambers of commerce, the wide, well-lit streets – only arrived at a sooty common somewhere on the margins, near factories where the machines ran twenty-four hours a day, a marketplace where handbills could be distributed and food bought cheap, a district for the working people where the houses were poky and the windows small, waste running in the middle of the alleys. If takings had been good, Conjuror put up Lily and Mrs Mo in lodgings for a night or two, sought out a respectable house where they could bathe in front of a fire, sleep on a feather mattress, eat hot rolls for breakfast. Mrs Mo relished these occasions. She walked around the meanest, smallest rooms examining the furnishings, exclaiming at the large space, the high ceilings, set up a chair by the window to watch the jossers going about their business.

For now, Lily preferred the van. She'd grown accustomed to stepping down barefoot into dewy grass early in the morning, bathing in warmed-up rainwater perfumed by woodsmoke, falling asleep in the velvety darkness to the sound of tawny owls, the creak of the van as the wind rocked it. There had been shocking sights. At a fairground in Stoke-on-Trent, a gang of drunken men set upon a fellow one night and with their steel-capped clogs kicked the life out of him. Another time, they came upon a stiff, stacked pile of dead horses, the corpses charred and half burned. The ponies dug in their hooves, backing their haunches into the van, refusing to pass the grisly hill. Conjuror had whispered in their ears, turned them around and found another route. Approaching a *tober* outside Sheffield, they'd narrowly avoided an escaped elephant rampaging through a field of ripe corn with its trunk in the air and a broken shackle still attached to one foot, the clank of iron mixing with the creature's hoarse bellows.

In Darlington, on the last night of the fair, three men had broken into the van where the bearded lady stayed. Two had held her down while the other tried to raise her skirts. Her screams were mighty and the Strong Man was fetched; he lifted the jossers out of the van with his bare hands, threw them down the steps and threatened to flatten them if he ever saw their miserable mugs again. Fairground people were quick to fight between themselves if they perceived a slight or an injustice, but when faced with a threat from outsiders, they stuck together. Conjuror and Mrs Mo were always Gyptians, even though they'd both been brought from their country as young children. Lily was a josser, because she hadn't been born into the fair, but few held it against her. She was generally agreed to be a born freak, Violet had told her.

They walked on in a companionable silence, Lily on one side of the horses and Conjuror on the other. The broad green hillsides were treeless, dotted with grazing sheep and wild ponies, divided by low walls made of pieces of stone fitted together like puzzles, the gaps filled with slivers of slate. Overhead, grand, impervious clouds traversed the sky, like steam ships departing for round-the-world voyages. Walking – breathing the clean, sweet air, feeling the strength and resilience of her body – Lily found it easier to think. Often, she thought about her daughter. Grace would be sitting up, crawling probably and reaching for things that caught her eye. Laughing at what amused her. Lisping a few words perhaps. Calling Faye her *Mama*.

Lily picked up a windfall apple and bit into it. She still searched for the Salts at every new fair but she'd lost her early confidence that she would find them. Back then, she hadn't understood how large England was, how expansive, how many countries were contained in one country – the west country; the black country; the north country. The world was bigger than she'd known and herself small as an apple pip.

Conjuror laid his hand on the lead horse's withers and Porter pricked his ears, walked more briskly for a few steps then resumed his steady pace, labouring up an incline, his coat under the old leather harness slicked with foam.

'What ails you, Walad?' Conjuror said.

Lily contemplated unburdening herself to the magician, telling him that she had disgraced her mother, failed her child, forfeited her dreams. That she was lost and afraid, a stranger in her own strange land, with nowhere to call home. She held out the apple core, felt the horse's soft muzzle, his breath and spittle on her palm.

'Nothing,' she said.

'Whatever it is,' said Conjuror, 'it shall soon be over.' And he waved his arm like a wand over her head and incanted something in his language, half speaking and half singing, words that sounded like a lament, that mingled with the calls of the birds and the lowing of the sheep; the sighs of the wind.

There were thirty miles still to cover before they reached Newcastle. On the edge of a small town, at dusk, they found a stopping place, bounded on one side by the railway and on the other by a scruffy hedge of bramble. Beyond the railway line, the great iron structure of a gasworks loomed like a giant crinoline. It was a mild, still evening in late September and when the van was parked, the horses unharnessed, Mrs Mo and Conjuror sat around a fire, Conjuror whittling a length of hazel with a knife, paring the bark from the stick in strips, the wood underneath white and smooth. Mrs Mo sat with a basin in her lap, picking over blackberries from the hedgerow.

A train came storming by, twin streams of smoke and

steam pluming into the sky. Lily watched as it passed, saw the blurred ovals of ghostly faces at the windows. The trails of vapour and smoke stretched and thinned and the sound died away. Bidding the old couple goodnight, she got into the van and sprang up to the top bunk, lay there listening to the sound of the horses tearing at the grass, sheep calling in the gloaming for their lost lambs.

Fifty-Six

Sheets billowed on hedges, horses cantered in fields, rivers chased their way to the sea. On the other side of the window, life rushed past, fleeting and insubstantial as the trail of steam and smoke. Grace pawed at the train window then began to struggle and Faye let her down to balance on her feet. She stood unsteadily on the straw-strewn floor, holding Faye's knees.

It was mid-afternoon and Faye felt weary to the point of exhaustion. Erasmus had left two days earlier, departed by road in advance of the theatre, impatient to get to the next fairground. Her brother had made Faye promise on the baby's life that she would bring it to Newcastle-Upon-Tyne. 'Why, Erasmus,' Faye had said, her tone cool and measured, 'you demonstrate such concern! Anyone might think you considered the child your own flesh and blood.' Erasmus had opened his mouth but hadn't uttered a word and again Faye had confirmation of her new understanding.

Grace dropped her doll and a widow sitting opposite

peered over her prayer book with a disapproving look on her face. Faye picked it up and stowed it in the valise that contained water for Grace and a paper bag of rusks, half a dozen clean napkins and the crocheted once-white blanket that was now little more than a grubby handful of wool but without which Grace couldn't settle.

'Ma'am! Your little girl.'

Grace was sitting on the floor, eating straw. 'No, Grace. That is dirty.'

Faye pulled her up onto her lap and held her, rummaging in the bag for her blanket. The little girl held it to her nose, sucking her thumb, and the tears ceased. For a short while, they both slept. Faye woke to see that in the seat opposite, the widow was chortling, her prayer book put aside for a penny dreadful. A whistle shrilled and another train passed close by, thundering in the other direction, heading south.

Erasmus met them at the train station, brought them to new lodgings. Written in capital letters, on a card hanging from a sputtering gas mantle, was a list of regulations. Clad in black from head to toe, the landladies looked at each other and then turned their gaze to Faye. Grace wriggled in her arms and Faye shifted her weight against her shoulder. The pram had been lost at Darlington, stolen from the hallway of the inn. When they got home, she would replace it. Wheel Grace through the lanes. Her childhood could begin.

'My sister, Mrs Brown. Widowed,' Erasmus said,

staring past the ladies at a narrow staircase covered in a red carpet.

Faye removed her glove to display the brass wedding ring she'd purchased for Lily Bell and now wore herself. Her clothes in their muted colours could pass as half-mourning but she refused to wear an armband, a bracelet of plaited hair. The sisters looked her up and down with dubious eyes, then turned to each other, a mute communication seeming to pass between them.

'Seven shillings and six the week,' said the older.

Faye opened her mouth to protest at the price but Erasmus was already peeling off notes from a wad, handing them over. He had grown careless of money since the show had become a commercial success. Upstairs in the room, a framed sampler hung aslant on the wall, over three beds of different heights and lengths; a low chest of drawers had been pushed up under a high window. Grace was still grizzling. She'd only had rusks to eat all day, Faye remembered.

'Can you provide warm milk? An egg?'

'I'll send something up. Don't mind my sister,' said the younger landlady, glancing over her shoulder.

The door closed behind her. Faye sat Grace at the back of a low chair and removed her outer clothes. Kneeling in front of her, she unlaced her kid bootees then gently pulled the child's thumb from her mouth, held her small soft hands. 'We are in Newcastle, Grace. You've never been here before and nor have I.' Grace looked at her doubtfully, her eyes those not of a baby but of an old soul, weary of the world and its duplicitous inhabitants. She refused the watery milk when it came, the bowl of congealed rice pudding, and it was all Faye could do to get her to take a few drops of boiled water.

For the rest of the evening, Grace seemed irritable and out of sorts, neither asleep nor awake, crying and arching her back, holding out her arms to be picked up from the bed, then struggling to be put down. Faye walked up and down the room with her, trying to comfort her, the window open to admit the air. Later, she sat in the rocking chair, the baby in her arms, singing nursery rhymes to her, trying to erase from her mind one that rang in her ears from long ago, that she hadn't known she knew. 'My baby is weeping, for want of good keeping. Oh, I fear my poor baby will die.'

By midnight, a rash had appeared on Grace's cheeks and forehead. Faye got out the cold cream and dabbed it on the flushed skin, trying to subdue a feeling of panic. By three in the morning, the child's body was burning, her face and body dotted with raised red spots. She began fitting, her small body stiffening then growing limp, her eyes glassy. Pulling on her mantle over her nightdress, Faye went along the landing to Erasmus's room, banging on the door.

Erasmus opened the door, rubbing his eyes.

'She is ill, Ras. Get the doctor.'

'Can't it wait?'

'Get the doctor. I'll do it, if you won't.'

The landladies were roused, a boy was sent with a note, and after what seemed to Faye like hours, the doctor arrived. Shrugging off his coat, warming his great hands in front of the spirit lamp, he examined Grace. The rash covered her back, her arms and legs, the soles of her feet.

The doctor laid her down in the cot and addressed Erasmus who was standing by the open door.

'Scarlet fever.' He turned to Faye. 'Oat baths, twice daily, to soothe the skin. Assuming she survives the night.' He looked around the room, frowning. 'I would take her home, if I were you.'

By morning, the worst of the crisis appeared to have passed. Grace lay in a heavy, hot sleep and Faye sat by the bedside, willing her to return to health, talking to her. 'We have one more fair to get through, Grace, and then I will take you home. You will live in the countryside. You can have a kitten, or a puppy, to play with. Would you like that?' The day that Arkwright's Travelling Theatre was taken down in Newcastle, the raked benches dismantled and the huge sheet of mirror secured in its wooden frame, then with or without Erasmus's agreement, she would take Grace to Nether Hall. 'We are going home, Grace. You will be my daughter. I will adopt you as my own precious child.'

Looking up, she saw the sampler hung above the child's bed. The colours had faded, the ground was a rough hessian, but the cross stitch was painstakingly formed, the words clear. *The Lord Giveth and the Lord Taketh Away*. Faye stood up and with a sudden, violent gesture, turned it to face the wall.

Fifty-Seven

A person lingered close by. It took Tom a minute to recognise the oddly dressed figure, with a grotesque wig on his head, as the gasman. Another to attempt to damp down the flare of hope that rose in him.

'Balthazar! I see life has been treating you well.'

Balthazar smirked; he rearranged the purple cravat he wore at his neck, flicked a piece of lint from the arm of his pea green coat. The buttons were tight over his pot belly and under the broadened shoulders his arms strained the seams of the sleeves. He had an expectant air, as if he had an announcement to make.

'Have you seen any of our old acquaintances?' Tom said, unable to contain his impatience. 'You were looking for Miss Bell, as I recall.'

Balthazar's lip curled. He tilted back his head, so that he seemed to look down his nose and then issued a strange cry like a peacock. Thrusting a hand inside the jacket, he pulled out an envelope in a violent shade of mauve. Pressed it against his heart.

'You want a letter read,' Tom said, trying to disguise his disappointment. 'From one of your lady friends, I suppose?'

Balthazar stared in front of him, his complexion darkening.

'Only jesting. Give it to me, Balthazar, and I will read it to you.'

Balthazar smirked again. He held out the envelope and Tom saw his own name on the front of it.

'Well. This is a surprise!'

Tom's heart somersaulted. If Balthazar had brought him a letter, it could only be from one person. She hadn't received his last letter but that might not have been the gasman's doing. It might have been intercepted by force, by Salt. The man was capable of any act of evil. Without looking at it, Tom took the envelope and tucked it inside his coat. He wouldn't read it here, in plain sight, his absurd happiness evident to all.

'It seems as if you are the one doing me a kindness. Accept my apologies, Mr Pook.'

He offered his hand but Balthazar, maintaining his sulky expression, kept his thumbs tucked into his waistcoat.

'Oh! Of course.'

Tom Ames felt in his pocket for a sixpence. Held out the coin.

'Where is Miss Bell staying?' he said, lightly. 'Where did you encounter her?'

Balthazar gave him a long, cunning look and Tom dug

again, found another. Then another. 'Is she well?' Balthazar pocketed one and six, turned on his heel and stalked off in the direction of Birdcage Walk. 'Come back tomorrow,' Tom called after him. 'I'll have an answer ready.'

Back in World's End, Tom climbed the ladder and ducked through the door, staggering on his feet. He sat down under the slanting window. He'd stopped for a pint of beer on the way back, for Dutch courage, and had several. He had thought a great deal about Lily since they had last met. He'd continued to go to the park every Sunday afternoon. If she had not come to find him, he hoped it must be because she had gone to find her child. He'd searched his heart and asked himself if he was able to love a woman that had borne a child already, whether he could love that child. He had decided that he would, that he could. That he wanted nothing more in this world than to do just that. If Lily had found her child and was ready to unite with him, he would go to her, wherever she was. If she wanted his help to look for the infant, he was ready.

Tom drew out the letter. The handwriting was a surprise – untidy and irregular, leaning forwards then backwards, the letters of his name scored into the coarse fibre of the envelope. Breaking the seal, he unfolded a single sheet of paper and from it something dropped. He picked it up, examined a scrap of dirty cotton, once blue and white; just visible beneath the grime were the remnants of a pattern of polka dots.

Dear Mister Ames,

I met Mister Pook on his travels and he reminded me of our old aqayntance. I write to inform you of what he cannot – that I have started a new life. I have married a gentleman from abroad, a master of magick, and can never again associate with my old friends. Nor would I wish to.

Be assured I shall never return to Ramsgit on the coast. The little place holds no charm for me now and I have no wish ever to go there again in my lifetime.

If you wish me well, then send me no word, and forget that you ever new me. I shall do the same. Mr Pook has keindly agreed to deliver this message and as proof it is from my own fare hand I enclose the remains of a kerchief you once lent me.

Sincerely 'Late Lily Bell'

Tom read the letter for a second time, willing it to say something different. Refolding it, he sat very still. He felt winded, as if he'd had a punch to the solar plexus. Later, rising from the chair, taking Professor Hoffmann's book, opening the well-thumbed volume, he slid the letter between its pages, thus by the simplest of methods causing it to disappear.

*

Tom woke in the morning and boiled up a strong pot of coffee. As he drank it, his head cleared. Remembering the way the letters leaned back and forward like drunks, the coarse paper and expression, he didn't need to look at it again to know that the letter was a forgery. Balthazar intended to keep him away from Miss Bell. The gasman and his boss meant her harm. Lily was in danger. But where was she? Finishing the coffee, he went out, looking for Balthazar Pook. Not finding him in the park, he went north to Soho, called in at the tavern where he'd met him once by chance, asked the landlord if he'd seen the little fellow. He'd been there, the man said, the previous evening. Tom walked all day, searching for Balthazar and that night, back in the confines of his room, as he paced around it, trying to think, a line from the note returned to him. *Nor will I ever return to Ramsgit on the coast.* Why would the gasman have written that if not in a crude attempt to throw him off the scent? Lily must be there. Or if she was not there now, she must be expected there. Dragging his spare shirts off the rope strung along the length of the room, collecting the packs of playing cards, the cups and balls and ribbons of his trade, the folded suit of evening dress with the special deep pockets known as *profondes*, for losing things in the tails of the coat, the smaller *pochettes* for producing items from the back of the trousers, stuffing them into his trunk, Tom prepared to go after her.

Fifty-Eight

The track leading to the *tober* was rutted; the living van lurched from side to side and a crash of china echoed from inside, followed by a cry from Mrs Mo. She had toothache and at Conjuror's insistence had ridden inside. With the van parked, while Conjuror saw to the horses, and Mrs Mo rewrapped the flannel around her jaw, Lily crouched on the stool, feeding twigs into the stove, pumping the bellows, spooning tea into the kettle. She waited while the water boiled, breathing in the smell of clove oil and incipient rain, then poured a cup for the old lady, stirred in three spoons of sugar.

'Think I'll take a walk around,' Lily said, as Mrs Mo sipped her tea. For some reason, she didn't know what it might be, Lily felt nervous. Splashing her face with cold water, she glanced at herself in the mirror that she still kept in her breeches pocket. Her hair – recently shorn again, this time by Mrs Mo – lay on her head like the fur of a cat. Her cheeks were browned by the sun as well as bearing the residue of the stage paint she wore for performances. Her eyes, with short hair, appeared larger. Their expression was wary.

Jamming her cap down over her ears, thrusting her hands into her pockets, Lily jumped down from the van. Conjuror was outside, feeding the doves ears of wheat from his fingertips. 'Going for a look around,' she said. 'Back in a while.'

'*In'shallah*,' he said as she walked past him. It meant – if God willed it. Conjuror took nothing for granted. He lived each day as if it was his last, enjoying the fragrant cigarettes he rolled for himself, his *kaffee*, the sun on his face as he sat on the steps of the van carving the new wand he was making. Sometimes Lily wondered what her life would have been if she'd had the conjuror for a stepfather instead of Mr Bell.

Moving through the fairground, letting her feet carry her where they would, she stopped to watch the India Rubber Girl rehearsing. Dressed in orange silk pyjamas, the girl was bending backwards from her waist to pass under a low pole, the ends of her hair sweeping the grass as she passed beneath the bamboo. She straightened up and waved at Lily. Tom Thumb sat on the steps of his van, polishing his tiny shoes. The Pig-Faced Lady was chained by an iron collar around her neck to a tree. Unshaven, out of her voluminous dress, she looked like what she was – a grizzled and elderly bear, greying around the muzzle and with mournful eyes. Lily approached and spoke soft words to her; she wanted to pat her, but the bear let out a long, low growl and she thought better of it.

Humbug Sally hobbled towards her, an angular figure swathed in a ragged Indian shawl, her basket on her arm. 'Hey, Sal! How're you keeping?' Lily kept her voice as low-pitched as she could make it, her manner gauche and shy. Fumbling in her breeches pocket, she brought out a penny. She had money, tied up in a piece of cloth in the van; Conjuror paid her wages after every fair, counting out the coins with satisfaction. The woman lifted the check cloth on the basket, pressed a twist of barley sugar into Lily's hand, looking up at her with sharp blue eyes. 'You keep yer coppers, miss. Till you find what you're looking for.'

Lily turned her head away. Kindness was hard to bear, she didn't know why.

'Ta, Sal. Not looking for nothing. Not any more.'

It was true. She had given up hope of encountering the Salts. Finding Grace again. Taking her back. She didn't know now how she'd ever believed that any of those things were possible. How she could have trusted that wanting it with all her heart and might, acting on it as best she could, would be enough to make it happen. Life wasn't like that.

Jagged snatches of barrel organ music pierced the air, stopping and starting as the grinders checked and oiled their machines. Black Jack rehearsed his monkey, prodding him to make him dance and then take off his cap and hold it out for his reward of groundnuts. The strong man groaned as he hoisted a bar with weights on each end of it, his arms bulging, face purple. Violet sat on the steps of his caravan, watching, stroking her beard.

'Evening, miss.' Lily tipped her cap.

'Evening, master.' Violet winked.

It was getting late but the day seemed reluctant to end, the darkness unwilling to descend. The light was eerie, neither day nor night, and the ground and the figures that walked around it were lit with a reflected, lingering luminosity. At the edge of the *tober*, a great oak had been struck by lightning. It lay on its side, felled and bleached, its branches leafless, trunk carved with dates, the initials of lovers, hearts joined. Sitting down on it, Lily drew her striped waistcoat more tightly around her. Mr Ames had not answered her letter. Was married by now, probably, to a normal woman, a good-hearted virgin with no secrets behind her smooth white forehead. She wished she hadn't written to him. She should forget him as he had forgotten her.

Lily had started back in the direction of the van, walking around the other side of the ground, when something in the distance caught her attention. It was bigger than the usual booths, large, like a barn, but not a barn. Drawing closer, she saw a vast wooden structure – forty feet long and twenty or more feet wide – with a canvas snapping over the top of it in the wind, men driving pegs into the ground all around and securing guy ropes. More men carried scaffolding in through a side door and from inside came the echoing thud of hammers. At the front was an ornate façade, supported by four fluted columns, and underneath it an outer parade where a boy strode up and down, beating on a drum.

It was a travelling theatre. Feeling confused, walking nearer to the great structure, Lily made her way around to the side, where a huge painted canvas was being put up, hung along the wooden shuttering. She couldn't at first make out what the image depicted, and had to step back in order to be able to see it, back and then back again.

The background was midnight blue, scattered with silver stars. In the centre of the canvas was a baby, eight or ten feet tall. Dressed in a simple white shift, she sat on the ground looking up, her lips parted as if she spoke. Bright, auburn curls formed a cloud around her head and from her back sprouted a pair of feathery wings. 'Salt's Ghost' proclaimed the words painted in a silver arc beneath her. 'An infant late of this world.'

Lily's head began to spin. The sky at last grew dark, the snatches of hurdy-gurdy music speeded up and grew deafeningly loud. She stood there, dazed, uncertain what to do and two children swarmed around her, a boy and a girl, their pale faces grimy, their lank hair uncombed. Lily recognised them as the Tantric Twins, born freaks who could read each other's minds.

'Told you,' said the boy, prodding her in the ribs with a stick. 'He's a boy.'

'She,' said the girl. Reaching up, slipping her hand

inside the waistcoat, the girl pinched Lily's breast. 'It's a she.'

A man dressed in tweeds and a deerstalker approached, flapping his hands.

'Clear off, you little oiks! Scarper!' Peering at Lily, he held out a handbill in a great ham of a hand, breathed a gust of onions over her.

'Care to see the little ghost, master? She comes only at the summons of the ghost professor.'

'Yes. I do.' Her voice came out girlish, the voice not of the conjuror's assistant but of Lily Bell. She bought a ticket and the man handed it over, looked at her incuriously and moved on. 'The infant ghost ... Summoned from the afterlife ... See her with your own eyes.'

The wooden doors of the theatre opened and the snaking queue that had formed over an hour became, in seconds, a scrum. Forcing herself forward, her cap pulled over her forehead, Lily thrust her ticket towards the man in tweeds. He admitted her without a second glance. The auditorium was damp and dim and the seats raked, raised up on wooden scaffolding. Hurrying to the front row, Lily sat down in the centre of it, barely aware of the people teeming in around her, the shuffle of boots on the sacking laid on the earth, the hubbub of anticipation.

The benches filled; bodies pressed against her from both sides. Lily stared at the wooden partition underneath the raised stage, picturing behind it a room – small and square, low-ceilinged, the walls lined with dusty black velvet. In the room, a woman preparing herself for her performance, walking to and fro by the glow of a rush light, her hair silver, her face and neck whitened, her eyes darkened. In her arms: Grace. Thinking about the child, her warmth and weight, the smell of her skin and the trust in her eyes, Lily felt as if she might burst from some internal pressure, as if her body was too flimsy a vessel to contain her feelings. She rubbed her knees, the thinning cloth of her breeches, with the palms of her hands and tried to breathe. It seemed as if she'd spent all of her life on this hard plank, breathing in the smell of canvas and crushed grass, as if no other place or time before this one had ever been real in the way that this was real.

The violinists began to play. As the music reached a crescendo, a ripple of excitement ran along the benches and a familiar figure walked onto the stage. He looked out at the crowd, smoothed back his head of faded auburn hair with one hand and bowed. Fear and disgust rose in Lily in equal measure; she shrank on the seat.

'Tonight,' he said. 'You will see the greatest marvel in the fair. In the country of England. In the world…' The people stirred and rustled, shivering like trees in a forest. 'At my summons, the ghost maiden will present herself to you.' He lowered his voice. 'And, if we are fortunate, she will bring with her that little innocent, the infant ghost.'

Making a bow, spreading his hands to indicate the need for quiet, he left the stage. The red velvet curtain rose to reveal a painted attic room with a full moon shining through the window. The background was the same one that Lily had appeared in front of in Ramsgate. Looking at the canvas from her place in the audience, Lily saw what she'd never seen when she performed in the blue room. The canvas was one of her stepfather's, his handiwork unmistakable.

At the back of the stage, a man dressed in widower's weeds sat with his head in his hands, a bottle labelled with a skull and crossbones next to him on the table. As the strains of the violins died away, the man rose and walked forward to the front of the stage, wringing his hands, looking from right to left with a piteous expression on his face. 'My beloved wife is no more,' he said. 'Our one and only child, a babe in arms, departed this world alongside her. Perished in a fire.'

A sigh swished through the auditorium and despite the close atmosphere, the crush of bodies, Lily felt chills running down her spine. The actor moved to the back of the stage, held up the flask of poison and fell to his knees. 'I have no cause to continue in this vale of sorrows. I will join them in that better place.'

'Drink it down,' someone shouted. 'Let's see the ghosts.'

With a melodramatic gesture, the man drew the cork from the bottle. As he did so, somewhere to the right of the stage, Salt tapped his stick, masking the sound with his voice. 'Lily!' he incanted. 'Late Lily Bell! Come to us.' Lily's skin contracted under her clothes. The lights around the edge of the stage dimmed and within moments, at the back, a figure appeared as if from the ether. It was a woman, in a halo of bright light, clad in a silver gown, a boa around her neck. Silence fell in the auditorium, punctuated by gasps and moans.

The ghost was dazzling, the vision compelling. But the woman was alone. There was no baby in her arms. No infant sat beside her, clutched at her hem. Lily held her breath.

'Wife,' cried the man on stage. 'Where is she? Where is our daughter?'

The gas lamps dimmed further. 'Come, child!' called Salt, in a soft voice. 'Have no fear. Come to us here on earth. We long for you.' Shortly – and it was impossible to say how, or from where – a second figure appeared. A tiny girl, in a white dress, sat at the feet of the ghost, her body propped against a cushion. Her curls were lit in a halo around her head; her little feet and ankles were bare and the wings on her back appeared poised for flight. Her expression was dazed. The actress reached down and touched her and the ghost baby flinched; her arms moved and she looked towards the audience as if confused.

Lily moaned and gasped, felt the dig of an elbow in her ribs. 'Hush,' a woman hissed.

'Farewell,' said the actress, stooping for the infant and picking her up. 'We must leave you now.'

The little ghost struggled in her arms and as the air thickened with a familiar, gassy fug, both of them disappeared. The footlights rose to show the widower alone again, striking his breast and lamenting his cruel fate. Twice more, at the summons from the professor, the ghosts appeared. Twice more, they vanished. The widower dispatched himself and with a spurt of pig's blood, the cameo was at an end. The violins struck up at a lively tempo, the swagged curtain was lowered and as the audience roared – calling for encores, weeping and pleading, begging the professor to summon their own lost children – Lily rose from the bench, slipped through the side doors and walked out into the night.

Fifty-Nine

Erasmus threw off his coat and began to pace up and down the sisters' cheerless drawing room, knocking into the backs of chairs, rucking up the rug, making the palm plant tremble.

'Looked everywhere for her,' he said.

'For who?' Faye said.

'She ain't here.'

'Who's not here?'

'And tomorrow is the last day. The fair will be over.'

Her brother poured himself a brandy. Swirling it around the glass, he took a gulp. He set down the glass and sighed, his anger seeming to have dissipated.

'Who?' Faye repeated. 'Who's not here?'

'Lily Bell, that's who,' he said, his voice flat. 'My ghost.'

Faye looked down at the work on her lap. She felt unbalanced, as if she was not in the parlour of a terraced house in Newcastle-upon-Tyne but out at sea, on a small boat buffeted by large waves, the horizon tilting violently.

'Of course she is not.' She forced a laugh. 'The girl could not be anywhere near.'

'She was here, all right,' said her brother. 'Had it on good information.'

The dizziness came more strongly and for a moment Faye thought she would faint. She took a breath and tried to steady her voice.

'What are you talking about?'

'Balthazar.' He picked up a porcelain shepherdess from the mantel, looked under its skirts. 'He found her at York. Said she'd be here.'

'What fine nonsense,' Faye said, pulling an end of embroidery thread through the bodice of the smock she was making, knotting it with shaking fingers. 'He must have been mistaken.'

Putting away the sewing, she bade Erasmus good-night and left the room, closing the door behind her. In the dark hallway, Faye lingered, as if in that unlit and unwarmed in-between place she might be able to undo the words her brother had uttered. Unsee the sight she had seen, a day earlier.

She'd been walking with Etta Arkwright around the fairground, the baby between them, each of them holding one of Grace's hands, swinging her for short distances across puddles while endeavouring to keep her little shoes dry. For the first time since she began her convalescence, Grace had been laughing, and a lad leaning on a tree, his hands pushed deep into his pockets, clothed in black breeches and a dark jacket had stiffened, seemed to flinch at the sound. From underneath a cap, he stared, his slack pose transformed to a sinewy attention. Grace landed with both feet in a puddle, her screams momentarily distracted Faye, and when she looked again, he'd turned and was walking away.

As she watched him go, Lily Bell had sprung like an acrobat into Faye's mind, landing on both feet and straightening up, whole and present. The set of the young man's head on his shoulders, his slight build, his way of walking, all recalled her. Lily had brothers, she'd spoken of them, and Faye would have sworn on her life that this must be one of them.

'Are you unwell?' Etta had said. 'You're white as a sheet, ma'am. You look as if you've seen a ghost.'

'I am quite well,' she'd said, her voice weak. By an effort of will, Faye had put the incident out of mind for the rest of the day. Lying in bed later, unable to sleep, she convinced herself that she had been mistaken. Now, standing in the dim chill of the hallway, she felt as if Lily's ghost had passed through the walls of the house and stood beside her, looking at her in mute reproach, her empty arms outstretched.

Pulling herself up the stairs by the bannister rail, fatigued to her bones, Faye let herself into the bedroom. Grace slept in her bed, her arms flung wide on the pillow, her skin still rough with little scabs. She stirred as Faye straightened the covers, placed the unsleeping doll on the pillow. Kneeling on the floor by the bed, Faye inhaled her smell of milk and sleep and soap, her soft breath and the flutter of her lashes.

'She's come, Grace,' she whispered. 'Your mama has come for you.'

Rising from her knees, turning up the lamp, the wick flaring to illuminate the walls, she walked around the room, holding the light up to the corners, checking inside the front-mirrored wardrobe. Wind rattled the sashes and the curtains billowed out, subsided and billowed again. Faye tightened the catch on the windows. Locked the door. She sat down at the table with her journal but didn't open it, or pick up her pen, only stared at the form of the child sleeping in the bed.

Sixty

Lily dragged the clothes chest from the props van and heaved it into the living van. She rummaged through it, pulling out a primrose yellow summer dress, a pink and blue striped skirt, a pale green challis, rejecting all of them. She sat back on her heels, empty-handed. Mrs Mo had been watching. Tapping out her pipe, dragging a trunk from under her bunk, Mrs Mo opened it and began to unroll a dress from sheets of brown paper. It was ivory-coloured, satin, long-sleeved and high-necked, the bodice stitched with hundreds of tiny glass beads. She held it out to Lily.

'How did you know?' breathed Lily, staring at the dress. 'It is perfect.'

Mrs Mo produced a matching shawl then unlocked a concealed compartment in the lid of the box and brought out a wig of long hair, pale as moonlight. From another section of the box, she retrieved a pair of fine white stockings, a circlet of wax orange blossom flowers.

'These were yours, weren't they?'

Mrs Mo patted her on the shoulder, her brown eyes soft. She left the van and, watched by the doves, Lily stripped off her shirt and trousers. She washed all over in cold water, scrubbing her body with a scrap of loofah until her skin smarted and turned pink. She slipped her old chemise over her head and donned the loose drawers of her sex. Trying on her stays, discovering she couldn't breathe or bend, she cast them aside. She stepped into the petticoats, pulled the drawstring tight around her waist and secured it with a reef knot. The dress hung from the top bunk. Lily tunnelled into it from the bottom of the skirts; she got her arms through the sleeves, tugged the tight-fitting bodice down over her breasts, buttoned it from the waist up to the throat. The bodice fitted like a glove, showed the shape of the muscles she'd acquired in her arms, the resumed narrowness of her waist. Sitting on the edge of the bunk, she pulled on her old boots over the white stockings. The long miles had worn holes in both soles but recently Conjuror had had them mended, in a pit village they'd passed through.

Running her fingers through the wig's long tresses, she pulled it onto her head, secured it with a pin and arranged over it the circlet, the white veil. Mrs Mo came back inside and began a strange, ululating cry from the back of her throat. Turning Lily round, examining her from all angles, she smoothed the skirts over Lily's hips, adjusted the shoulders of the bodice, fastened an overlooked button. From a carved box brought down from one of the shelves, she produced a small pair of lace gloves, a silver brooch in the shape of a sickle moon that she pinned at Lily's throat. Finally, she handed Lily a white parasol, lined with silk and fringed, the long ferrule tipped with iron. Lily took it. Mrs Mo gave her hand a squeeze and Lily hugged her. She stood between the bunks and the doves' cages, the old van familiar and safe as a nutshell, closed her eyes and prepared herself to walk out on stage.

Exiting the van, taking the wooden steps slowly, one by one, holding up her skirts, accepting the broad hand the conjuror offered to steady her, she stepped down onto the grass.

'I cannot assist you tonight, Conjuror,' Lily said. 'There is something important that I must do.'

Conjuror bowed. '*In'shallah*, you will succeed.'

The days were growing shorter. The grass was dry after the long summer, brown, fragrant as hay. With the white veil concealing her face, Lily walked with her head up, her gaze set not on the ruts beneath her feet but on the horizon, where a great fiery sun was slipping behind a row of oak trees, lighting their branches with red and gold. The hem of the dress touched the ground behind her; her legs, unbreeched underneath the weight of petticoats, felt naked. Violet Spratt hurried by without giving her a second glance. The strong man, practising by the side of his booth, put down his dumbbell and swivelled his head, let out an ear-splitting whistle. Only the bear moaned her recognition, watching with sad eyes from under her tree as Lily passed by.

The outline of the great travelling theatre loomed out of the dusk like a castle, the front lit by flares illuminating a hand-painted sign. Arkwright's Travelling Theatre. On a raised parade beside the entrance, the man in tweeds paced up and down, roared through a megaphone. 'Roll up, roll up! Last return of the infant ghost! See her now or see her never!' Below it, a milling crowd pressed and jostled around a wooden turnstile. Women with bowls of quartered oranges, roasted nuts and displays of souvenirs and trinkets did brisk business; Humbug Sally hurried by, her tray empty.

Skirting the back of the queue, Lily walked past the theatre. She carried on, picking her way through the crowds, ignoring obscene comments and lewd invitations, to the far edge of the ground, the great felled tree trunk carved with hearts and dates and the names of lovers. Sitting on the trunk, half hidden by branches, she watched the people around the theatre as if she was in the audience of a play. Soon, the scrum thinned; the theatre swallowed the people; the great doors closed. Violin music drifted out, floating on the air. Stepping out from behind the tree, a spectral figure in the luminous dusk, Lily made her way towards the back of the theatre.

Sixty-One

The performance was sold out. Punters were crammed onto the bench seats, crowded into the standing area at the back and sides, like passengers on a London bus. Arkwright, by dint of ordering the planks to be taken down and bolted closer together, had contrived five extra rows and still there were more people outside, banging on the wooden doors, agitating to get in.

Erasmus took a generous nip of brandy from his hip flask. He'd quarrelled earlier with Faye. At five o' clock, just as they were due to leave the lodgings for the fairground, the hansom waiting outside, she'd come down the stairs in her nightdress. Grace was in her arms – in the costume and ready to go, dosed with the drops – but Faye had claimed a migraine and refused to leave the house. 'You'll have to take her to the theatre yourself, Erasmus,' she'd said. 'I cannot help you.' Erasmus had first offered her a brandy, then ordered her to take her salts and get ready without wasting any more time, but his sister had refused. She'd been overwrought and, fearing an attack of hysteria and unfounded accusations, he'd taken the child.

She'd followed him out onto the pavement, thrust a bag containing milk, rusks and apples into the hansom. The kid was fast asleep. In the cab, Erasmus noticed a scrap of blanket sewn to the bodice of the costume. Tried and failed to rip it off. When they got to the theatre, he had laced the jar of milk with extra drops and instructed Etta Arkwright to administer it. Without Faye present to calm her, the brat might wrench at her wings, struggle and kick in Etta's arms or – as had occurred the previous night – start bawling.

Erasmus drank again from the flask. Women were the source of most of the problems in this world. He was livid at not having found Lily Bell at the fair. Intended to have words with Balthazar when he saw him next. The fellow wouldn't see another penny until the girl was captured and the deed was done. Erasmus hadn't prayed since he was twelve years old and learnt the fruitlessness of prayer but, sitting in his reserved seat on the edge of the front row of Arkwright's Travelling Theatre, as the violins struck up, he vehemently *wished* that he might see the infant back in the arms of his first and most beautiful ghost, Lily Bell. Brandy burned in his throat, his chest, and as the red curtains went up, he took another slug.

The actor began his nightly lament for his lost wife and daughter. Distracted by his troublesome thoughts, Erasmus gave the gasman's cue late but the ghost, when she appeared in response to his summons, for once stood in the right spot. The child was a vision – her hair the colour of fire, her childish hand gleaming ivory; she made no protest, put up no struggle, but moved her arms and head as if in a ballet. The extra drops had proved their efficacy.

After the requisite build-up, in which the excitement of the audience grew fevered, the ghosts again appeared and disappeared at Erasmus's command. The third act commenced and soon the end of the cameo approached. On stage, the stricken widower expressed the desire to follow his wife and child, to be reunited with them forever. From his position by the pit, Erasmus rose to his feet. 'Come to us,' he called out, tapping three times on the partition under the stage, concealing the noise with his sonorous voice. 'Do not be afraid. We beseech you – let us see you one last time!' He resumed his seat to watch the effects of his summons.

The infant appeared, sitting on the boards against the backdrop of a starry night sky. She was alone. Etta Arkwright, who ought to have been holding her, was nowhere to be seen. The child's wings were lopsided; she looked confused, clutching the rag to her cheek. Cursing under his breath, Erasmus reached out his stick and rapped urgently on the partition.

'Late Lily Bell,' he intoned, as if from the pulpit. 'We beseech you to appear to us.'

'Grace,' came a soft voice. 'I am here.'

The gas chandelier over the stage dimmed further, the hidden limes blazed brighter and from nowhere the ghost of a woman appeared. Not the broad form of Arkwright's daughter but a slight, strong figure, clad in tight satin, her pale hair cascading to her narrow waist, her lips a vivid gash in her alabaster face. Erasmus's mouth fell open. He was transfixed. For a single, blissful moment, he believed that God had heard him. His prayer had been answered.

Then he saw her feet. Visible under the hem of the wedding dress, the ghost's feet were clad not in satin slippers but in buttoned boots. In one sure movement she gathered up the child into her arms, holding her against her breast, kissing her again and again. Erasmus opened his mouth to protest, to order the stage lights be raised, the theatre doors locked, but no words emerged. Tossing her silver hair over her shoulders, the brilliant, shining spirit turned to face the audience, looking directly at him. 'I have come for my child,' she said, her white face possessed with fearful purpose. 'We shall return no more. Do not search for us for you can never hope to find us. Farewell.'

Women moaned and sighed; sobbing erupted around the auditorium. Erasmus struggled to his feet. Reaching forward, he thumped with his stick on the partition, the noise lost in the roars of the crowd as with the limes still flaring the ghost did not fade, did not disappear into the ether, but walked off-stage, carrying the child.

'Stop her,' Erasmus shouted, his voice now that it had arrived drowned out by the screech of strings, the cries and prayers of women. 'Stop the bitch.'

Sixty-Two

After a meal of bread and cheese, improved by a pint and a pickled onion, Tom bought a third-class train ticket to the south coast. Dark clouds thickened the sky as he boarded the train; by the time it reached Ramsgate, passing through the tunnel that went under the little town, emerging at the terminus down on the beach, the weather was stormy. Winds whipped in from the north-east; white-topped waves crashed against the harbour wall, sending up mountains of water.

The flag on the parade ground flew at half-mast. Black crape festooned the door knockers, streamed from the railings and the narrow first-floor balconies. Wellington, the iron duke, the last great Englishman, was dead. It was unsettling, Tom thought as he walked up to the East Cliff, to live in this new world where the old ways were being swept away but the new ones had yet to be established.

Near his old lodgings, in the street called Plains of Waterloo, he found an attic room to let, installed his trunk and, in the driving rain, went out looking for Lily. He came back late, drenched with salty rain but more determined than ever. In the morning, in the daylight, he would start again. He'd searched for her before and found her. He would find her again.

Tom had long since perfected the Handkerchief Cut Up and Restored – he needed to work on new tricks. Opening the battered copy of Hoffman's *Modern Magic*, the letter supposed to be from Lily fell out from between the pages. He pulled the paper from inside the lurid envelope, unfolded it. Looking at the cold words, the press of the pen onto the coarse paper, Tom considered the possibility that the gasman had tricked him again, lured him to Ramsgate on a false premise. Tearing up the letter, he threw it into the grate. This was the place to be, he felt certain.

Sixty-Three

Sunlight filtered around the edges of the curtains. Outside, on the landing, a broom knocked against the skirting boards; a maid sang to herself. For a minute, Faye knew only the warmth of her body between the sheets, the play of the light on the wall. It was the day on which she'd intended to take Grace to Nether Hall. Their box stood on the floor, packed and ready to go. The atmosphere in the room was still and vacant.

Knowing what she would find, Faye got out of bed. Grace's little bed was as she had left it – turned down, the top sheet folded cleanly over the blanket, the feather pillow plumped. The bed was empty. It was as it should be. She would not scream Grace's name. Would not succumb to searching under the beds and inside drawers, throwing up sash windows, running screeching onto the landing, banging on every door in the house, tearing her hair, threatening, if Grace was not found immediately and returned, to leap from the window. To do any of these things would be to fail the gravity of the situation.

She remained where she was, stranded in the unbearable moment, staring at the sampler on the wall. It had been turned around again and faced outwards, the words implacable in their truth. *The Lord Giveth and the Lord Taketh Away.*

By the roadside, human bundles stirred and stretched in the hedgerows. The verge was dense with tramps, some booted and bearded, others clad in rags, no more than skin and bone. There were women amongst them – wearing men's jackets over their skirts, their faces dark with sun and wind, expressions so bold and brazen that they seemed neither man nor woman but some third sex.

The horses raced south, past inns and farms, cottages and coalmines, past countrywomen selling marrows and cobnuts and apples from their front gates. Faye clung to the hand strap as the coach slowed at junctions and Erasmus leaned out of the open window, bellowing at travellers, carters, milkmaids, pedlars or any other person he saw.

'Seen a ghost? Two ghosts? A woman and her infant, all dressed in white? I am searching for them and must find them.' Some people stared, open-mouthed. Others jeered or cursed him for a fool, made the sign of the cross. None had seen a ghost woman and her ghost child, flitting in white gowns across the fields and orchards, disappearing into the dawn. 'They are my ghosts,' he shouted, pulling up the window, collapsing back onto the seat. 'They belong to me.'

Faye pulled her mantle up around her face. Closed her eyes. By the time she'd got to the fairground at the town moor, most of the booths had been dismantled. The theatre was coming down like a card house, men slinging hoardings onto the back of flatbed carts, throwing scaffolding poles along a human chain. The great mirror had been dropped, either that or someone had taken a hammer to it; it lay shattered on the ground in a thousand glinting pieces, reflecting a fractured, fallen sky. In the cabin that they used for a box office, Erasmus sprawled drunk on a bench. Harry Arkwright was talking to a police officer. The officer could barely contain his mirth as Henrietta Arkwright swore that a real ghost had appeared to her in the blue room, materialised from nowhere, dressed all in white, her face concealed by a lace veil. The ghost instructed her to leave the theatre and if she knew what was good for her to never come back. Frightened almost out of her wits, Etta had obeyed immediately. She couldn't be persuaded by her father to describe the ghost to the officer, or indicate in which direction she and the child had fled. Only stared at Faye, whey-faced, and repeated that it had been a real spirit, that she would never again play a ghost or so much as set foot in the blue room, that it had been a wicked enterprise all along and she ought never to have agreed to it.

The Arkwrights had left for York, Mr Arkwright first unlocking the safe and removing most of the contents, leaving the door hanging open. Faye slipped half of the several bundles of notes that remained into her valise before rousing Erasmus.

'We shall go after them,' he said, when he came round. He found a coach and four to take them up, ranting about his ghosts. Sitting in the back of the carriage, racing out of the city and through a landscape tinged with rust and gold, Faye went over in her mind the last hour she had spent with Grace, in the room at the lodgings. She had bathed her and fed her, sewn the last scraps of the crocheted blanket to the bodice of the costume, talking to her all the while. 'One day, Grace, we will meet again. Although we might travel far from each other, wherever life may take you, your aunt's love will follow you.' Grace had sat quietly, playing with a fan, opening it and closing it, chuckling. After dressing her in the lace gown, Faye kissed her fingers and cheeks, her forehead, and said goodbye; even before she was gone she had missed Grace with a dull, physical ache.

The chaise slowed to walking pace. Erasmus cursed the driver, banged on the roof with his fist, then dragged down the window and leaned his head out. The road had narrowed and they were stuck behind two caravans pulled by a pair of sturdy cobs. It appeared that the entourage belonged to fairground people; the larger caravan was painted with a picture of an Oriental in a red cloak brandishing a wand. A man in a greatcoat trudged by the horses' heads.

'Hey, you!' shouted Erasmus, when finally the road widened and their carriage drew level. 'D'you speak

English?' The man moved his head in what might have indicated either assent or dissent. 'I am looking for a woman and child. They are runaways and must be found for their own good. Have you seen them?'

The man stroked his black beard, fixed Erasmus with piercing eyes. 'There are those amongst us that are not to be seen by mortal men,' he said. 'You may see 'em, and yet you may see 'em not.'

'Speaking in riddles,' Erasmus said, drawing his head back inside the coach. 'Bloody fool.' He sucked from a brandy bottle, stuck it back in his pocket, his face set. 'I shall find her, Faye. Take Grace back. The child is mine. I know it. Miss Bell knows it.' He laughed to himself then stopped and looked at Faye, his eyes cunning and cold. 'And you know it. Don't you, Faye?' Faye couldn't speak. 'Don't you?' he said again, his expression murderous.

Groping inside her collar for the locket around her neck, Faye enclosed it in the palm of her hand. The image of her mother, the enamelled miniature of her as a small girl, had always been her talisman; comforted her in times of trouble. Helped her to know what she must do. 'Yes, Erasmus,' she whispered as the driver whipped the horses onwards, sending up a cloud of dust. 'I know it.'

Sixty-Four

It was dusk and the fishermen were lighting their lamps ready to set sail; a collection of small lights bloomed against the gathering darkness. The night was cold as if in a premonition of winter, wind howled in across the water from the east. Springing down from the box of the stagecoach, his nose lifted as if he scented a trail, Balthazar looked around the deserted quayside. Salt had telegrammed, instructed him to be ready. As soon as he captured the little *runaway*, he would bring her here for a *breath of sea air*.

The room he took on the third floor of the Mariner's Hotel suited his mood and his purpose. The bed was narrow, the view from the window of rows of crooked chimney pots. There was no one to see or be seen by. Hanging his greatcoat in the wardrobe, Balthazar lay down on the bed for a half hour then went down to the public bar where he ate fried fish served with boiled potatoes, drank two pints of draught beer and indicated with regret to the landlord that he was a mute, unable to answer his inquiries.

Next morning, he rose late. Balthazar had left his pea green suit, his *syrup*, in London; he wore the patched, plain clothes and greasy flat cap in which he could disappear at will into the mass of working men. Curling the cheese wire into a neat circle, because it never hurt to be prepared, he slid it into his trouser pocket alongside the gimlet and left the hotel. It was market day and the streets were choked with carts piled high with turnips and swedes, stalks of Brussels sprouts, bales of cloth, tin bowls and buckets. Costers called out their wares in Kentish lilts; children sat with jugs outside taverns, waiting for them to open their doors.

He stopped at a pastrycook's for an apple turnover, bought a half pint of tea from an old woman sitting on her doorstep with a kettle. Drinking the last of the tea, wiping flakes of pastry from his mouth, he set off for a stroll about the resort. Balthazar made his way down to the beach and walked along the sands to a pillar of chalk cliff that time and tides had separated from the mainland. It reared up from the sands like a great natural monument. He put his hand in his pocket and flexed the wire in his palm. Tested the point of the gimlet. He hoped not to employ either. It would be simplest if Miss Bell departed this earth in the manner indicated on her headstone, and *slipped from a cliff*. There would be no evidence, no blood on his hands and it would be over before she knew it.

Leaning one shoulder against the chalk stack, as the wind blew into his ears and seawater seeped into his boots, he looked out with great happiness at the horizon. A *monkey*, he repeated softly to himself. A *monkey* for Balthazar Pook.

Sixty-Five

Cocooned in the living van with Grace, on the long
journey south, Lily had made a plan. They were heading
for the south coast anyway and the kind old couple had
agreed to take her and Grace to Ramsgate. Lily had
spent nothing of her wages from Conjuror and she still
had the money she'd been paid for her hair, and most
of what she'd got for the opal ring. She would ask Mrs
Ali to permit her and Grace to lodge with her, while
she got to know her daughter again, and consider what
to do next. Mrs Ali had greeted Lily and Grace with
surprise and pleasure. She recognised Conjuror and Mrs
Mo immediately as fellow Gyptians, insisted they stay
for a few days as her guests. Next morning, after making
a bowl of bread and warm milk for Grace, Lily left
Conjuror and the two women talking in their language,
and took the child out for a walk.

It was a windy day; Lily wore a blue-striped skirt
from the properties box, a wide-sleeved green velvet
jacket and a felt hat embroidered with poppies. It was

still peculiar to her to be perceived by the world as a woman. She had left off her stays, determined to retain some aspects of her months as a boy, and with Grace in her arms she walked with a long, easy stride, aware of the strength in her arms and her heart, unafraid to raise her eyes and look around her, see what she saw.

At the harbour, by the Obelisk, was a familiar barrow topped with a striped umbrella. Signor Pelosi didn't recognise Lily with her face uncovered. He greeted her as *signora*, presented the little *signorina* with a dab of vanilla ice cream in a scallop shell. Grace too was dressed from the props chest, in a red velvet shift, a short coat adorned with a brooch in the shape of a cat. They sat in the wind shelter while Grace ate the ice cream with her fingers.

'So you like ice cream, Grace?' Lily said as Grace licked the palms of her hands.

Her daughter had protested when she woke in the caravan from her long sleep. She had cried, briefly and wildly, then been distracted by the doves, fluttering out of their open cages over her head, landing in front of her and bowing to her. Her cheeks still wet, she had begun to laugh. 'Mama,' she had said, catching hold of Lily's ear. 'Mama.' The motion of the van had soothed her and at night, when they stopped to rest the horses, she had lain on the bunk with her thumb in her mouth, the little scrap of blanket held to her nose. Her eyes open.

Grace dropped the shell. Lily wiped her daughter's face, returned the scallop shell to the Italian and they went down onto the sand. Lily walked slowly, following the child as she crawled, stopping with her to look at feathers and rounded pebbles of green glass, shells as small and pink as her own fingernails. Picking up Grace, kissing her curls – how beautiful they were – brushing sand off her hands and knees, Lily went up the steps near the Belle Vue Hotel. As the child fell asleep on her shoulder, Lily walked along past the marble skating rink and on to where the cliff was wild and untamed, the wind blowing in straight from the Continent. She did not see the figure that followed behind her at a distance of thirty yards or more, moving silently, stealthily, maintaining the same distance between them, as if attached to her by an invisible wire.

As Grace slept, Lily walked to the edge of the cliff, looking out over the shining, disturbed sea, banded on the horizon with indigo and granite and aquamarine. She remembered the day when she had intended to throw herself down onto the rocks below, hoping to end two lives, and made a silent apology to her daughter. 'I'll never leave you again, Grace,' she said aloud, her words caught on the wind. 'I will try to be a worthy mother to you.'

Balthazar stepped forward, his feet silent on the tussocky grass. He was not ten yards away from her, could have reached her in seconds and with a single shove dispatched her over the edge. The problem was the kid. He wouldn't have cared, might be best for it if it met its end with its mother. But Salt had been insistent. No harm must come to it. *Not a hair on its head.* He couldn't risk the monkey. Clenching and unclenching his fists, hissing to himself, Balthazar willed Miss Bell to put the child down on the grass.

Down on the beach, near the line of bathing machines, a small crowd had gathered. Grace was growing heavy. Shifting the weight of the child to her other shoulder, shading her eyes against the brilliant light, Lily looked down at them. The hope had never entirely left her that, one day, in some out-of-the-way place, she would come across a figure with his face tipped back to the heavens, red leather balls flying like birds from his hands. The crowd dispersed and revealed a tall figure, down on one knee, packing his bag. He stood up, his hair blowing in the wind and his shirt.

'Mr Ames,' Lily shouted, her voice carried away. 'Mr Ames!' She waved her arm in the air and he looked up, standing perfectly still, as if turned to stone. He did not wave back. Lily turned away from the edge of the cliff and set off along the cliff-top path towards the steps. Retreating behind the thicket of brambles, Balthazar cursed, shouting into the wind, stamping his foot on the grass.

By the time she got down to the beach, the circle had broken up, the bystanders drifted away. Tom walked towards her, stopped at a little distance and bowed.

'Miss Bell,' he said. 'Thank God you are safe. This must be Grace.'

'I shall never be parted from her,' Lily said.

'I know.' He held out his arm to Lily. 'Let's walk. I have something I'd like to show you.'

The inside of the cave was damp and glistening green, the letters Tom had carved clear and unchanged. Grace woke and Lily sat her down on the sand, by a pool of seawater. Tom kneeled by her, on the wet sand, showed her how to make milk with chalk, rubbing the stones together in the pool, turning it white.

'Will you be with me, Lily? You and your daughter? Will you live with me and be my loves?'

'We will,' she said.

Grace laughed and splashed her hands in the pool as Tom set to work with his pocketknife, added Grace's name to his and Lily's initials, enclosed all three in a single, capacious heart. Only then did he tell her who he had seen standing behind her on the cliff top.

Sixty-Six

❦

It had taken days to reach London, Erasmus stopping the coach at tollgates and coaching inns, questioning carters and shepherds and shoeshine boys and police officers. They arrived at the coaching inn by the river, and that evening they waited in the snug, Erasmus pacing the confines of the small room. He stopped in front of the fire, kicked the fender. 'He's late. Let him dare to pretend he doesn't know where his daughter is.'

'Stepdaughter,' Faye corrected him, from her place in the corner under an empty birdcage. Erasmus banged his glass down on the table. 'Never mind that. I'll find them, Faye.' He looked at her. 'You might as well know. I am to demonstrate the marvel to the Next World Society conference. I will call Lily Bell back in spirit. And if not her –' his eyes gleamed brighter '– then it will be her daughter.'

'Erasmus,' Faye said. 'Lily Bell does not wish to appear as the ghost. She doesn't wish Grace to be on stage either.'

Erasmus smiled. 'What Miss Bell *wishes* is not important. The infant belongs to me.'

'It is a terrible thing,' Faye said, her voice trembling, 'for a child to be deprived of her mother.'

Erasmus crossed the snug to where she sat and stood in front of her.

'Don't she need her father?'

Faye felt for the locket around her neck, held it in her palm. 'Yes, Erasmus,' she said. 'She needs her father.'

Her brother's face relaxed. He spoke softly. 'I knew I could rely on you, Faye. You will be my witness. You know the truth.'

At that moment, Alfred Bell arrived. He looked thinner and older, as if time had galloped forward, dragging him with it.

'Where is she?' Erasmus said.

Mr Bell blinked. 'If you're talking about Lily, I don't know where she is. Haven't seen hide nor hair of her since her mother died.'

'You must have some idea. Is there an aunt? A cousin?'

Alfred Bell shook his head. 'Sharper than a serpent's tooth. I'd tell you if I knew. Could do with the funds.'

'I'll take up no more of your time in that case.'

Bell left and for some time Erasmus sat without speaking. He ordered and emptied more glasses of brandy. As they sat there, the clerk came up with a telegram. Faye watched as Erasmus read it.

'Balthazar Pook has found her,' he said, aloud, linking

347

his fingers, causing the knuckles to crack. 'She's there with her fancy man.'

'She's where?'

He looked at her distractedly. 'Ramsgate. Of course.'

'But, Erasmus—' Faye said.

'Be ready early.'

The air was rank with the smell of seaweed. A chill wind lifted the mantle from Faye's shoulders, made her shiver. Erasmus looked around him, his eyes gleaming by the light of the harbour lamps. Balthazar stepped out of the shadows, groaning a greeting. He began a clowning routine but seeing the expression on Erasmus's face appeared to think better of it, and saluted.

'Where is she?' Erasmus said, his voice menacing.

The gasman stepped back, indicating with grunts and hand gestures that she was here, nearby. Erasmus stood for a minute, staring at him.

'Mrs Ali's,' he said. 'The old woman.'

'Ras, stop—'

Her brother ignored her. He set off down the slipway and along the sands towards the cottage, with Balthazar following. With a sense of dread, Faye hurried behind, trying to keep up. The tide was flooding in, waves running up the beach, the wrinkled surface of the water like the skin of a great beast about to pounce. Her foot plunged into a puddle of seawater and cold seeped through her stocking.

Lights gleamed in the windows of the little house

under the cliff. Erasmus kicked open the door and walked in, Balthazar on his heels. In the parlour, the table was laid as if for a celebration, with a platter of meat, green leaves and fruits, a pile of flatbreads. Many candles were lit. Mrs Ali and another old woman who resembled her stood close to each other, dressed in embroidered kaftans and with lines of gold bangles up their arms. At first, Faye didn't recognise the figure standing in the centre of the room. Lily looked wiry and strong; short hair, as if she was convalescing after an illness, framed her face. She wore a white dress, a white veil thrown back over her head. Tom Ames stood next to her, his hair in long soft tails over his shoulders, a red rose in the buttonhole of his jacket. In front of them, a tall, dark-skinned man, familiar from somewhere, was giving a benediction with a wand.

'Miss Bell,' said Erasmus, his voice menacing. 'What a pleasure to see you.'

Lily's face paled. Going to a crib in the corner, she picked up the sleeping baby.

'What are you doing here?' she said.

'Looking for you,' Erasmus said. 'And dear little Grace.'

From the doorway, Balthazar made a low unpleasant growl. Tom Ames moved to where Lily stood and put his arm around her shoulders.

'You're not welcome here, Salt,' he said. 'What do you want with us?'

349

'Want?' Erasmus sneered, moving towards them. 'I want my child.'

'You shall never have her,' Lily said. 'You won't lay a finger on her. Not while I draw breath.'

Erasmus laughed. 'She is mine. I shall take her now.'

He lunged at the child in Lily's arms. As if from nowhere a curved, jewelled dagger appeared in the conjuror's hand. The man seemed to have grown taller even than he had been and his hawk-like eyes were fixed on Erasmus, the bevelled blade glinting in the candlelight, an inch from the jugular. Erasmus shrank back, his hands falling by his sides.

'Tell them, Faye,' he breathed. 'Tell them that the child is mine. Speak up, for God's sake.'

Faye stepped into the centre of the room. Reaching into her valise, taking out a slim bundle of notebooks, she held them in the air. 'I have a record here of everything.'

'I knew I could rely on you,' Erasmus said, looking around the assembled company. 'She knows everything. My sister is my witness.'

Faye turned to Lily and bowed her head. 'My condolences for the loss of poor Mrs Bell. She must have spent her last months believing that you were lost to her. Please forgive me, Lily. May I?' Faye lifted Grace's hand and kissed it. 'I have missed you, Grace. I am glad to see you reunited with your mama.' Her voice broke as she turned to Tom Ames, drew herself up. 'And your papa,' she said. 'I misjudged you entirely, Mr Ames.'

'What the devil...' Erasmus rumbled from the corner. The conjuror shot a threatening look at him and, holding the notebooks up in the air again, it was the conjuror that Faye addressed. To tell the truth was not always the right thing. The godly thing. Sometimes, it was right to lie. 'Lily Bell and Tom Ames contracted a natural marriage in May last year. Grace is the fruit of their love. I have the date on which the two of them met alone, the record of Miss Bell's sorrow when Mr Ames was dismissed, and of her travails since. My brother has used her shamefully, and her little child.'

Erasmus bellowed and, returning her notebooks to her bag, closing it, Faye continued. 'You have deceived everybody, Erasmus,' she said, softly, shaking her head. 'Most of all, you have deceived yourself. Your ghosts are a sham. None of us will see the dead again.'

Tom Ames leaned forward and lifted Erasmus to his feet by the lapels of his coat. 'Get out, Salt,' he said, and after delivering a single punch to Salt's face, threw him out of the cottage door into the darkness.

Sixty-Seven

The great arched trees were waiting for them, their branches linked to form a vaulted tunnel of red and gold. Erasmus walked ahead of Faye, stumbling on the ruts in the lane, his shoulders bowed, one hand held to his swollen eye. He had lost or discarded his hat and walked bareheaded, mumbling to himself. Since the encounter in Mrs Ali's parlour, Erasmus had changed. His body appeared to have shrunk and deflated, as if some inner substance had deserted him, as if his bones gave way inside him; his authority and certainty had melted away and he had seemed to Faye more than anything like a small boy, the boy she had once known. Balthazar had agreed, by means of grunts and gestures, to come back to Nether Hall with them and take care of him. He had stayed behind at the railway station to arrange for their luggage to be transported to the house.

The way was empty, the hedges high on each side. A rabbit lolloped over the road and was gone. The birds had fallen silent and the only sound on the air was the trickling of an unseen stream. At the crossroads, near the old smithy, the air grew suddenly cold. Stopping, looking around her, Faye heard a woman scream, a muffled, desperate cry as if she was choking. 'Who is it?' she cried out. Erasmus turned and looked at her, dully. 'What?'

'I thought heard someone,' Faye said, pulling her mantle around her.

The cart arrived down the lane. Behind its blinkers, the horse shied and tried to back up, had to be coaxed by the carter into standing still. Balthazar helped Erasmus onto the back of the cart and – glancing around again – Faye got up by the driver and they carried on to Nether Hall.

Grass grew up around the iron gates and daisies had invaded the carriage drive, turned it into a long, low sweep of white. While Balthazar set about opening the padlock, Faye helped her brother over the stile. They went through the kitchen garden and on around the old stable block, Erasmus leaning on Faye's arm. The tower on the east wing stood square, the battlements empty, the lions each raising one front paw. Her brother stopped and looked up at the tower.

And he wept.

Having consigned Erasmus to the gasman's care, in her childhood bedroom, Faye sat down at the writing desk. She opened her notebook and wrote down the events of the last few days, including the journey south from Newcastle-upon-Tyne, the informal wedding she had witnessed in Mrs Ali's parlour. The story was not ended but this part of it was over. Opening the roll-top desk, putting away the pen and ink, Faye had a nagging sense that the unforgetting was not complete; that something evaded her. The memories came when they chose, she reminded herself; rose up in their own time, like springs from the ground.

When it grew light, she rose from her bed, repacked her valise and, leaving a note on the hall table stating that she would return shortly and taking some of the notes she still had from the safe, set off back to the station. Only she waited on the platform for the London train. The great engine ground to a halt and she opened the carriage door and got in, slamming the door behind her, gazing out of the window as the train gathered speed.

By two in the afternoon, she stood on the pavement outside the foundlings hospital, under the line of plane trees with scaling bark that formed strange shapes, maps of a world not yet encountered. Faye lingered there, aware that she was on the threshold of a new chapter in the book of her life, praying that she would be fit for what it asked of her.

She nodded at the porter, passed by the lodge and walked towards the long white building. The sun shone and from inside she could hear the sound of children's laughter. Picturing her daughter as she had seen her that day, engrossed in playing with her bricks, Faye felt she knew her, that the time they had spent apart had done little to separate them. Folded in her valise, wrapped in tissue paper, was a tiny white chemise, the date and place of her baby's birth and her name – Clara Valentina – stitched in red thread into the hem. The dress was an exact replica of the one she had dressed her baby in when she left her at the foundlings hospital. Faye felt peace, a sense of wholeness, as she sat down in the matron's private sitting room, took a sip of water and began to explain why and for whom she had come.

Epilogue

The last of the unforgetting occurred soon afterwards. I was in what used to be our mother's boudoir but was now turned into the nursery; the faded wallpaper had been stripped off and replaced with clean new paint, the floor polished and a woollen rug laid down. As always, Clara Valentina was near me – toddling around the room, singing to herself, playing with her doll. As I stood folding her clothes, smoothing a cotton dress with a pattern of yellow daisies on a blue background, the last memory rose in me.

After Maria Hedges disappeared, I had found the costume, our mother's old gown, in a heap on the floor in the dressing room. Had packed away the dress, the veil and gloves and feather boa, hastily, piling them into the chest, turning the key in the lock and rushing to my own room. That night, lying in my bed, my mind had raced with awful, unconscionable thoughts. At some time in the early hours, I rose from my bed and, lighting a candle, taking it with me, crept up to the attic. In the dim, dusty space I felt behind a roof beam for what I knew my hand would find. Pulled out a dark bundle. With that under my arm, I stole down the stairs and out of the back door of Nether Hall. No dogs barked as I made my way past the stables; my feet made no sound on the sandy ground as I slipped through the gate and into the kitchen garden. Neglected ever since our mother's disappearance, the neat rows of cabbages and onions, the flourishing potatoes, had long since been lost to bramble, nettles and tall grasses.

In the glasshouse, rusted tools hung in a line on the wall. The stove once used for heating, for producing in our mother's time oranges and peaches, gardenias for her to wear in her hair, still stood in the middle of the derelict space. Standing the candle on top of the stove, by its light I unrolled the bundle of Maria Hedges's clothes. Shook out the girl's pretty gown, the flowers studding the blue ground, held up her silky shawl. I could still smell her scent, Millefeuille, mixed with her perspiration as I dripped candle wax on the shawl and when enough had collected, set fire to it, dropping the smouldering bundle into the stove, closing the door, opening the flue so that the silk caught and flared in the updraft. Tearing the dress into sections, by means of a pair of rusty shears taken down from the wall, I burned that too. When a lively blaze crackled in the stove, most ghastly of all, I picked up one of her down-at-heel shoes, threw it onto the flames and watched through the alabaster door as it curled and contorted. Feeling on the ground for the other one, breathing in the stinging reproach of burning cloth and leather, I discovered it was missing. I waited until the clothes were no more than a pile of ashes, replaced the shears on the wall and returned to my bed.

If you, Clara Valentina, should one day read these words, wonder whether my account of those times might be a fiction, you must know that it is not. Search the attic here at Nether Hall, and you will find – hidden behind a roof beam – a single blue shoe that once belonged to the late Maria Hedges.

Acknowledgements

I'm deeply grateful to those friends, family and colleagues who gave encouragement and support in the writing of *The Unforgetting*.

In particular, I'd like to thank my agent Ivan Mulcahy for his unfailing vision, faith and friendship. My editors Clare Hey and Olivia Barber, and all the team at Orion, for their skill and creativity. My dear friends Essie Fox, Denise Meredith and Andie Lewenstein, for insights and inspiration writerly and otherwise.

During the gestation of the book, I benefitted from the Royal Literary Fund's university fellowship scheme for writers – an invaluable treasure. Many thanks to Steve Cook and everyone at the RLF.

Above all, my love and gratitude to my sons and my husband, for being there always.

Credits

Rose Black and Orion Fiction would like to thank everyone at Orion who worked on the publication of *The Unforgetting* in the UK.

Editorial
Clare Hey
Olivia Barber

Copy editor
Joanne Gledhill

Proof reader
Clare Wallis

Audio
Paul Stark
Amber Bates

Contracts
Anne Goddard
Paul Bulos
Jake Alderson

Design
Debbie Holmes
Joanna Ridley
Nick May

Editorial Management
Charlie Panayiotou
Jane Hughes
Alice Davis

Finance
Jasdip Nandra
Afeera Ahmed
Elizabeth Beaumont
Sue Baker

Production
Ruth Sharvell

Marketing
Brittany Sankey

Publicity
Francesca Pearce

Sales
Jen Wilson
Laura Fletcher
Esther Waters
Victoria Laws

Rachael Hum
Ellie Kyrke-Smith
Frances Doyle
Georgina Cutler

Operations
Jo Jacobs
Sharon Willis
Lisa Pryde
Lucy Brem